# THE ADVENTURES OF DANIEL BOOM AKA LOUD BOY

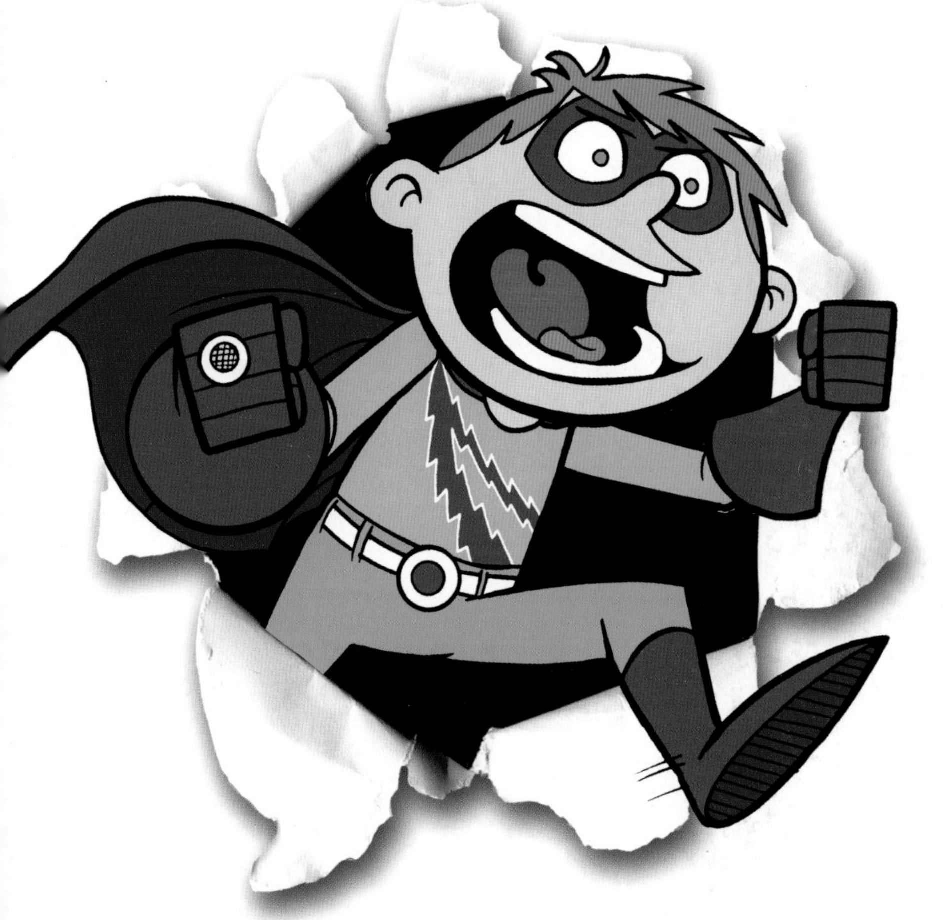

## GROW UP!

WRITTEN BY D. J. STEINBERG

ILLUSTRATED BY BRIAN SMITH

GROSSET & DUNLAP
AN IMPRINT OF PENGUIN GROUP (USA) INC.

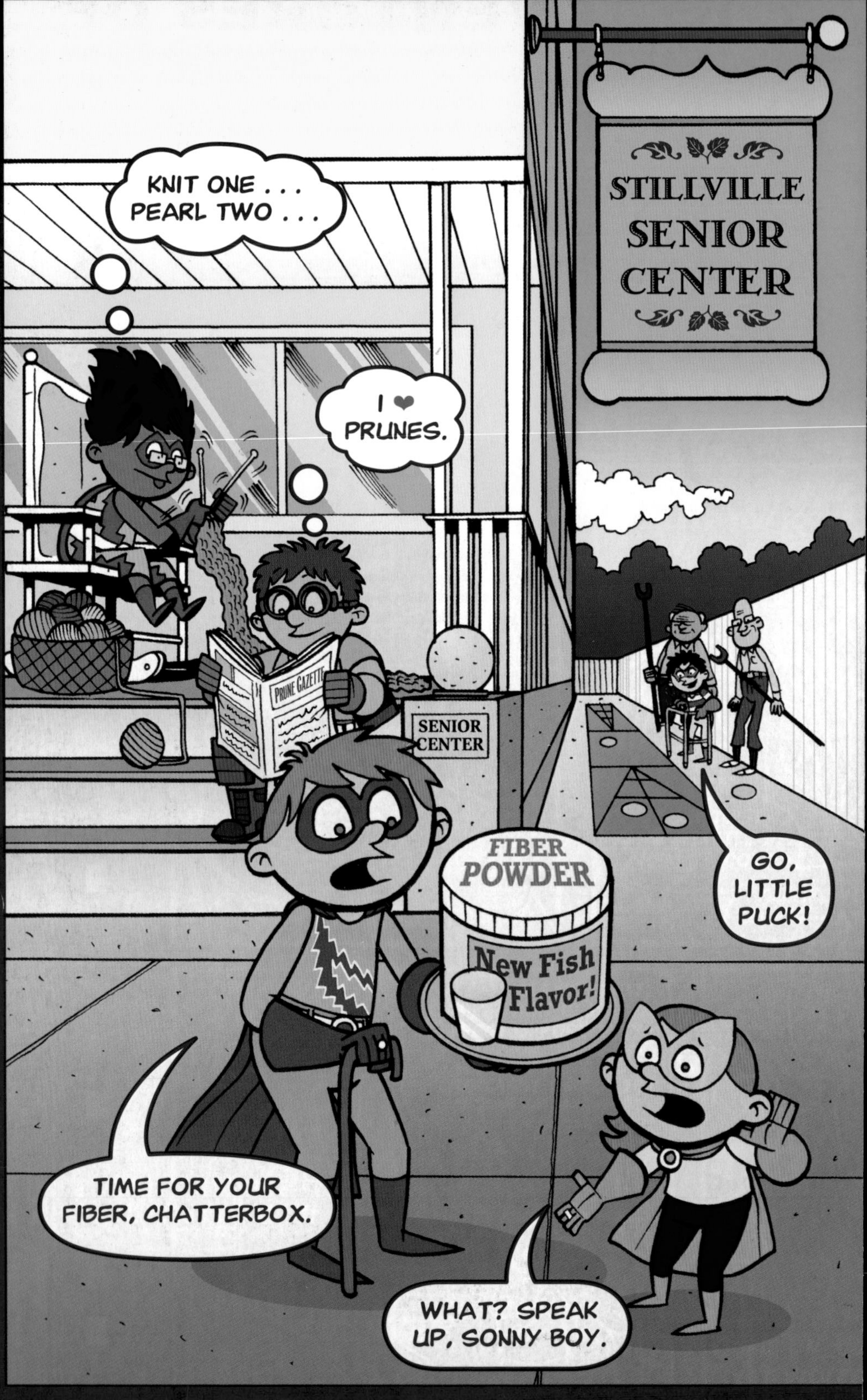
STILLVILLE SENIOR CENTER
KNIT ONE . . . PEARL TWO . . .
I ❤ PRUNES.
PRUNE GAZETTE
SENIOR CENTER
FIBER POWDER
New Fish Flavor!
GO, LITTLE PUCK!
TIME FOR YOUR FIBER, CHATTERBOX.
WHAT? SPEAK UP, SONNY BOY.

What are our five heroes doing?
They may look like Loud
Boy, Chatterbox, Tantrum
Girl, Destructo-Kid, and
Fidget, but—a CANE?
KNITTING NEEDLES?
SHUFFLEBOARD?
THE *PRUNE GAZETTE*?!
Why in the name of Pete are they
acting like a bunch of old people?

Something is WRONG here—very, very wrong . . .

Are these the same five kids who kaboshed bad guys everywhere with their youthful powers . . . ?

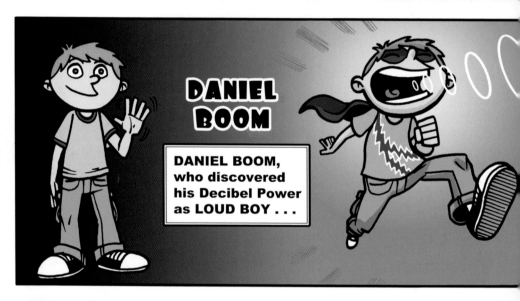

# DANIEL BOOM

DANIEL BOOM, who discovered his Decibel Power as LOUD BOY . . .

. . . his sister, JEANNIE S. BOOM, who discovered her Know-It-All Power as CHATTERBOX . . .

# JEANNIE S. BOOM

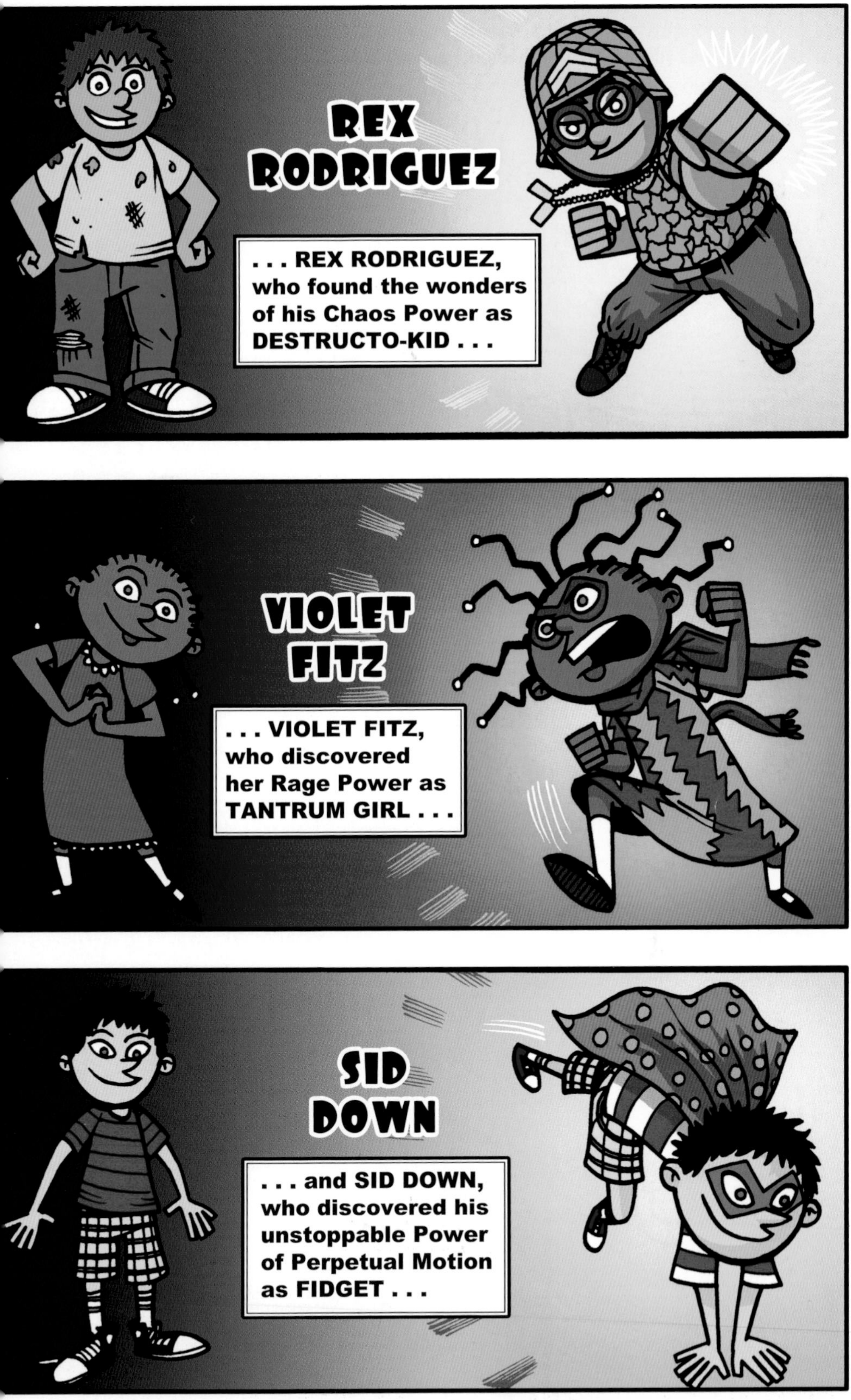
REX RODRIGUEZ
. . . REX RODRIGUEZ, who found the wonders of his Chaos Power as DESTRUCTO-KID . . .
VIOLET FITZ
. . . VIOLET FITZ, who discovered her Rage Power as TANTRUM GIRL . . .
SID DOWN
. . . and SID DOWN, who discovered his unstoppable Power of Perpetual Motion as FIDGET . . .

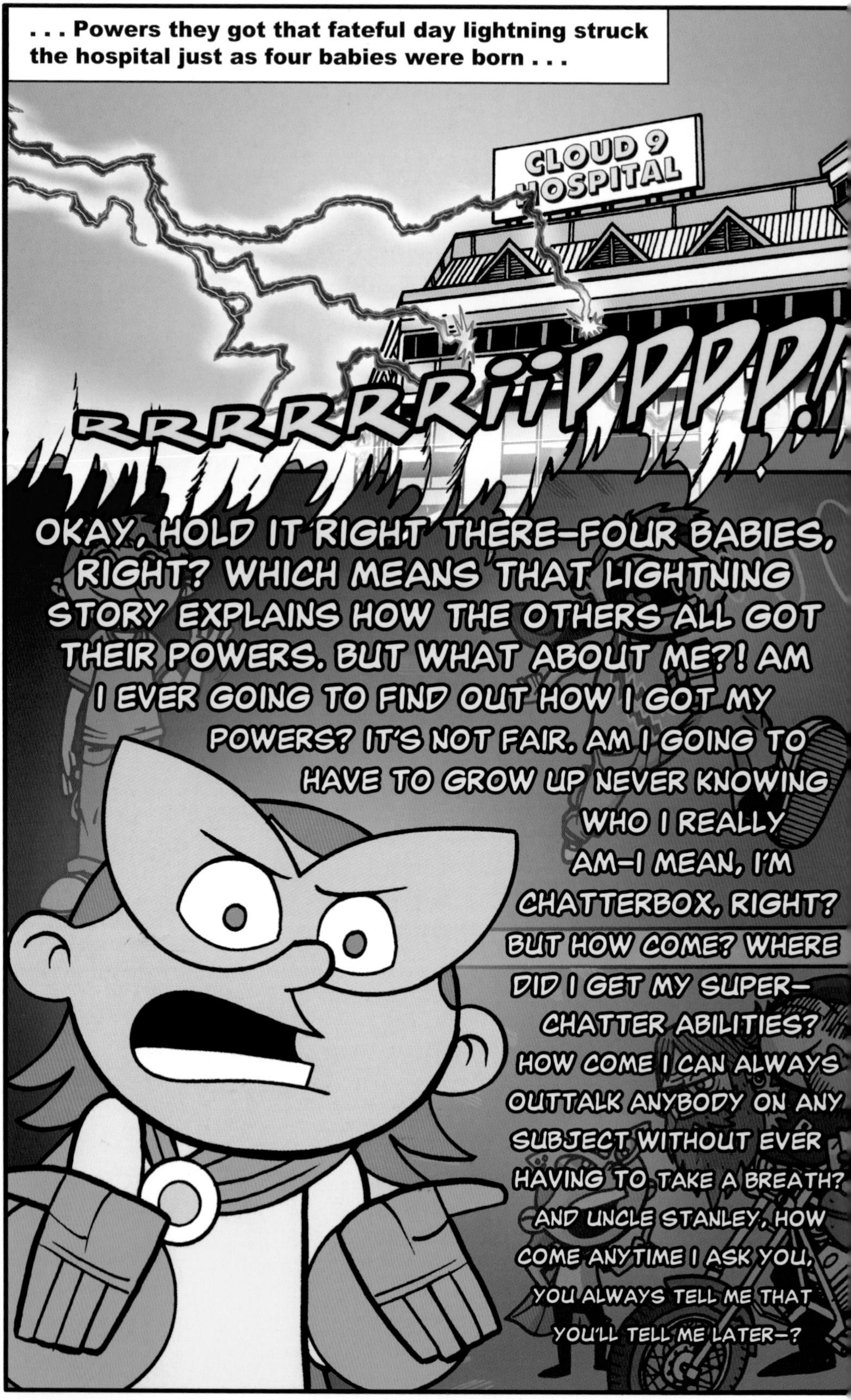
. . . Powers they got that fateful day lightning struck the hospital just as four babies were born . . .
CLOUD 9 HOSPITAL
RRRRRRiiPPPPP!
OKAY, HOLD IT RIGHT THERE–FOUR BABIES, RIGHT? WHICH MEANS THAT LIGHTNING STORY EXPLAINS HOW THE OTHERS ALL GOT THEIR POWERS. BUT WHAT ABOUT ME?! AM I EVER GOING TO FIND OUT HOW I GOT MY POWERS? IT'S NOT FAIR. AM I GOING TO HAVE TO GROW UP NEVER KNOWING WHO I REALLY AM–I MEAN, I'M CHATTERBOX, RIGHT? BUT HOW COME? WHERE DID I GET MY SUPER-CHATTER ABILITIES? HOW COME I CAN ALWAYS OUTTALK ANYBODY ON ANY SUBJECT WITHOUT EVER HAVING TO TAKE A BREATH? AND UNCLE STANLEY, HOW COME ANYTIME I ASK YOU, YOU ALWAYS TELL ME THAT YOU'LL TELL ME LATER–?

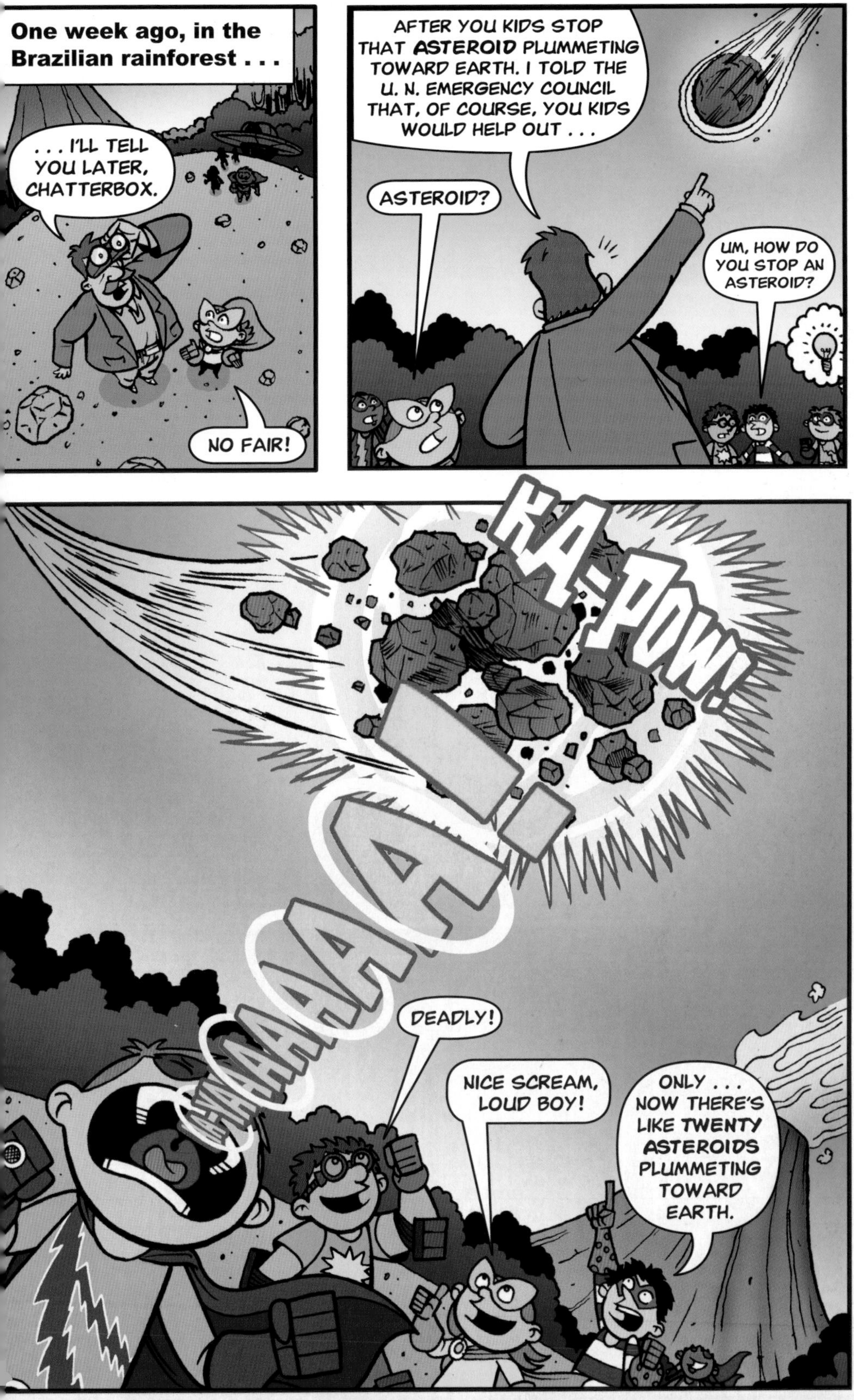
One week ago, in the Brazilian rainforest . . .
. . . I'LL TELL YOU LATER, CHATTERBOX.
NO FAIR!
AFTER YOU KIDS STOP THAT ASTEROID PLUMMETING TOWARD EARTH. I TOLD THE U. N. EMERGENCY COUNCIL THAT, OF COURSE, YOU KIDS WOULD HELP OUT . . .
ASTEROID?
UM, HOW DO YOU STOP AN ASTEROID?
KA-POW!
AAAAAAAA!!
DEADLY!
NICE SCREAM, LOUD BOY!
ONLY . . . NOW THERE'S LIKE TWENTY ASTEROIDS PLUMMETING TOWARD EARTH.

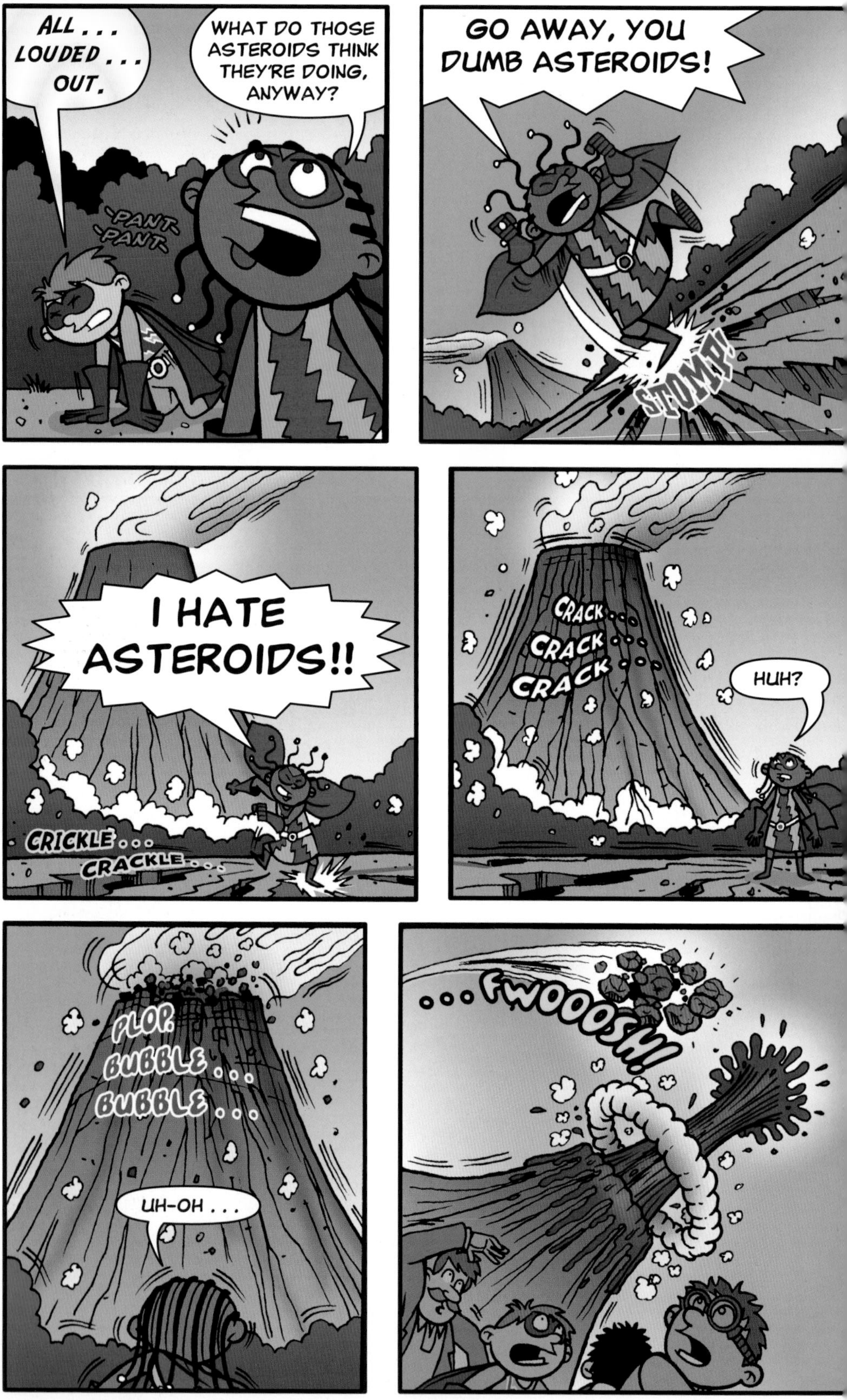
ALL . . . LOUDED . . . OUT.
WHAT DO THOSE ASTEROIDS THINK THEY'RE DOING, ANYWAY?
PANT PANT
GO AWAY, YOU DUMB ASTEROIDS!
STOMP!
I HATE ASTEROIDS!!
CRICKLE . . .
CRACKLE . . .
CRACK . . .
CRACK . . .
CRACK . . .
HUH?
PLOP.
BUBBLE . . .
BUBBLE . . .
UH-OH . . .
. . . FWOOOSH!

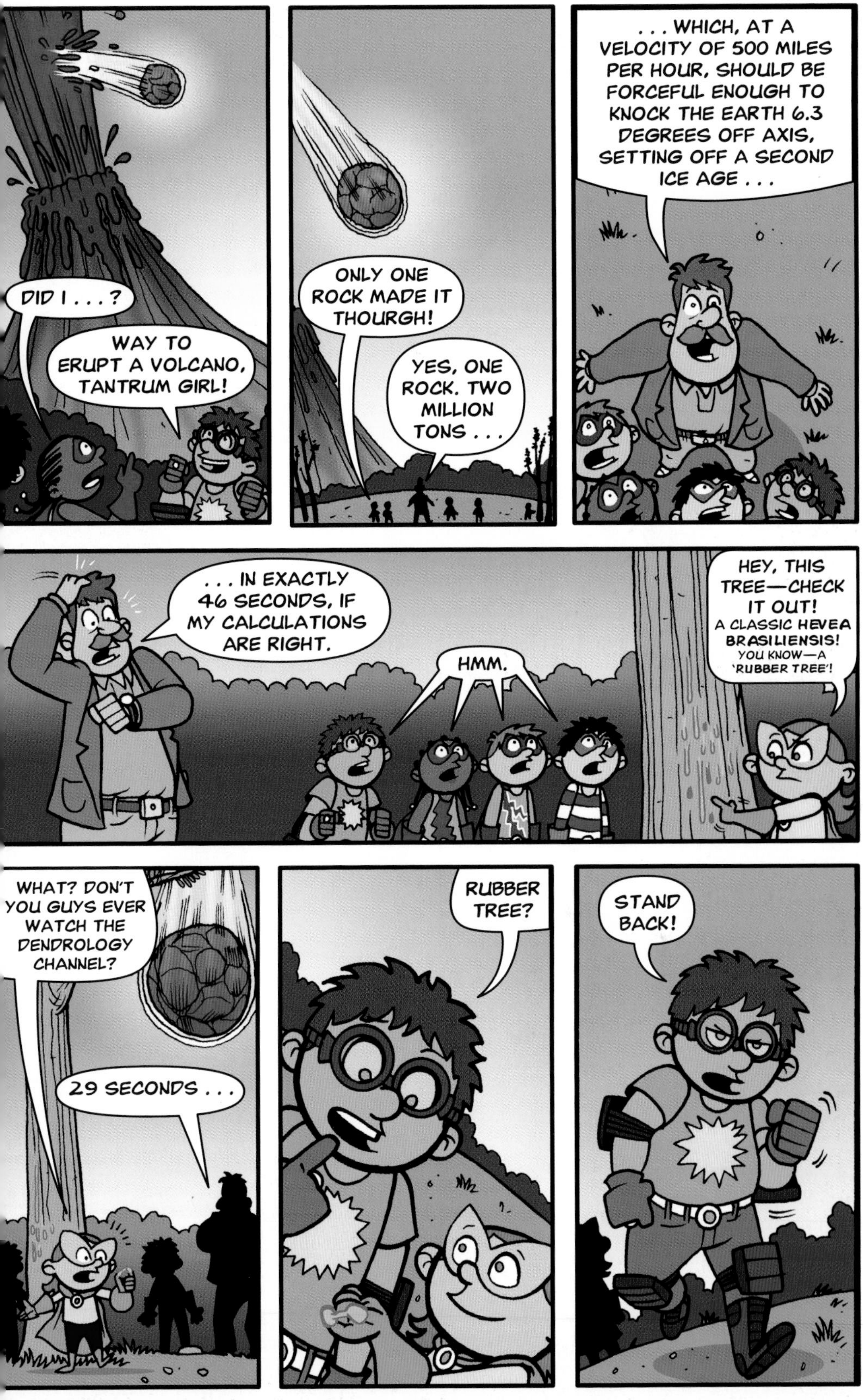
DID I . . . ?
WAY TO ERUPT A VOLCANO, TANTRUM GIRL!
ONLY ONE ROCK MADE IT THOURGH!
YES, ONE ROCK. TWO MILLION TONS . . .
. . . WHICH, AT A VELOCITY OF 500 MILES PER HOUR, SHOULD BE FORCEFUL ENOUGH TO KNOCK THE EARTH 6.3 DEGREES OFF AXIS, SETTING OFF A SECOND ICE AGE . . .
. . . IN EXACTLY 46 SECONDS, IF MY CALCULATIONS ARE RIGHT.
HMM.
HEY, THIS TREE—CHECK IT OUT! A CLASSIC HEVEA BRASILIENSIS! YOU KNOW—A 'RUBBER TREE'!
WHAT? DON'T YOU GUYS EVER WATCH THE DENDROLOGY CHANNEL?
29 SECONDS . . .
RUBBER TREE?
STAND BACK!

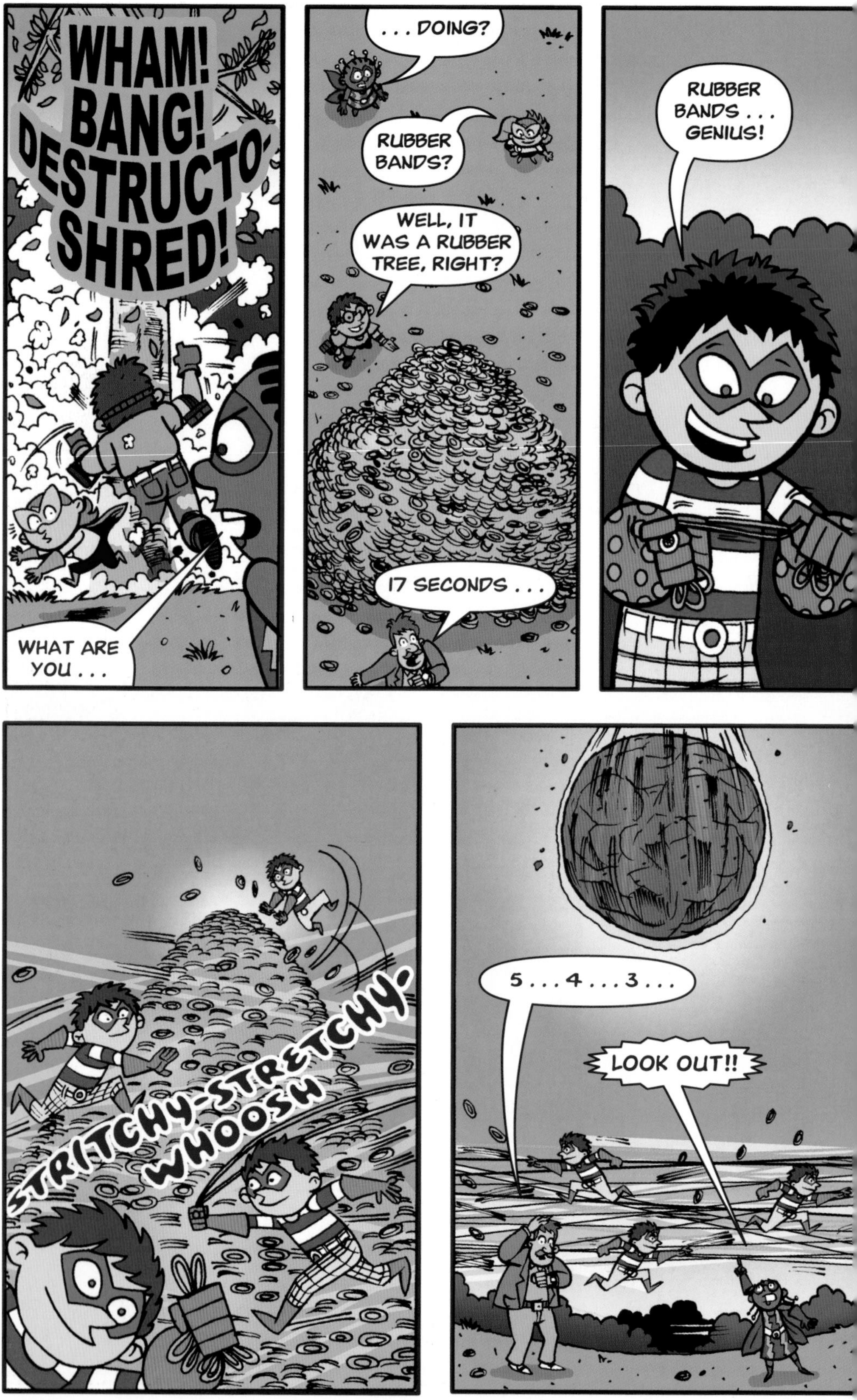
WHAM! BANG! DESTRUCTO-SHRED!
WHAT ARE YOU . . .
. . . DOING?
RUBBER BANDS?
WELL, IT WAS A RUBBER TREE, RIGHT?
17 SECONDS . . .
RUBBER BANDS . . . GENIUS!
STRITCHY-STRETCHY-STRETCHY-WHOOSH
5 . . . 4 . . . 3 . . .
LOOK OUT!!

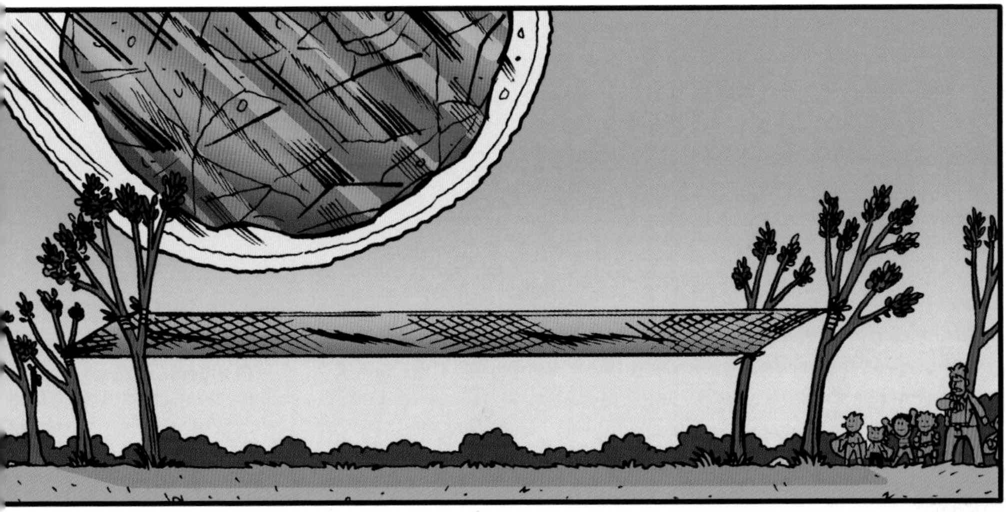

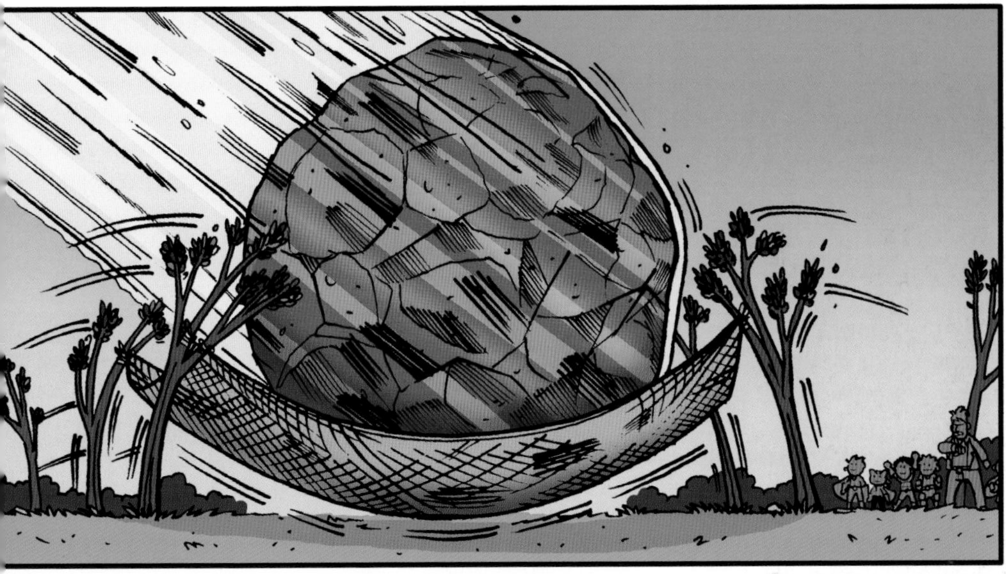

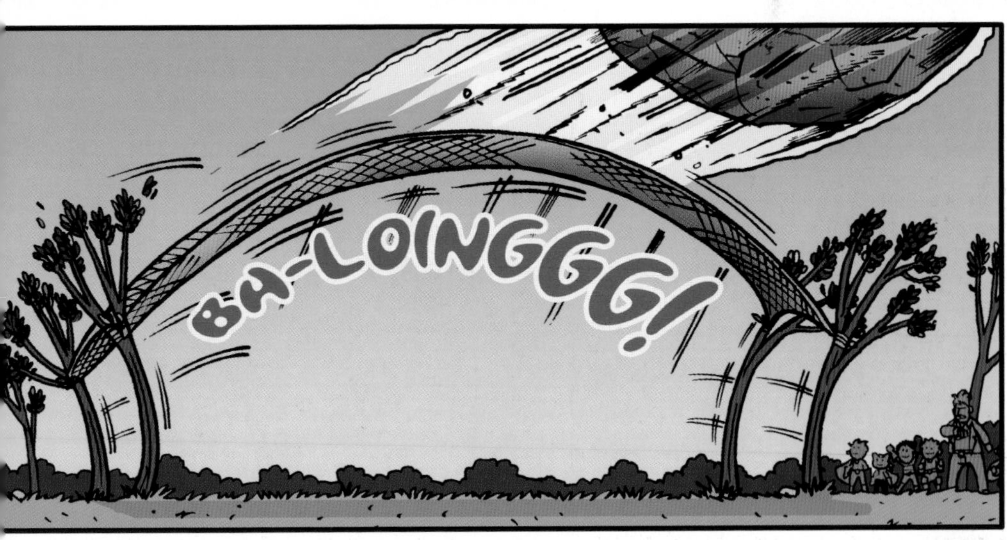

BA-LOINGGG!

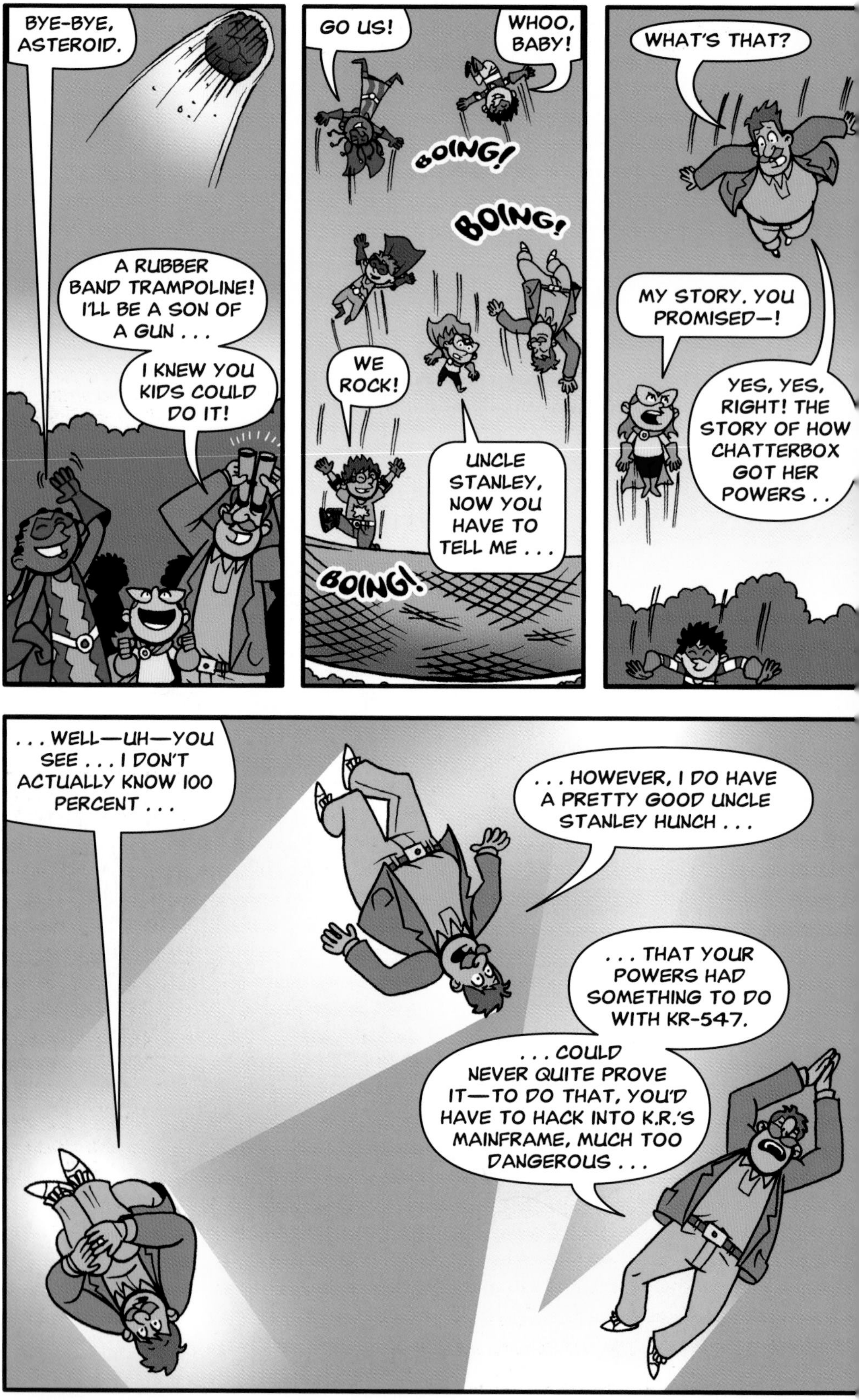
BYE-BYE, ASTEROID.
A RUBBER BAND TRAMPOLINE! I'LL BE A SON OF A GUN . . .
I KNEW YOU KIDS COULD DO IT!
GO US!
WHOO, BABY!
BOING!
BOING!
WE ROCK!
UNCLE STANLEY, NOW YOU HAVE TO TELL ME . . .
BOING!
WHAT'S THAT?
MY STORY. YOU PROMISED—!
YES, YES, RIGHT! THE STORY OF HOW CHATTERBOX GOT HER POWERS . .
. . . WELL—UH—YOU SEE . . . I DON'T ACTUALLY KNOW 100 PERCENT . . .
. . . HOWEVER, I DO HAVE A PRETTY GOOD UNCLE STANLEY HUNCH . . .
. . . THAT YOUR POWERS HAD SOMETHING TO DO WITH KR-547.
. . . COULD NEVER QUITE PROVE IT—TO DO THAT, YOU'D HAVE TO HACK INTO K.R.'S MAINFRAME, MUCH TOO DANGEROUS . . .

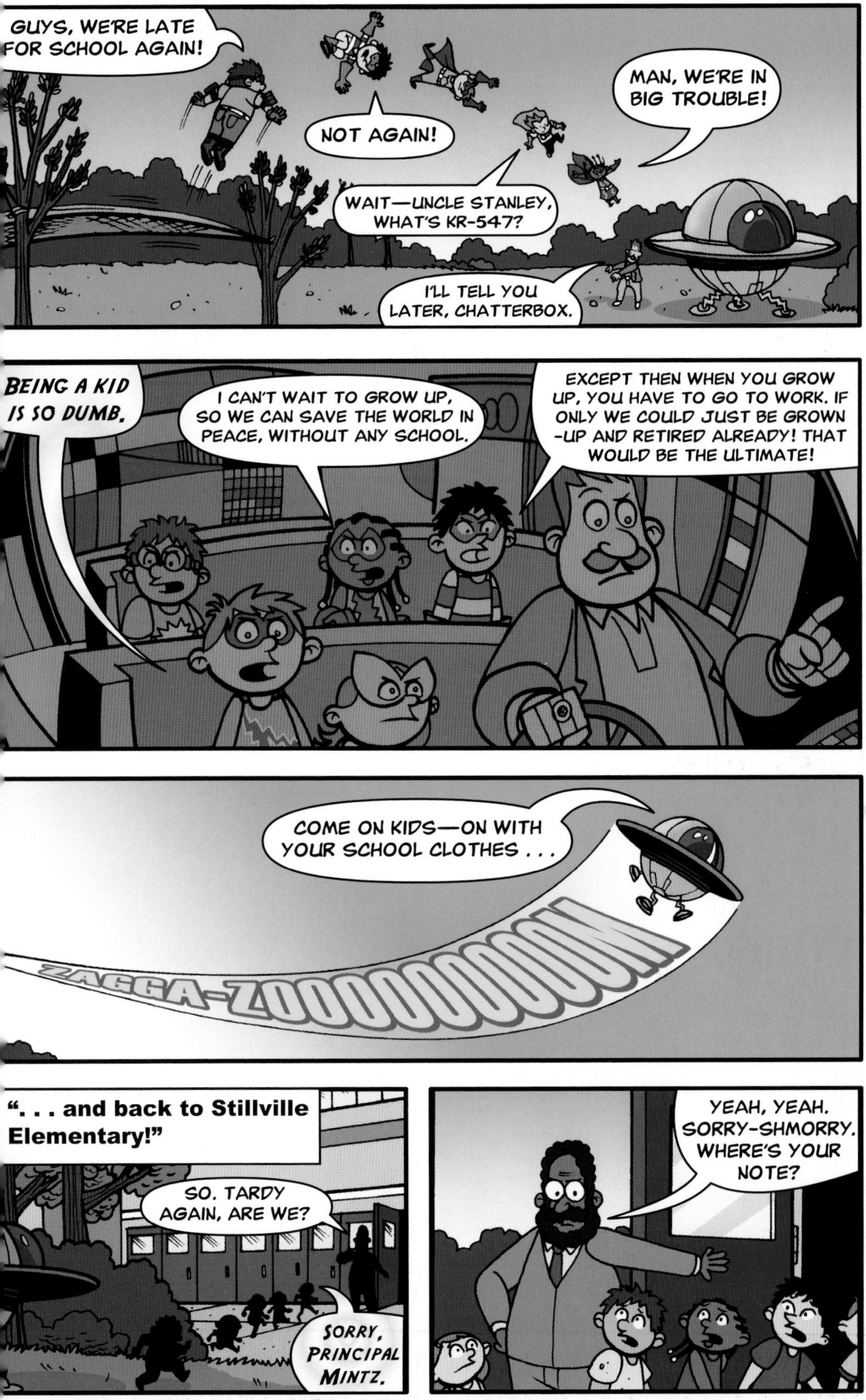
GUYS, WE'RE LATE FOR SCHOOL AGAIN!
NOT AGAIN!
MAN, WE'RE IN BIG TROUBLE!
WAIT—UNCLE STANLEY, WHAT'S KR-547?
I'LL TELL YOU LATER, CHATTERBOX.
BEING A KID IS SO DUMB.
I CAN'T WAIT TO GROW UP, SO WE CAN SAVE THE WORLD IN PEACE, WITHOUT ANY SCHOOL.
EXCEPT THEN WHEN YOU GROW UP, YOU HAVE TO GO TO WORK. IF ONLY WE COULD JUST BE GROWN-UP AND RETIRED ALREADY! THAT WOULD BE THE ULTIMATE!
COME ON KIDS—ON WITH YOUR SCHOOL CLOTHES . . .
ZAGGA-ZOOOOOOOOOM!
". . . and back to Stillville Elementary!"
SO. TARDY AGAIN, ARE WE?
SORRY, PRINCIPAL MINTZ.
YEAH, YEAH. SORRY-SHMORRY. WHERE'S YOUR NOTE?

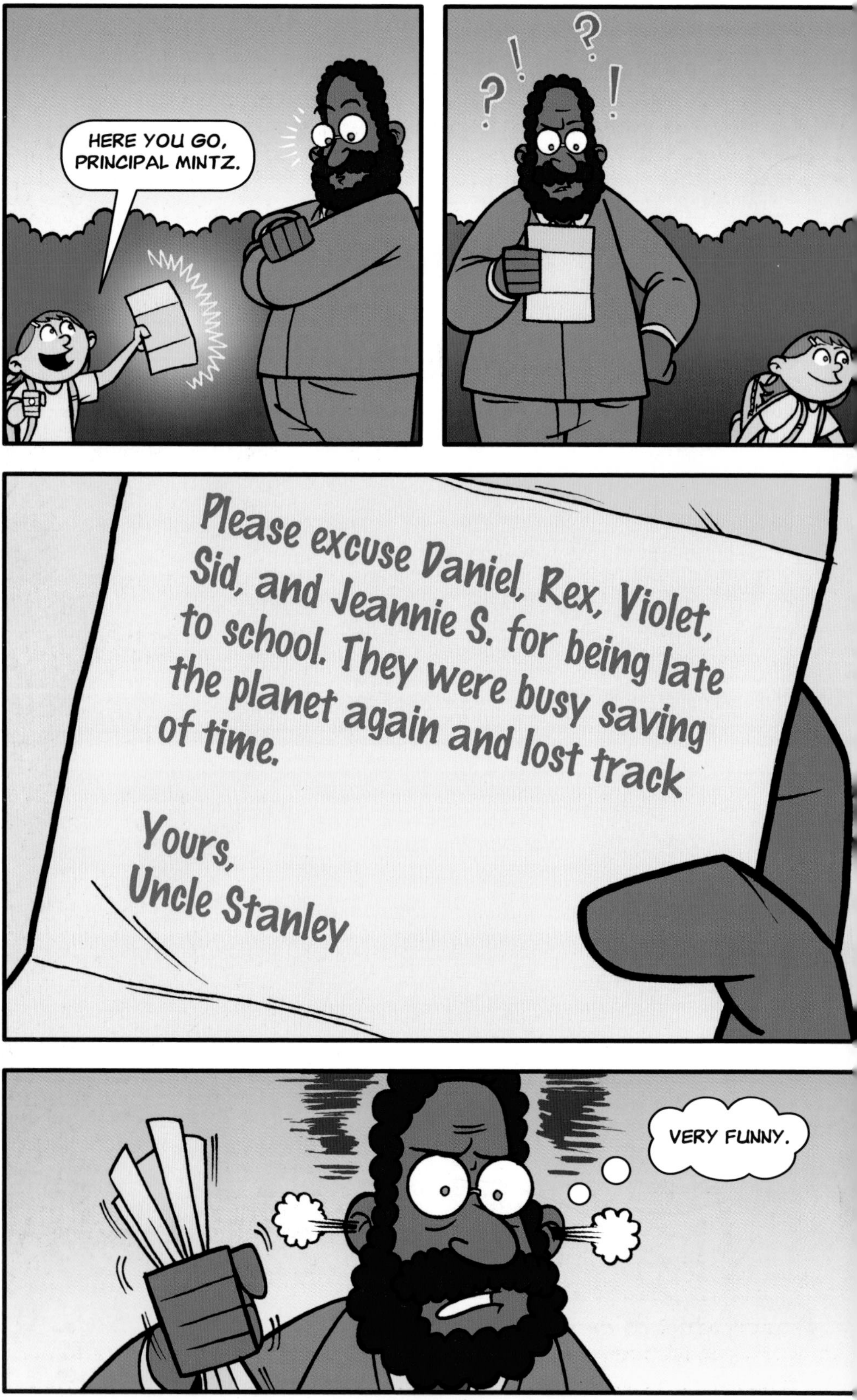
HERE YOU GO, PRINCIPAL MINTZ.
?!?!
Please excuse Daniel, Rex, Violet, Sid, and Jeannie S. for being late to school. They were busy saving the planet again and lost track of time.
Yours,
Uncle Stanley
VERY FUNNY.

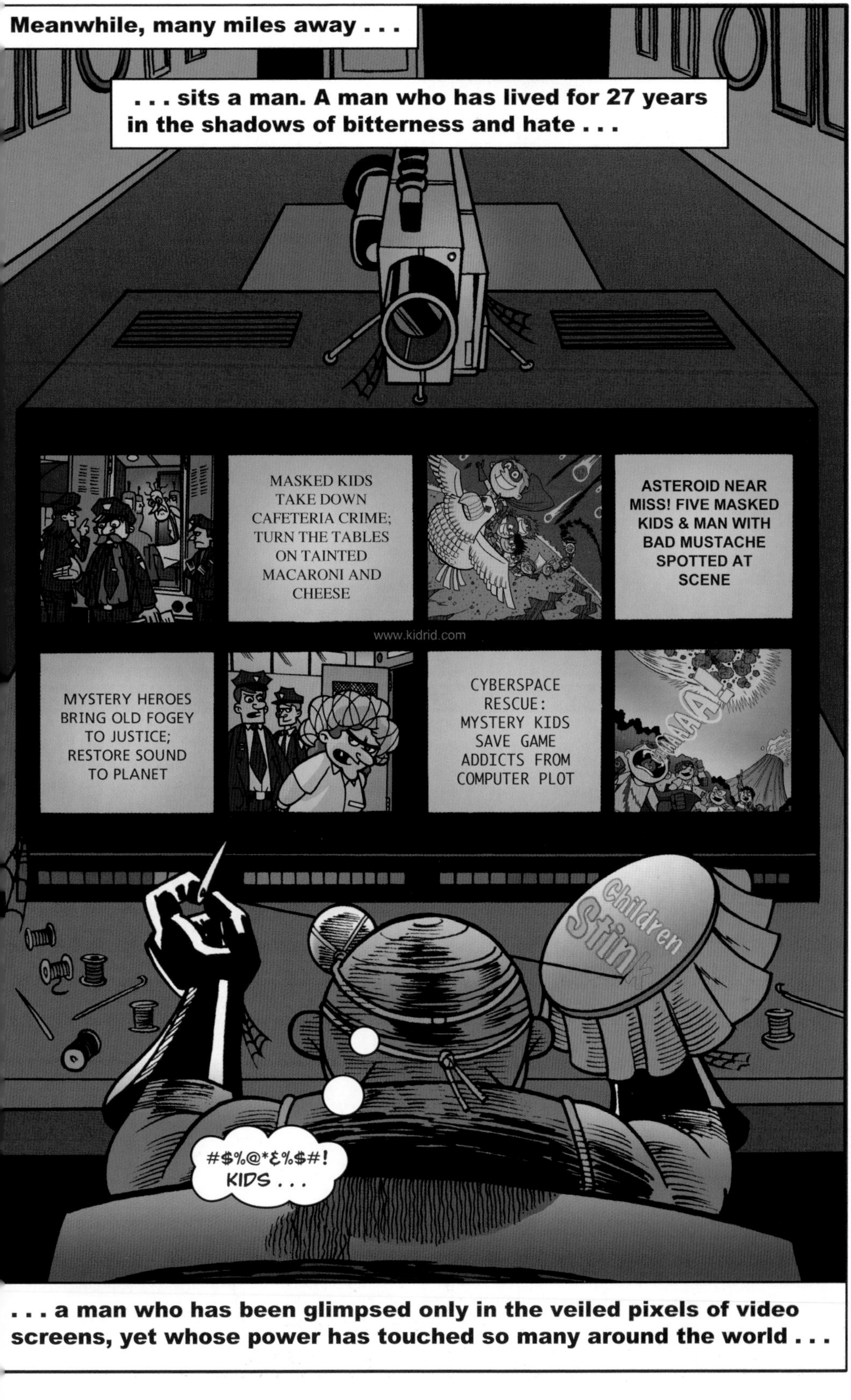
Meanwhile, many miles away . . .
. . . sits a man. A man who has lived for 27 years in the shadows of bitterness and hate . . .
MASKED KIDS TAKE DOWN CAFETERIA CRIME; TURN THE TABLES ON TAINTED MACARONI AND CHEESE
ASTEROID NEAR MISS! FIVE MASKED KIDS & MAN WITH BAD MUSTACHE SPOTTED AT SCENE
www.kidrid.com
MYSTERY HEROES BRING OLD FOGEY TO JUSTICE; RESTORE SOUND TO PLANET
CYBERSPACE RESCUE: MYSTERY KIDS SAVE GAME ADDICTS FROM COMPUTER PLOT
Children Stink
#$%@*&%$#! KIDS . . .
. . . a man who has been glimpsed only in the veiled pixels of video screens, yet whose power has touched so many around the world . . .

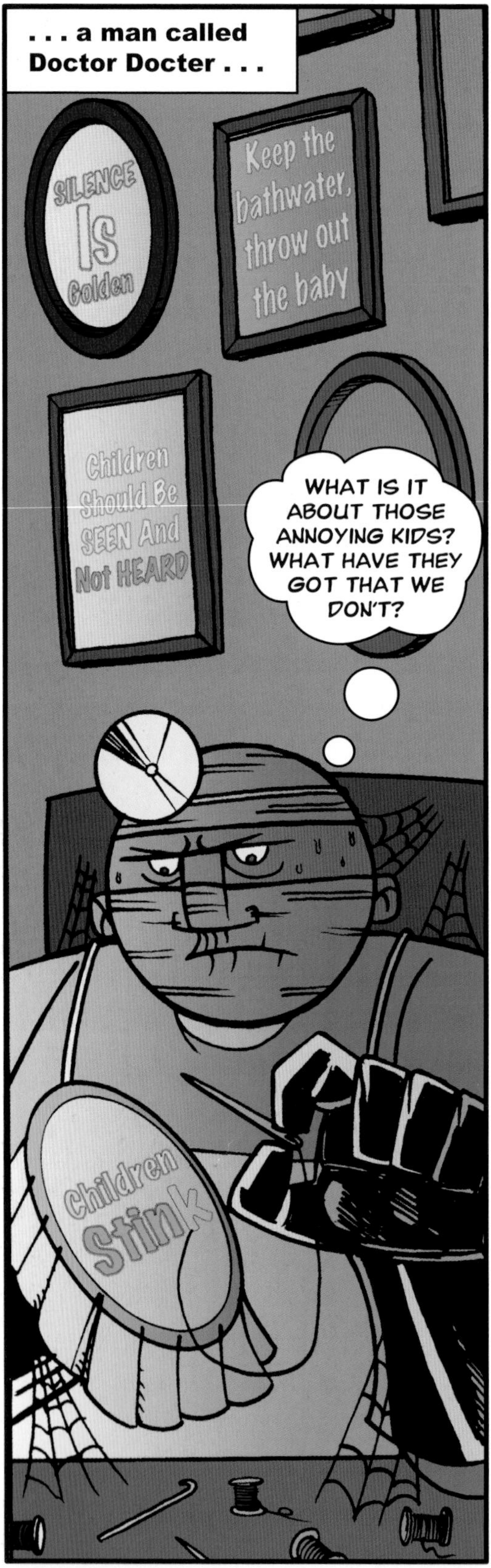
. . . a man called Doctor Docter . . .
SILENCE Is Golden
Keep the bathwater, throw out the baby
Children Should Be SEEN And Not HEARD
WHAT IS IT ABOUT THOSE ANNOYING KIDS? WHAT HAVE THEY GOT THAT WE DON'T?
Children Stink

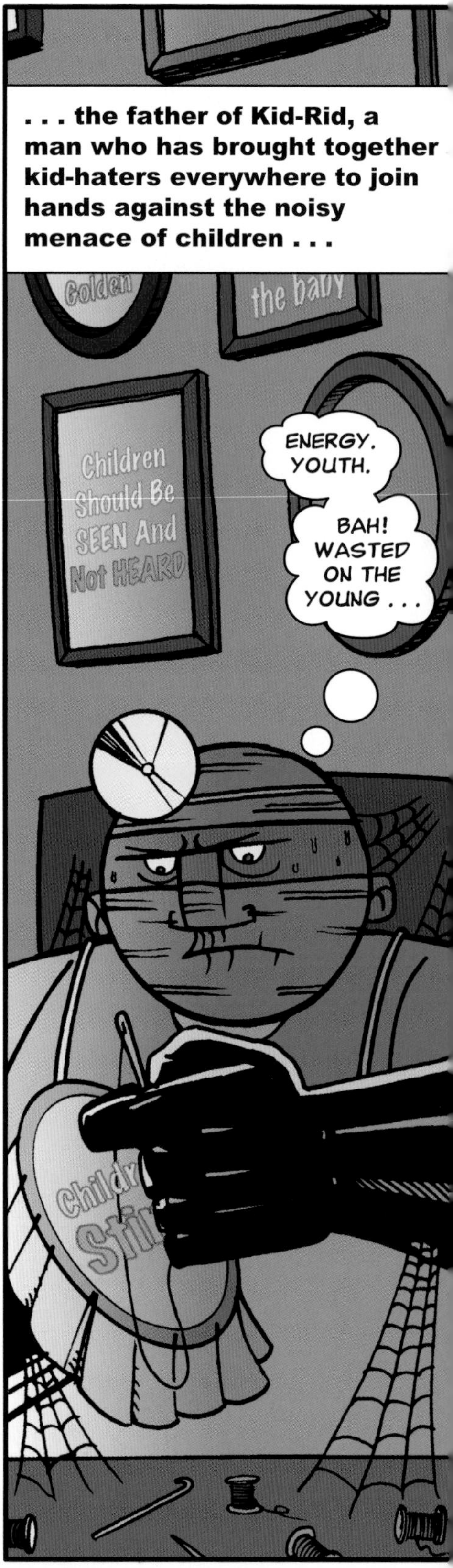
. . . the father of Kid-Rid, a man who has brought together kid-haters everywhere to join hands against the noisy menace of children . . .
Golden
the baby
Children Should Be SEEN And Not HEARD
ENERGY. YOUTH.
BAH! WASTED ON THE YOUNG . . .

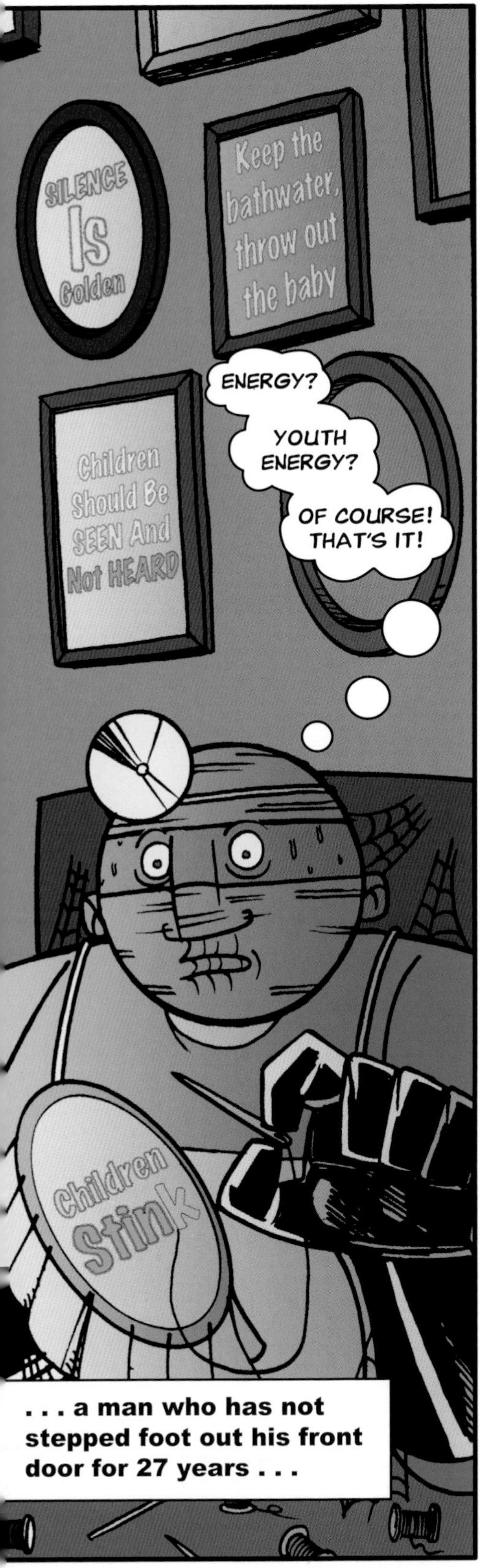
SILENCE Is Golden
Keep the bathwater, throw out the baby
Children Should Be SEEN And Not HEARD
ENERGY?
YOUTH ENERGY?
OF COURSE! THAT'S IT!
Children Stink
. . . a man who has not stepped foot out his front door for 27 years . . .

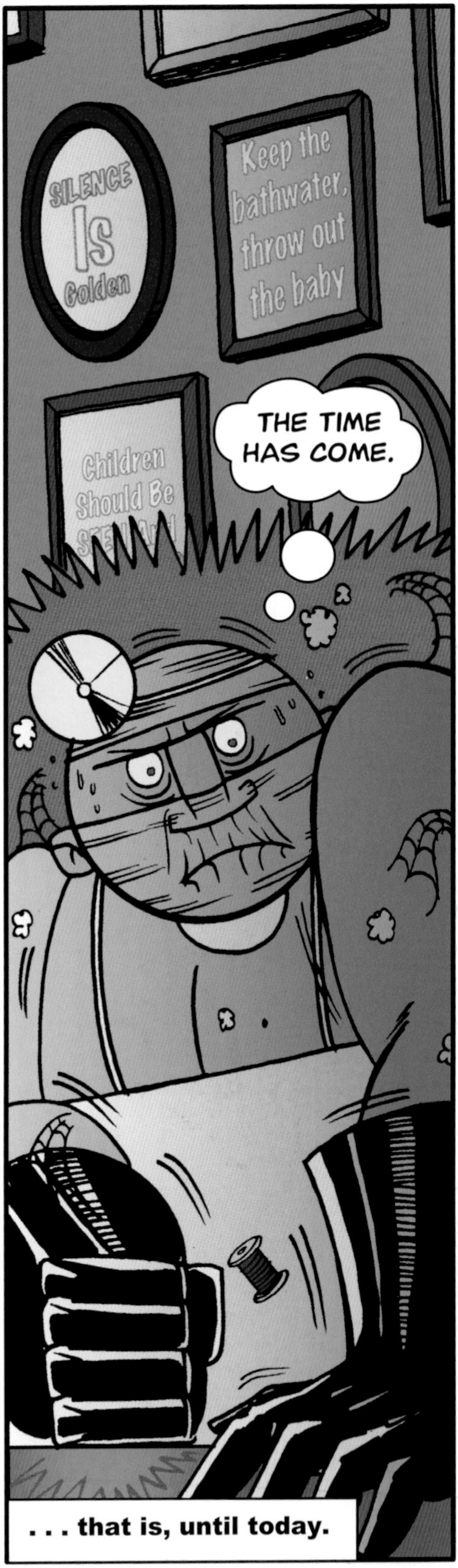
SILENCE Is Golden
Keep the bathwater, throw out the baby
THE TIME HAS COME.
. . . that is, until today.

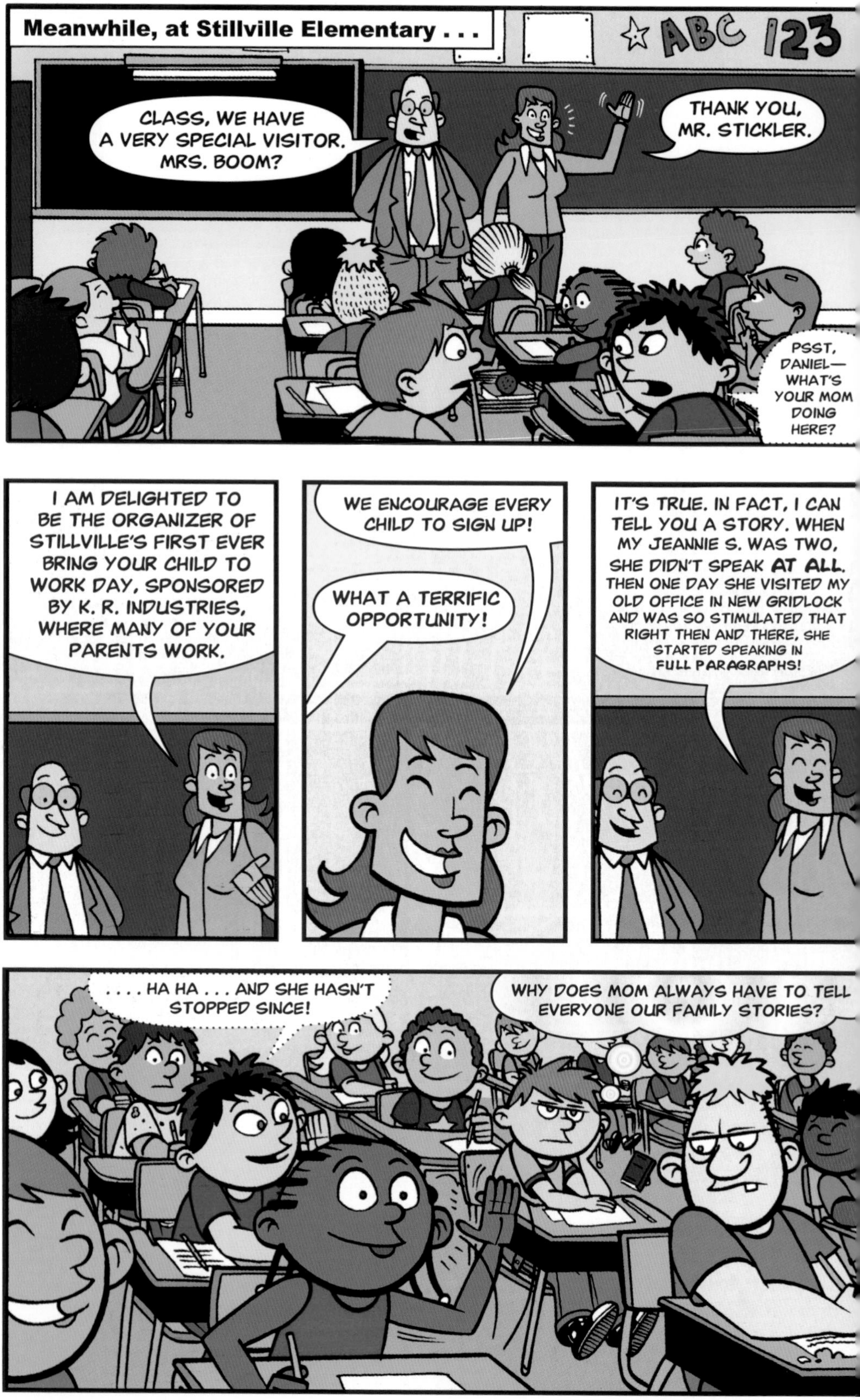
Meanwhile, at Stillville Elementary . . .
ABC 123
CLASS, WE HAVE A VERY SPECIAL VISITOR. MRS. BOOM?
THANK YOU, MR. STICKLER.
PSST, DANIEL— WHAT'S YOUR MOM DOING HERE?
I AM DELIGHTED TO BE THE ORGANIZER OF STILLVILLE'S FIRST EVER BRING YOUR CHILD TO WORK DAY, SPONSORED BY K. R. INDUSTRIES, WHERE MANY OF YOUR PARENTS WORK.
WE ENCOURAGE EVERY CHILD TO SIGN UP!
WHAT A TERRIFIC OPPORTUNITY!
IT'S TRUE. IN FACT, I CAN TELL YOU A STORY. WHEN MY JEANNIE S. WAS TWO, SHE DIDN'T SPEAK AT ALL. THEN ONE DAY SHE VISITED MY OLD OFFICE IN NEW GRIDLOCK AND WAS SO STIMULATED THAT RIGHT THEN AND THERE, SHE STARTED SPEAKING IN FULL PARAGRAPHS!
. . . . HA HA . . . AND SHE HASN'T STOPPED SINCE!
WHY DOES MOM ALWAYS HAVE TO TELL EVERYONE OUR FAMILY STORIES?

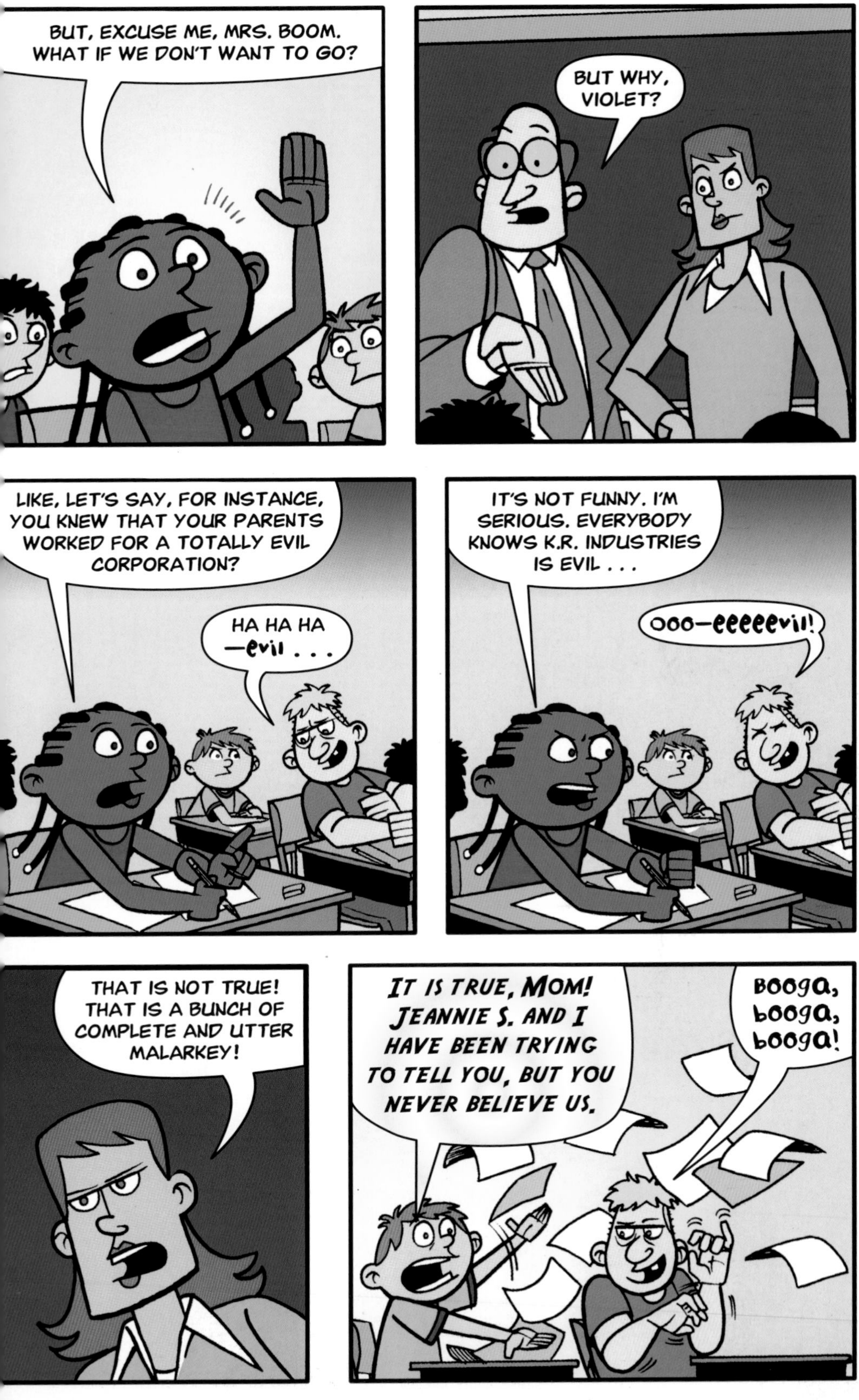
BUT, EXCUSE ME, MRS. BOOM. WHAT IF WE DON'T WANT TO GO?
BUT WHY, VIOLET?
LIKE, LET'S SAY, FOR INSTANCE, YOU KNEW THAT YOUR PARENTS WORKED FOR A TOTALLY EVIL CORPORATION?
HA HA HA —evil . . .
IT'S NOT FUNNY. I'M SERIOUS. EVERYBODY KNOWS K.R. INDUSTRIES IS EVIL . . .
OOO—eeeeevil!
THAT IS NOT TRUE! THAT IS A BUNCH OF COMPLETE AND UTTER MALARKEY!
IT IS TRUE, MOM! JEANNIE S. AND I HAVE BEEN TRYING TO TELL YOU, BUT YOU NEVER BELIEVE US.
Booga, booga, booga!

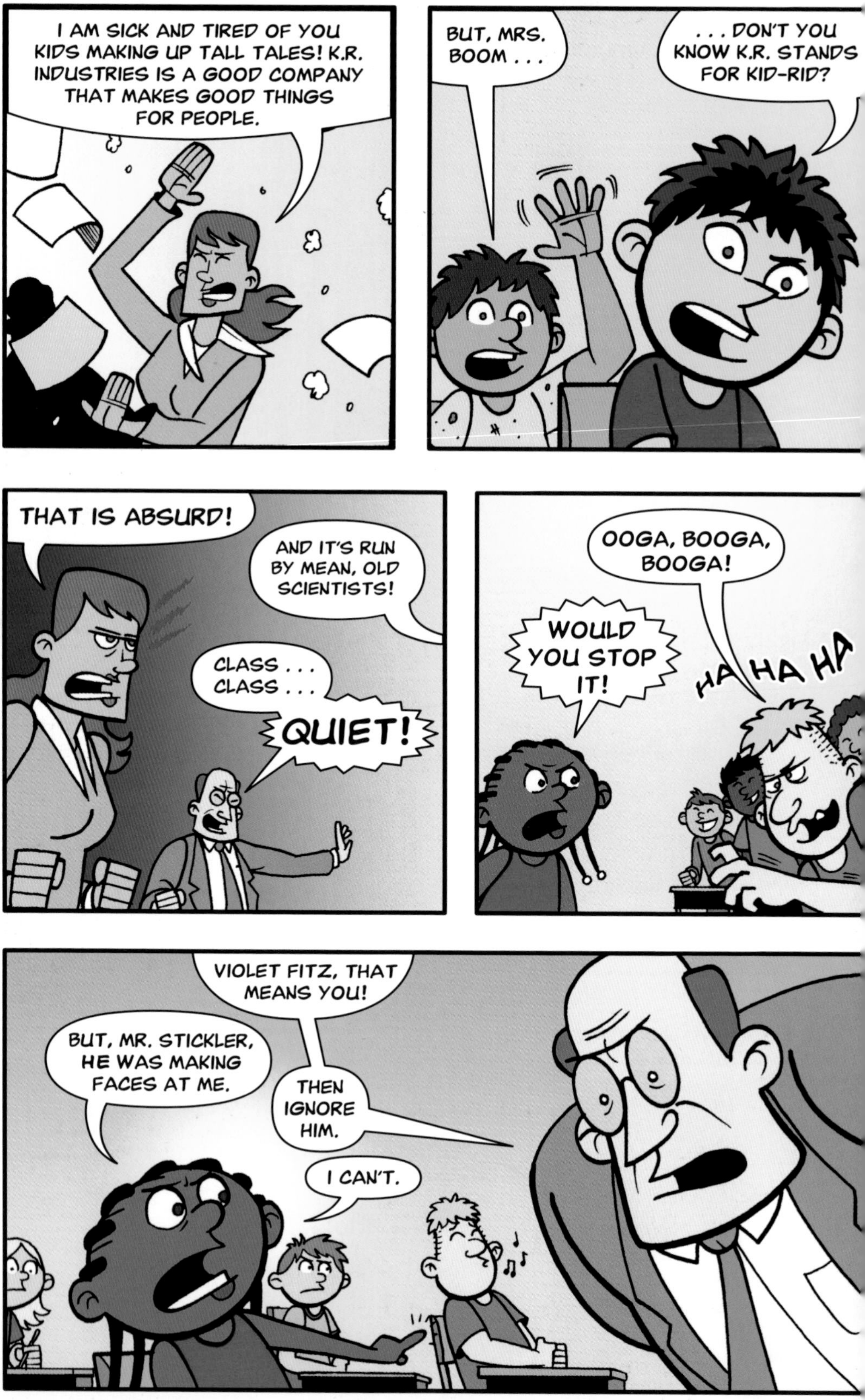
I AM SICK AND TIRED OF YOU KIDS MAKING UP TALL TALES! K.R. INDUSTRIES IS A GOOD COMPANY THAT MAKES GOOD THINGS FOR PEOPLE.
BUT, MRS. BOOM . . .
. . . DON'T YOU KNOW K.R. STANDS FOR KID-RID?
THAT IS ABSURD!
AND IT'S RUN BY MEAN, OLD SCIENTISTS!
CLASS . . . CLASS . . .
QUIET!
OOGA, BOOGA, BOOGA!
WOULD YOU STOP IT!
HA HA HA
VIOLET FITZ, THAT MEANS YOU!
BUT, MR. STICKLER, HE WAS MAKING FACES AT ME.
THEN IGNORE HIM.
I CAN'T.

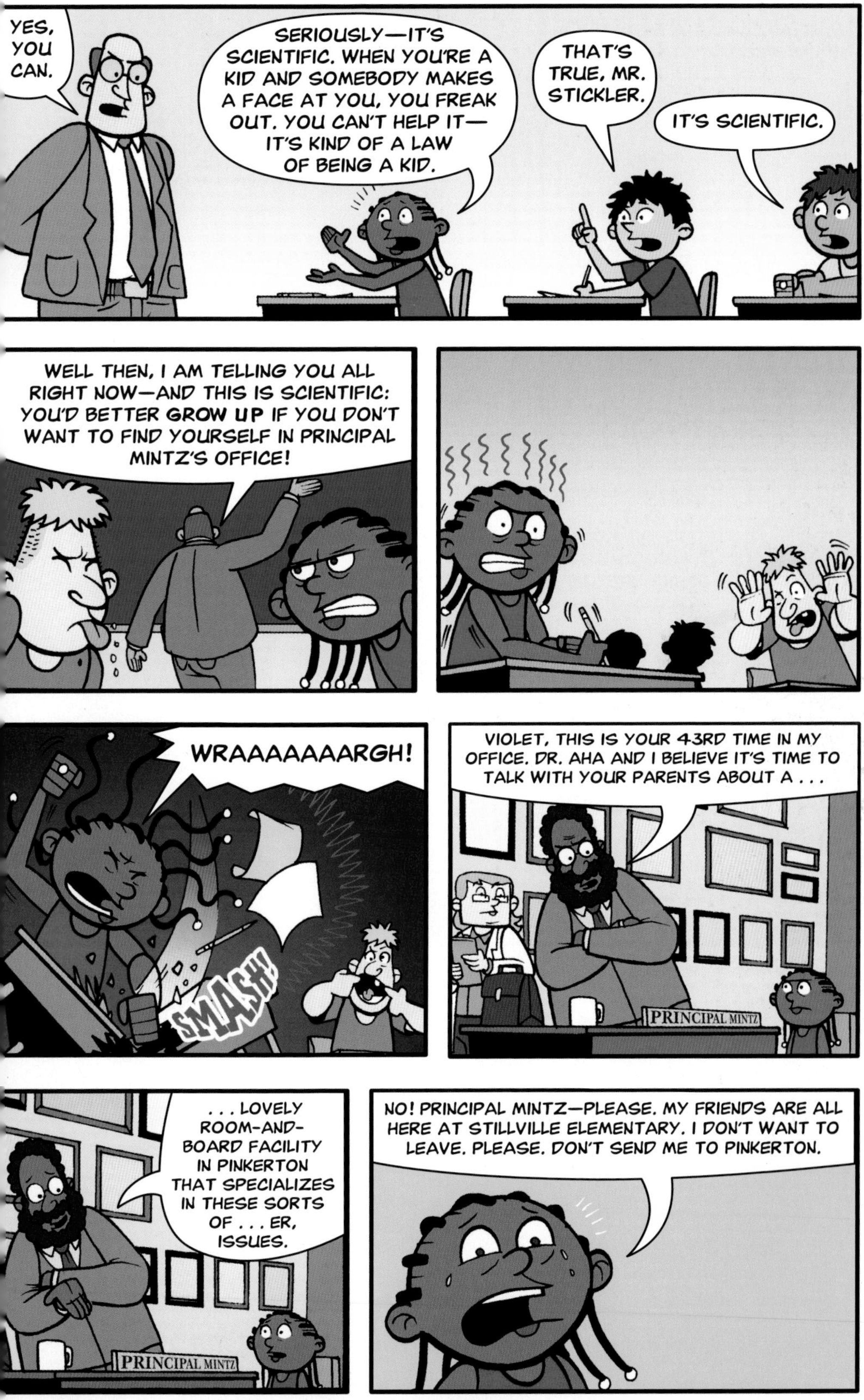
YES, YOU CAN.
SERIOUSLY—IT'S SCIENTIFIC. WHEN YOU'RE A KID AND SOMEBODY MAKES A FACE AT YOU, YOU FREAK OUT. YOU CAN'T HELP IT—IT'S KIND OF A LAW OF BEING A KID.
THAT'S TRUE, MR. STICKLER.
IT'S SCIENTIFIC.
WELL THEN, I AM TELLING YOU ALL RIGHT NOW—AND THIS IS SCIENTIFIC: YOU'D BETTER GROW UP IF YOU DON'T WANT TO FIND YOURSELF IN PRINCIPAL MINTZ'S OFFICE!
WRAAAAAAARGH!
SMASH!
VIOLET, THIS IS YOUR 43RD TIME IN MY OFFICE. DR. AHA AND I BELIEVE IT'S TIME TO TALK WITH YOUR PARENTS ABOUT A . . .
PRINCIPAL MINTZ
. . . LOVELY ROOM-AND-BOARD FACILITY IN PINKERTON THAT SPECIALIZES IN THESE SORTS OF . . . ER, ISSUES.
PRINCIPAL MINTZ
NO! PRINCIPAL MINTZ—PLEASE. MY FRIENDS ARE ALL HERE AT STILLVILLE ELEMENTARY. I DON'T WANT TO LEAVE. PLEASE. DON'T SEND ME TO PINKERTON.

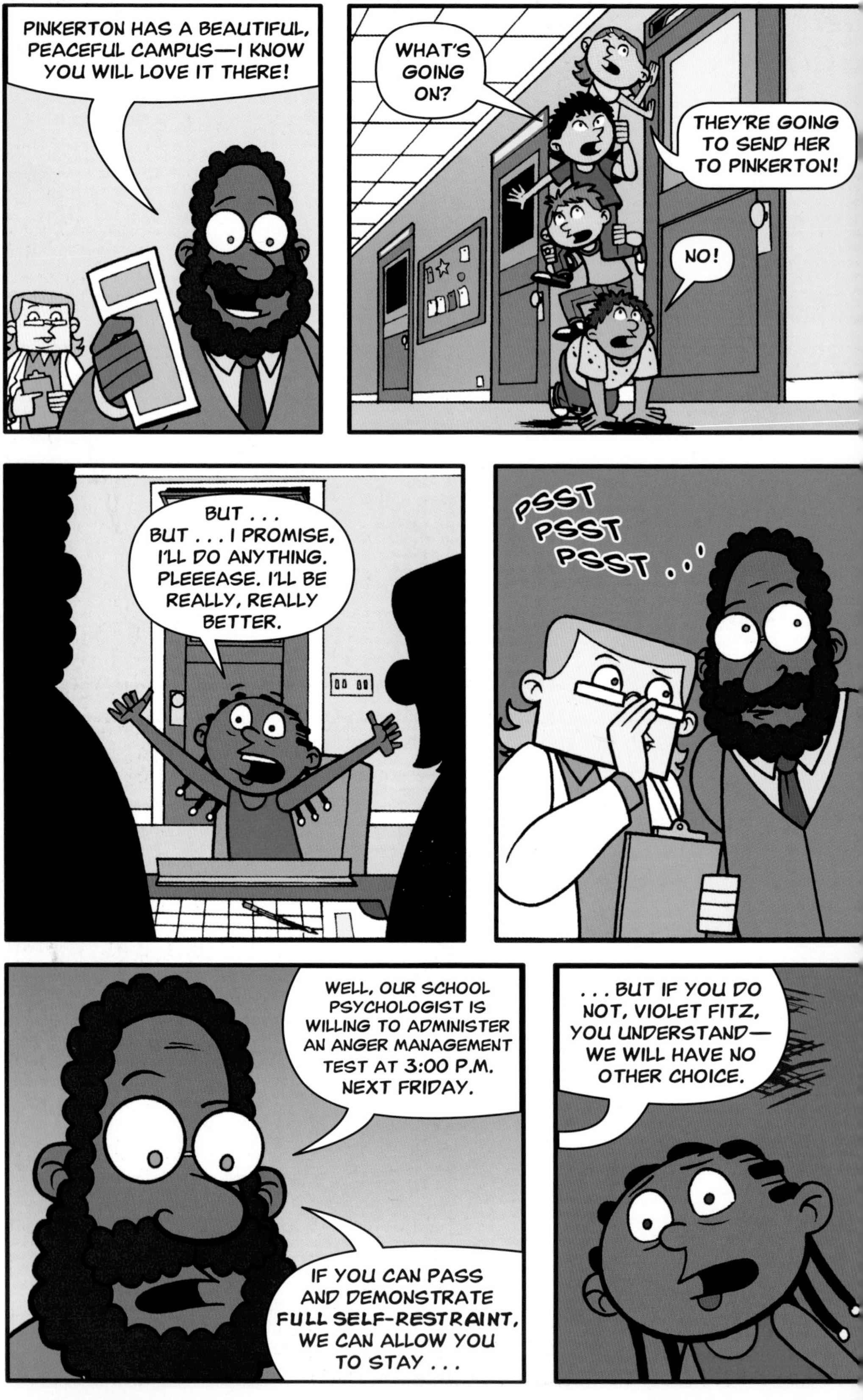
PINKERTON HAS A BEAUTIFUL, PEACEFUL CAMPUS—I KNOW YOU WILL LOVE IT THERE!
WHAT'S GOING ON?
THEY'RE GOING TO SEND HER TO PINKERTON!
NO!
BUT . . . BUT . . . I PROMISE, I'LL DO ANYTHING. PLEEEASE. I'LL BE REALLY, REALLY BETTER.
PSST PSST PSST . . .
WELL, OUR SCHOOL PSYCHOLOGIST IS WILLING TO ADMINISTER AN ANGER MANAGEMENT TEST AT 3:00 P.M. NEXT FRIDAY.
IF YOU CAN PASS AND DEMONSTRATE FULL SELF-RESTRAINT, WE CAN ALLOW YOU TO STAY . . .
. . . BUT IF YOU DO NOT, VIOLET FITZ, YOU UNDERSTAND—WE WILL HAVE NO OTHER CHOICE.

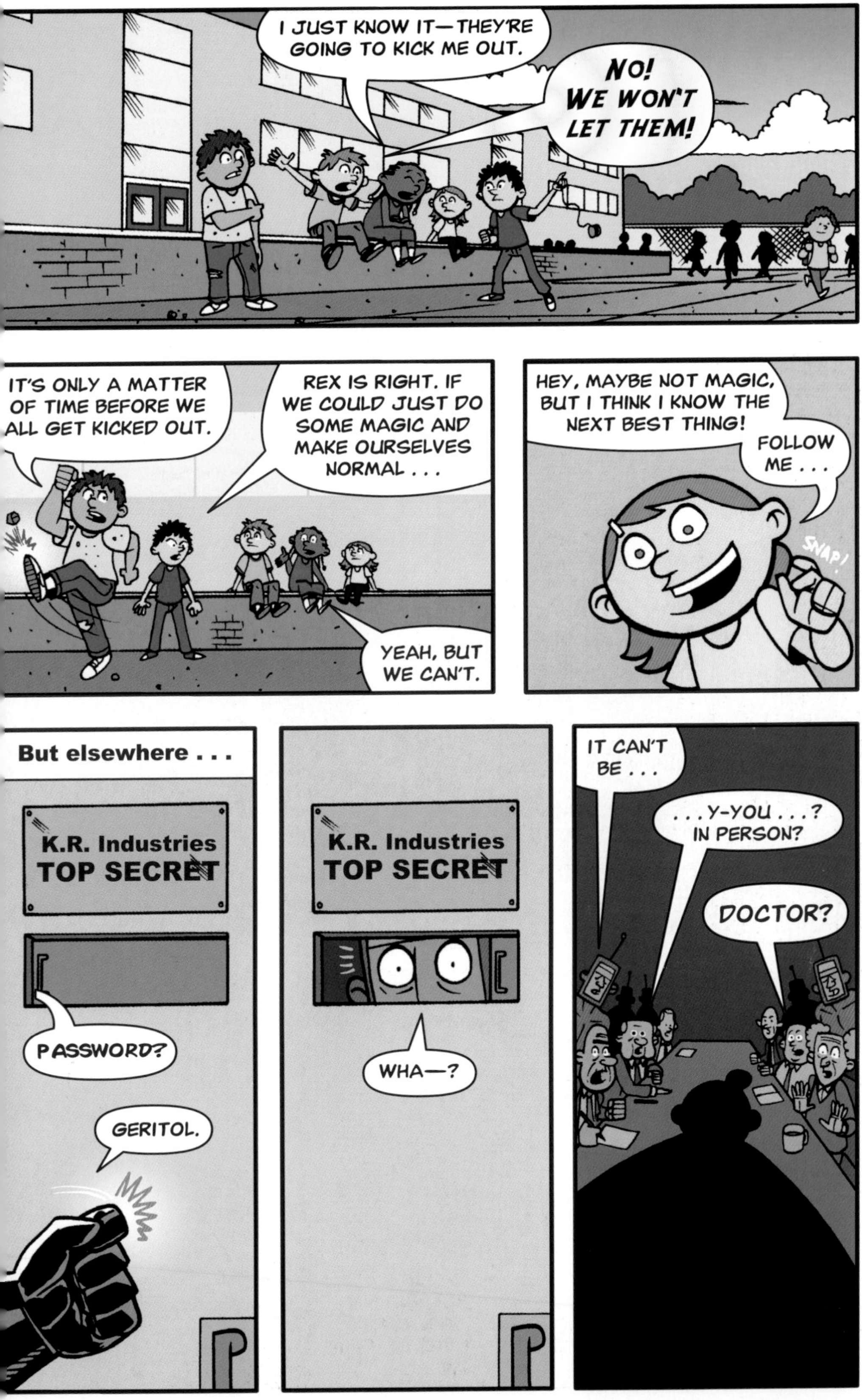
I JUST KNOW IT—THEY'RE GOING TO KICK ME OUT.
NO! WE WON'T LET THEM!
IT'S ONLY A MATTER OF TIME BEFORE WE ALL GET KICKED OUT.
REX IS RIGHT. IF WE COULD JUST DO SOME MAGIC AND MAKE OURSELVES NORMAL . . .
YEAH, BUT WE CAN'T.
HEY, MAYBE NOT MAGIC, BUT I THINK I KNOW THE NEXT BEST THING!
FOLLOW ME . . .
SNAP!
But elsewhere . . .
K.R. Industries TOP SECRET
PASSWORD?
GERITOL.
K.R. Industries TOP SECRET
WHA—?
IT CAN'T BE . . .
. . . Y-YOU . . .? IN PERSON?
DOCTOR?

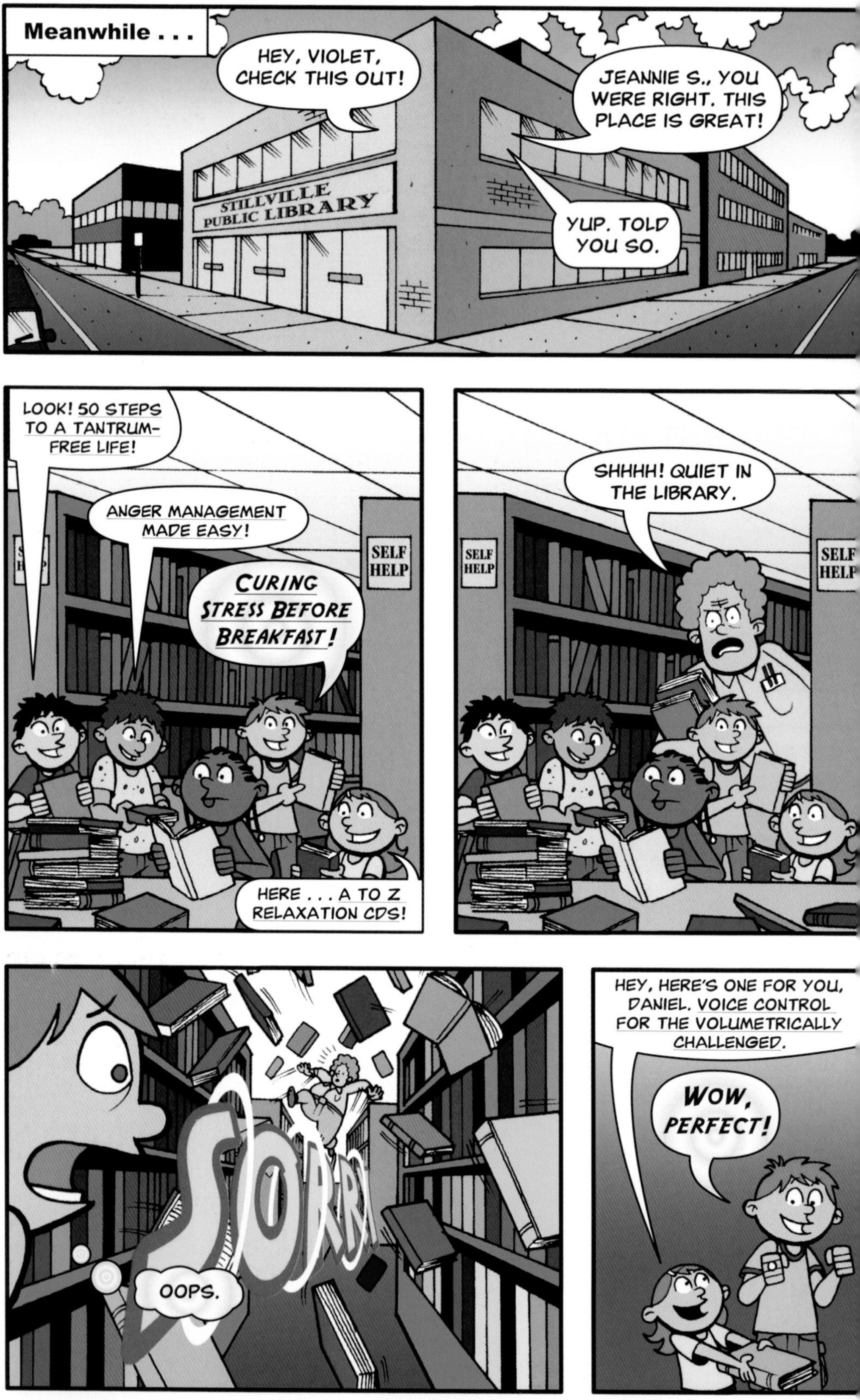
Meanwhile . . .
HEY, VIOLET, CHECK THIS OUT!
JEANNIE S., YOU WERE RIGHT. THIS PLACE IS GREAT!
STILLVILLE PUBLIC LIBRARY
YUP. TOLD YOU SO.
LOOK! 50 STEPS TO A TANTRUM-FREE LIFE!
ANGER MANAGEMENT MADE EASY!
SELF HELP
CURING STRESS BEFORE BREAKFAST!
HERE . . . A TO Z RELAXATION CDS!
SHHHH! QUIET IN THE LIBRARY.
SELF HELP
SELF HELP
SORRY
OOPS.
HEY, HERE'S ONE FOR YOU, DANIEL. VOICE CONTROL FOR THE VOLUMETRICALLY CHALLENGED.
WOW, PERFECT!

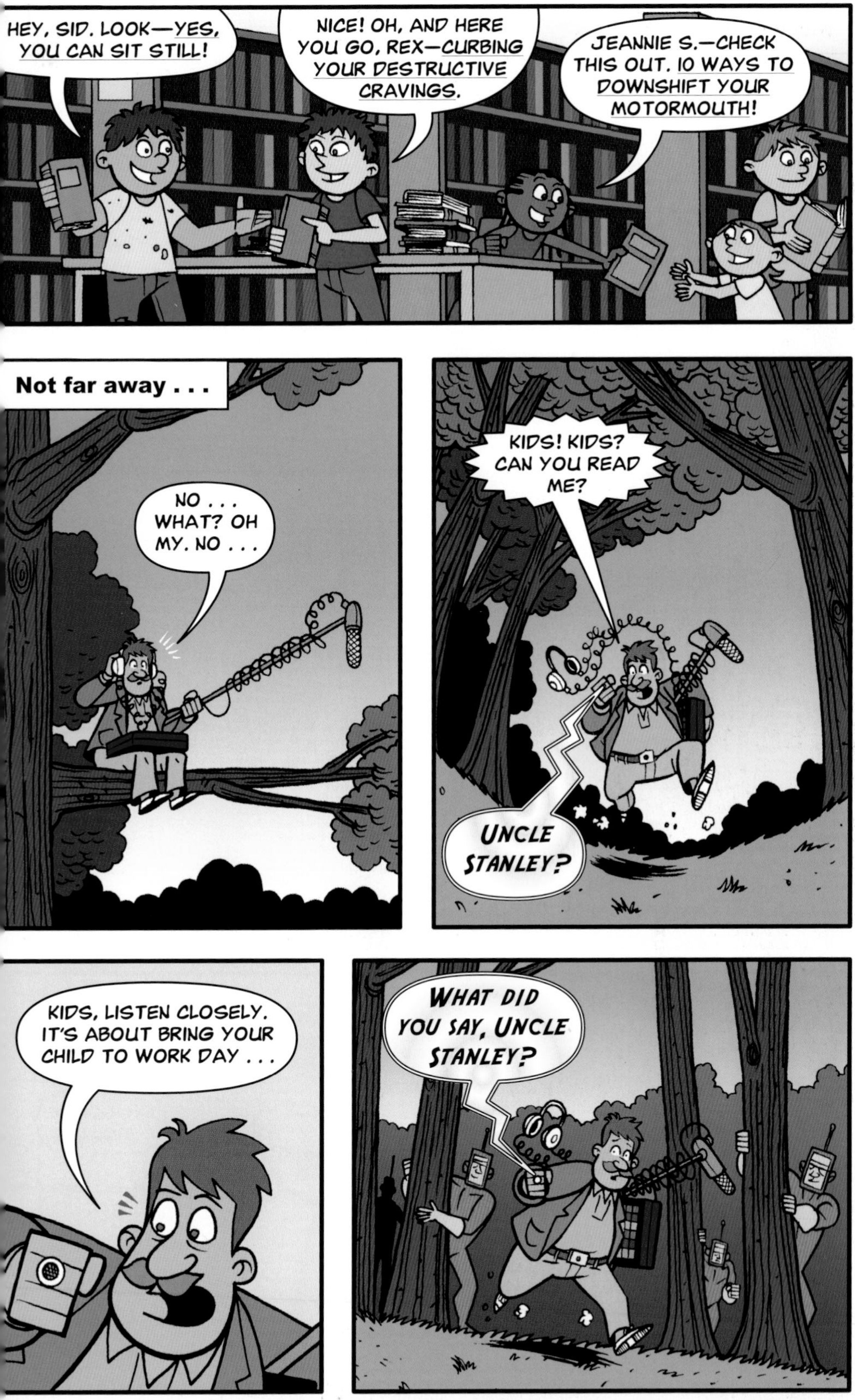
HEY, SID. LOOK—YES, YOU CAN SIT STILL!
NICE! OH, AND HERE YOU GO, REX—CURBING YOUR DESTRUCTIVE CRAVINGS.
JEANNIE S.—CHECK THIS OUT. 10 WAYS TO DOWNSHIFT YOUR MOTORMOUTH!
Not far away . . .
NO . . . WHAT? OH MY. NO . . .
KIDS! KIDS? CAN YOU READ ME?
UNCLE STANLEY?
KIDS, LISTEN CLOSELY. IT'S ABOUT BRING YOUR CHILD TO WORK DAY . . .
WHAT DID YOU SAY, UNCLE STANLEY?

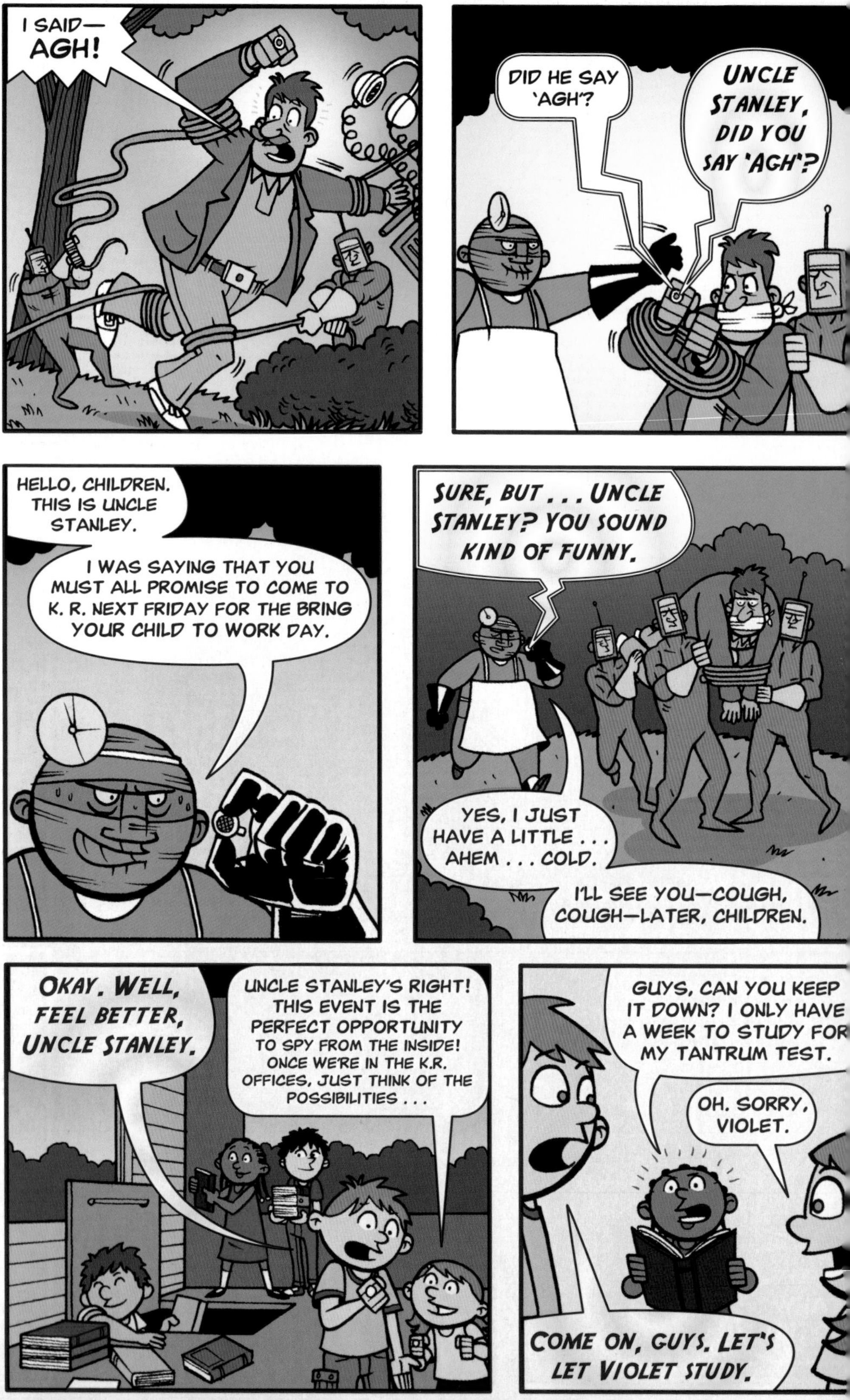
I SAID— AGH!
DID HE SAY 'AGH'?
UNCLE STANLEY, DID YOU SAY 'AGH'?
HELLO, CHILDREN. THIS IS UNCLE STANLEY.
I WAS SAYING THAT YOU MUST ALL PROMISE TO COME TO K. R. NEXT FRIDAY FOR THE BRING YOUR CHILD TO WORK DAY.
SURE, BUT . . . UNCLE STANLEY? YOU SOUND KIND OF FUNNY.
YES, I JUST HAVE A LITTLE . . . AHEM . . . COLD.
I'LL SEE YOU—COUGH, COUGH—LATER, CHILDREN.
OKAY. WELL, FEEL BETTER, UNCLE STANLEY.
UNCLE STANLEY'S RIGHT! THIS EVENT IS THE PERFECT OPPORTUNITY TO SPY FROM THE INSIDE! ONCE WE'RE IN THE K.R. OFFICES, JUST THINK OF THE POSSIBILITIES . . .
GUYS, CAN YOU KEEP IT DOWN? I ONLY HAVE A WEEK TO STUDY FOR MY TANTRUM TEST.
OH. SORRY, VIOLET.
COME ON, GUYS. LET'S LET VIOLET STUDY.

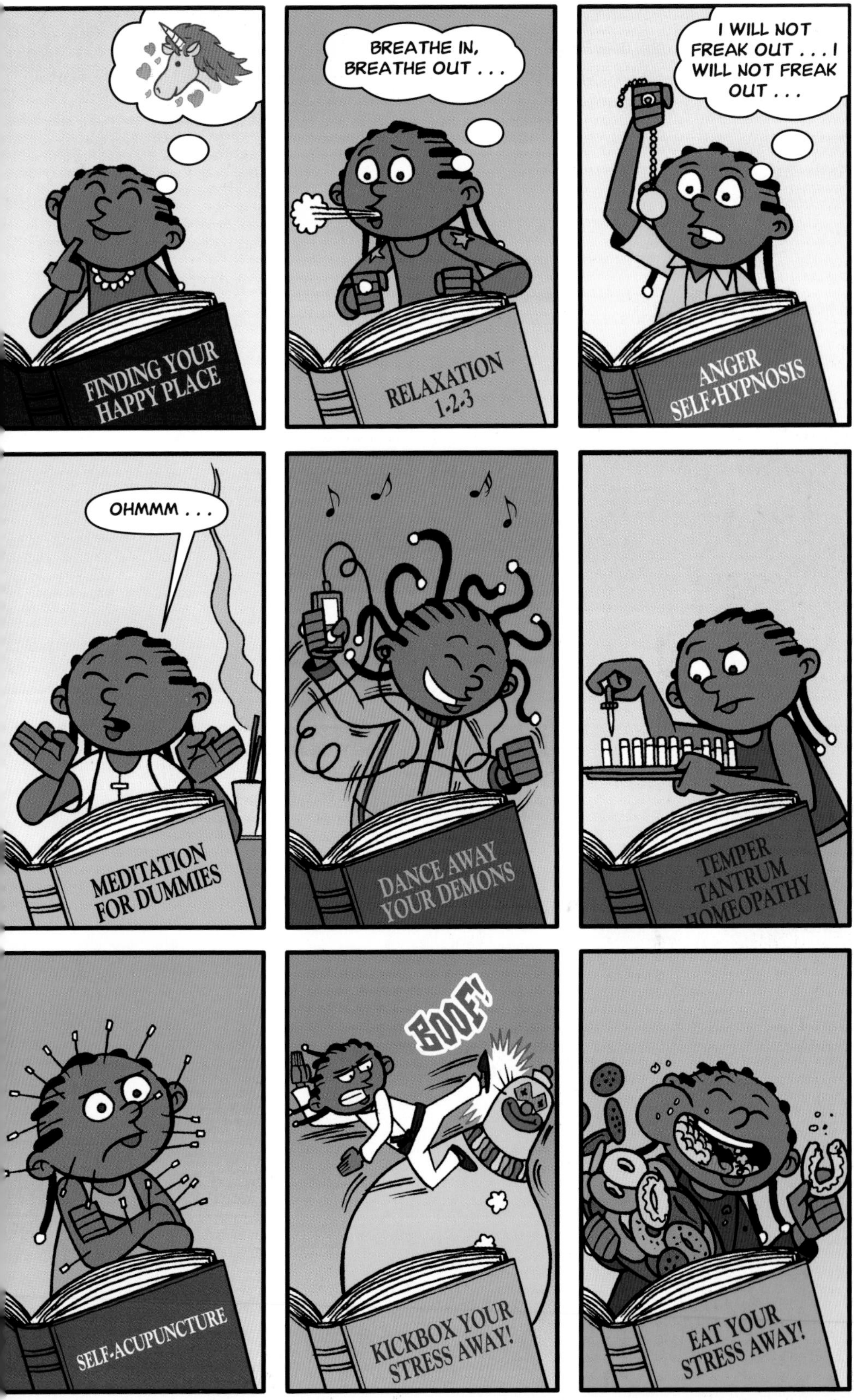
FINDING YOUR HAPPY PLACE
BREATHE IN, BREATHE OUT . . .
RELAXATION 1-2-3
I WILL NOT FREAK OUT . . . I WILL NOT FREAK OUT . . .
ANGER SELF-HYPNOSIS
OHMMM . . .
MEDITATION FOR DUMMIES
DANCE AWAY YOUR DEMONS
TEMPER TANTRUM HOMEOPATHY
SELF-ACUPUNCTURE
BOOF!
KICKBOX YOUR STRESS AWAY!
EAT YOUR STRESS AWAY!

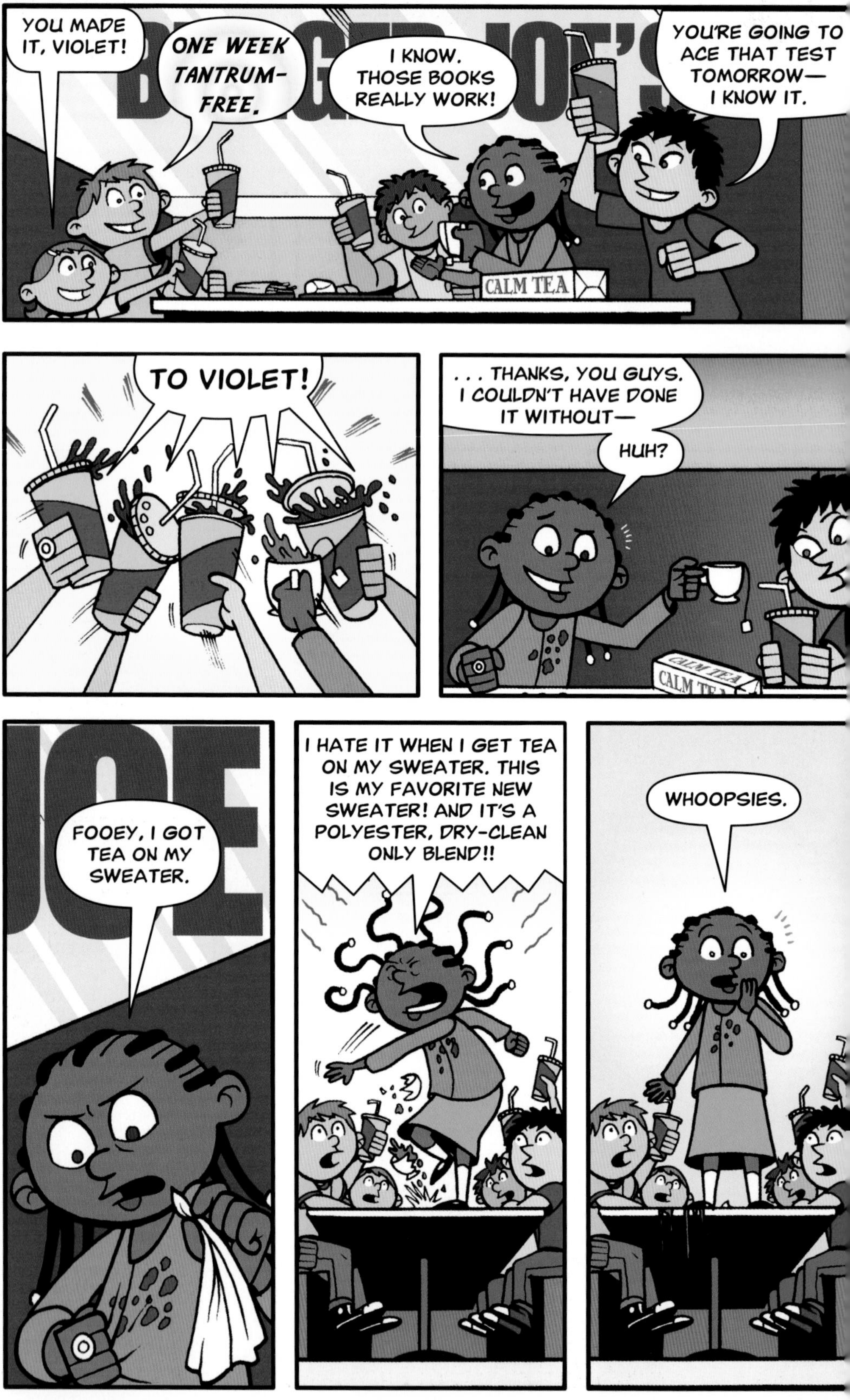
YOU MADE IT, VIOLET!
ONE WEEK TANTRUM-FREE.
I KNOW. THOSE BOOKS REALLY WORK!
YOU'RE GOING TO ACE THAT TEST TOMORROW— I KNOW IT.
CALM TEA
TO VIOLET!
. . . THANKS, YOU GUYS. I COULDN'T HAVE DONE IT WITHOUT—
HUH?
CALM TEA
FOOEY, I GOT TEA ON MY SWEATER.
I HATE IT WHEN I GET TEA ON MY SWEATER. THIS IS MY FAVORITE NEW SWEATER! AND IT'S A POLYESTER, DRY-CLEAN ONLY BLEND!!
WHOOPSIES.

IT'S OKAY. NO BIGGY.

JUST A LITTLE SLIP. DOESN'T MEAN ANYTHING.

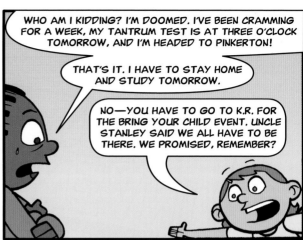

WHO AM I KIDDING? I'M DOOMED. I'VE BEEN CRAMMING FOR A WEEK, MY TANTRUM TEST IS AT THREE O'CLOCK TOMORROW, AND I'M HEADED TO PINKERTON!

THAT'S IT. I HAVE TO STAY HOME AND STUDY TOMORROW.

NO—YOU HAVE TO GO TO K.R. FOR THE BRING YOUR CHILD EVENT. UNCLE STANLEY SAID WE ALL HAVE TO BE THERE. WE PROMISED, REMEMBER?

I CAN'T.

YES, YOU CAN. JUST BRING YOUR NOTES ALONG TO THE FIELD TRIP. WE'LL BLOCK FOR YOU AND MAKE SURE YOU CAN STUDY.

REALLY? THINK THAT'LL WORK?

SURE THING!

YOU BET!

Next morning . . .

WELCOME, CHILDREN, TO THE WORLD-WIDE HEADQUARTERS OF K. R. INDUSTRIES FOR OUR FIRST EVER BRING YOUR CHILD TO WORK DAY.

K. R. INDUSTRIES

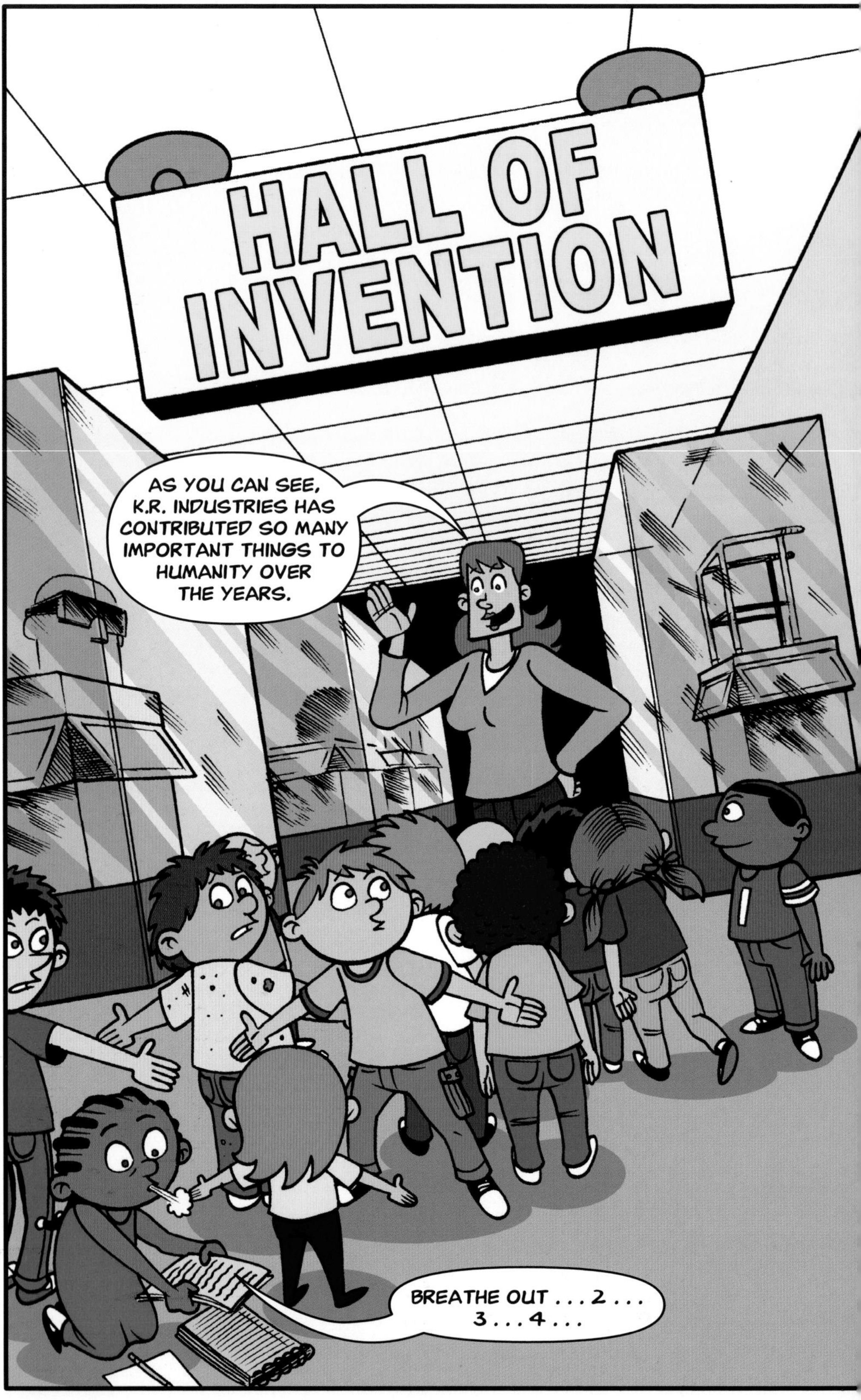
HALL OF INVENTION
AS YOU CAN SEE, K.R. INDUSTRIES HAS CONTRIBUTED SO MANY IMPORTANT THINGS TO HUMANITY OVER THE YEARS.
BREATHE OUT . . . 2 . . . 3 . . . 4 . . .

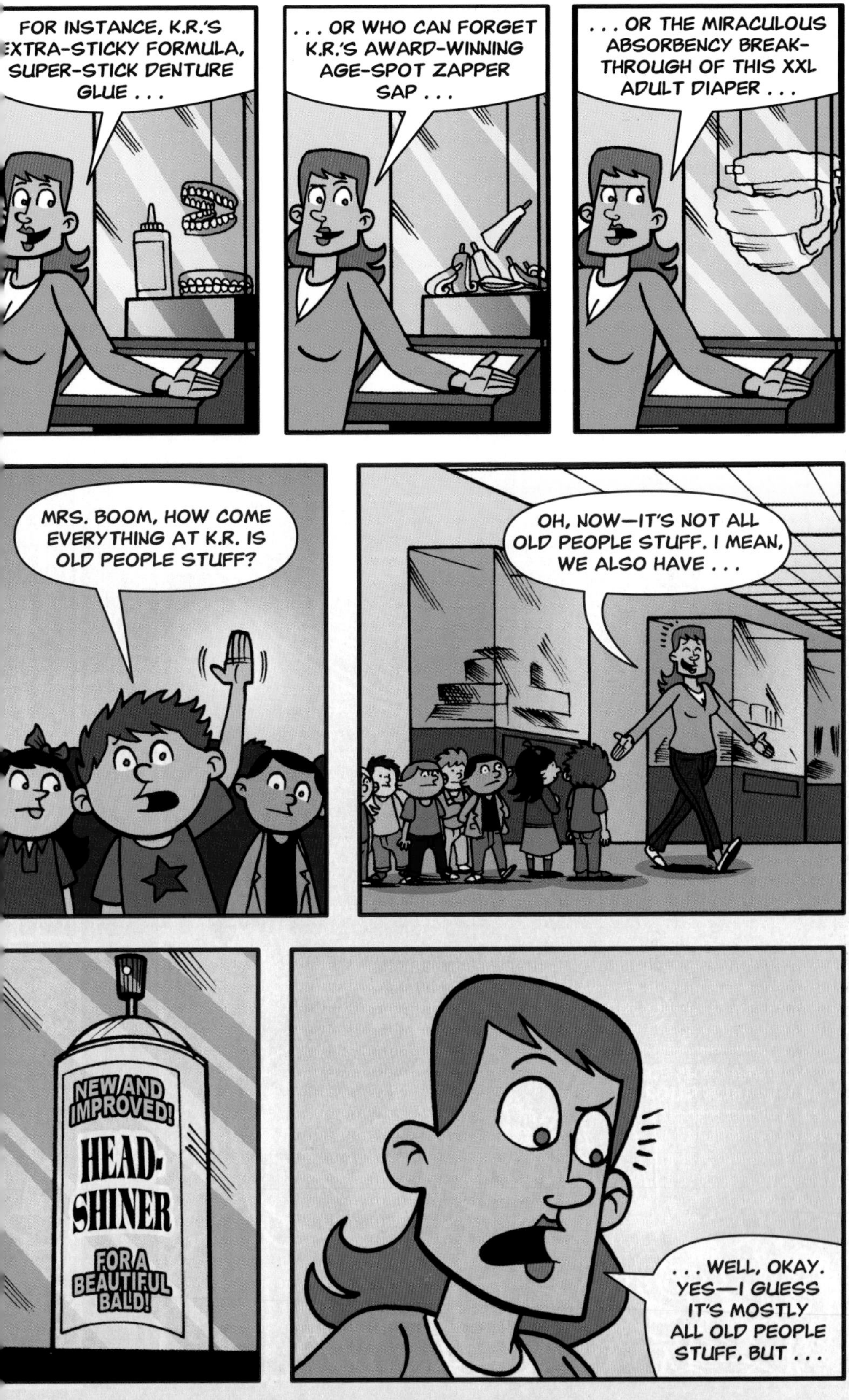
FOR INSTANCE, K.R.'S EXTRA-STICKY FORMULA, SUPER-STICK DENTURE GLUE . . .
. . . OR WHO CAN FORGET K.R.'S AWARD-WINNING AGE-SPOT ZAPPER SAP . . .
. . . OR THE MIRACULOUS ABSORBENCY BREAK-THROUGH OF THIS XXL ADULT DIAPER . . .
MRS. BOOM, HOW COME EVERYTHING AT K.R. IS OLD PEOPLE STUFF?
OH, NOW—IT'S NOT ALL OLD PEOPLE STUFF. I MEAN, WE ALSO HAVE . . .
NEW AND IMPROVED!
HEAD-SHINER
FOR A BEAUTIFUL BALD!
. . . WELL, OKAY. YES—I GUESS IT'S MOSTLY ALL OLD PEOPLE STUFF, BUT . . .

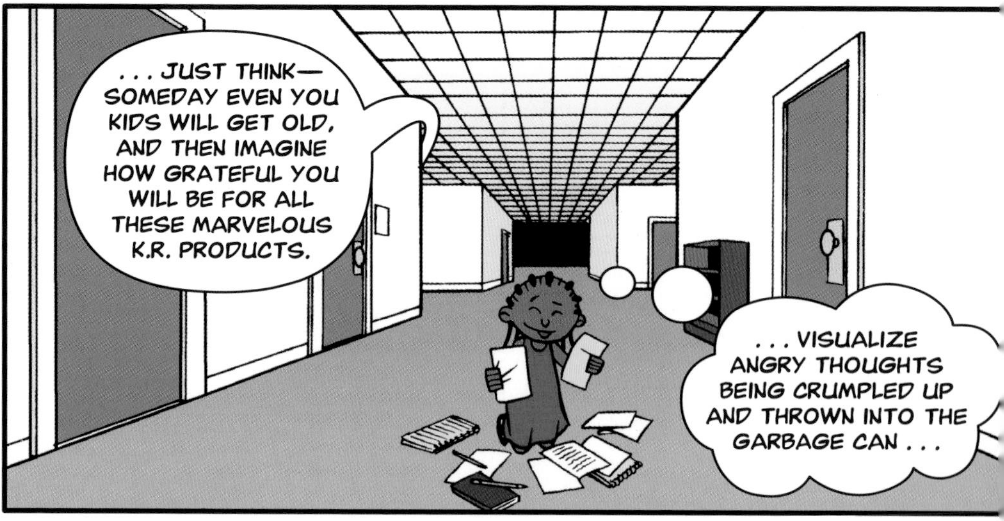
. . . JUST THINK—SOMEDAY EVEN YOU KIDS WILL GET OLD, AND THEN IMAGINE HOW GRATEFUL YOU WILL BE FOR ALL THESE MARVELOUS K.R. PRODUCTS.
. . . VISUALIZE ANGRY THOUGHTS BEING CRUMPLED UP AND THROWN INTO THE GARBAGE CAN . . .

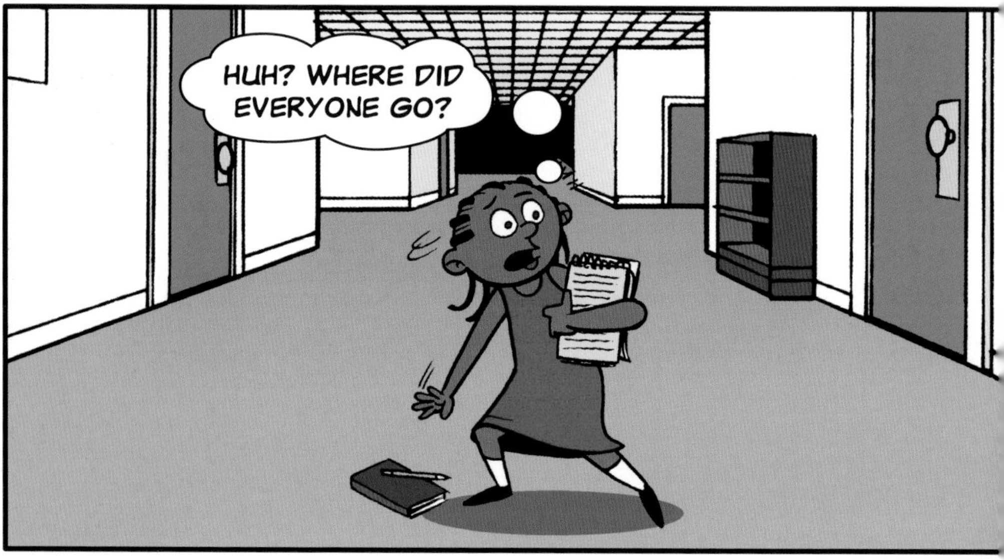
HUH? WHERE DID EVERYONE GO?

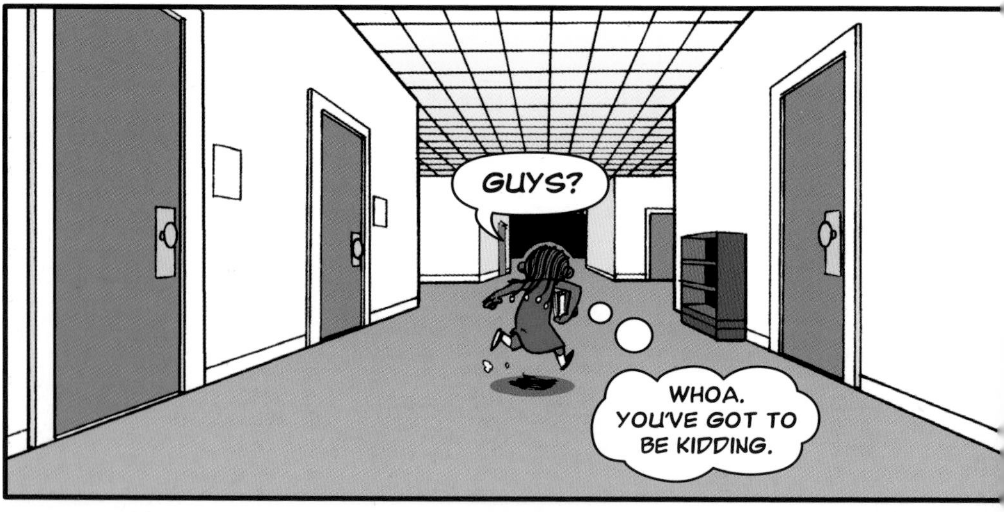
GUYS?
WHOA. YOU'VE GOT TO BE KIDDING.

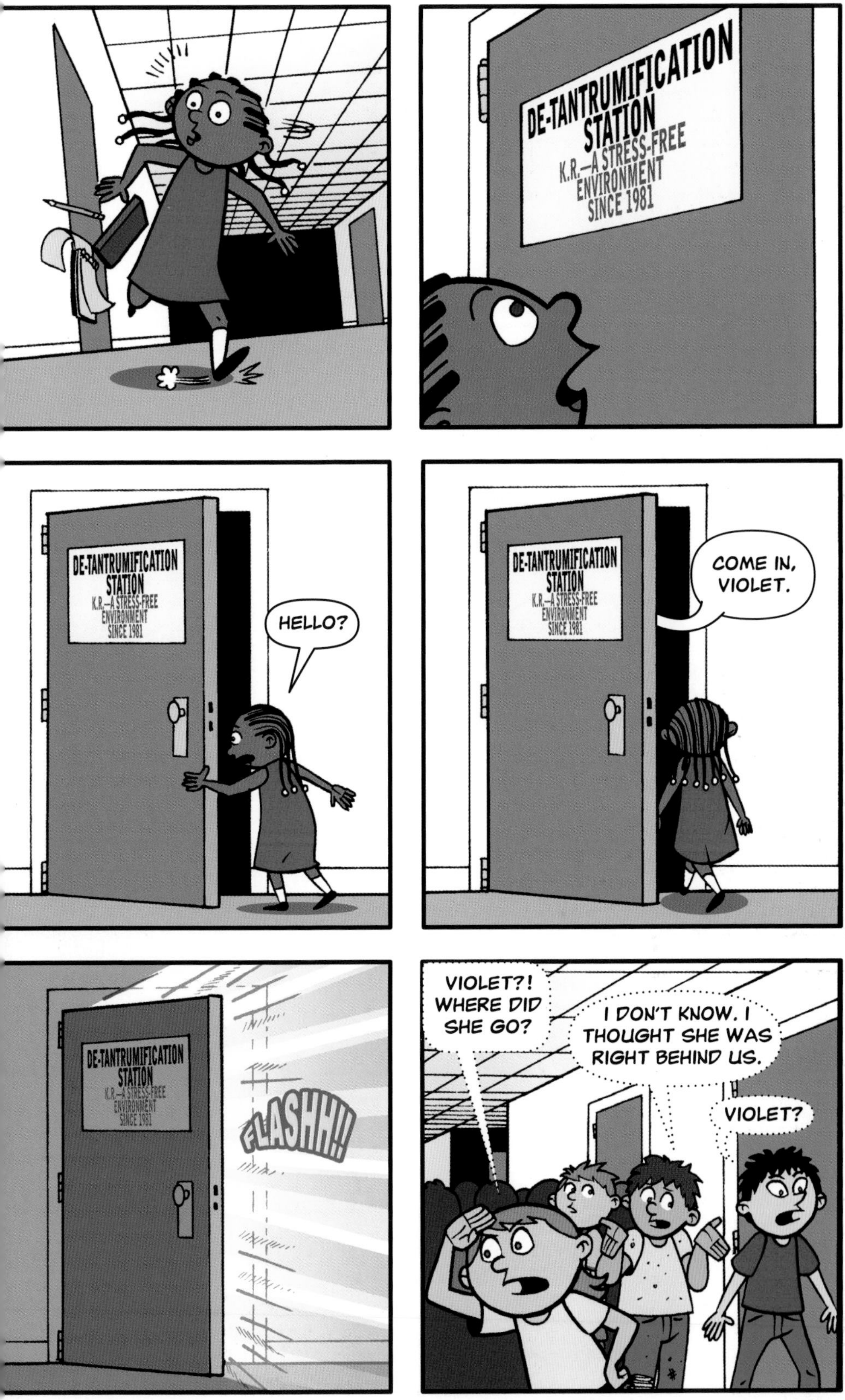

DE-TANTRUMIFICATION STATION
K.R.—A STRESS-FREE ENVIRONMENT SINCE 1981
HELLO?
COME IN, VIOLET.
FLASHH!!
VIOLET?! WHERE DID SHE GO?
I DON'T KNOW. I THOUGHT SHE WAS RIGHT BEHIND US.
VIOLET?

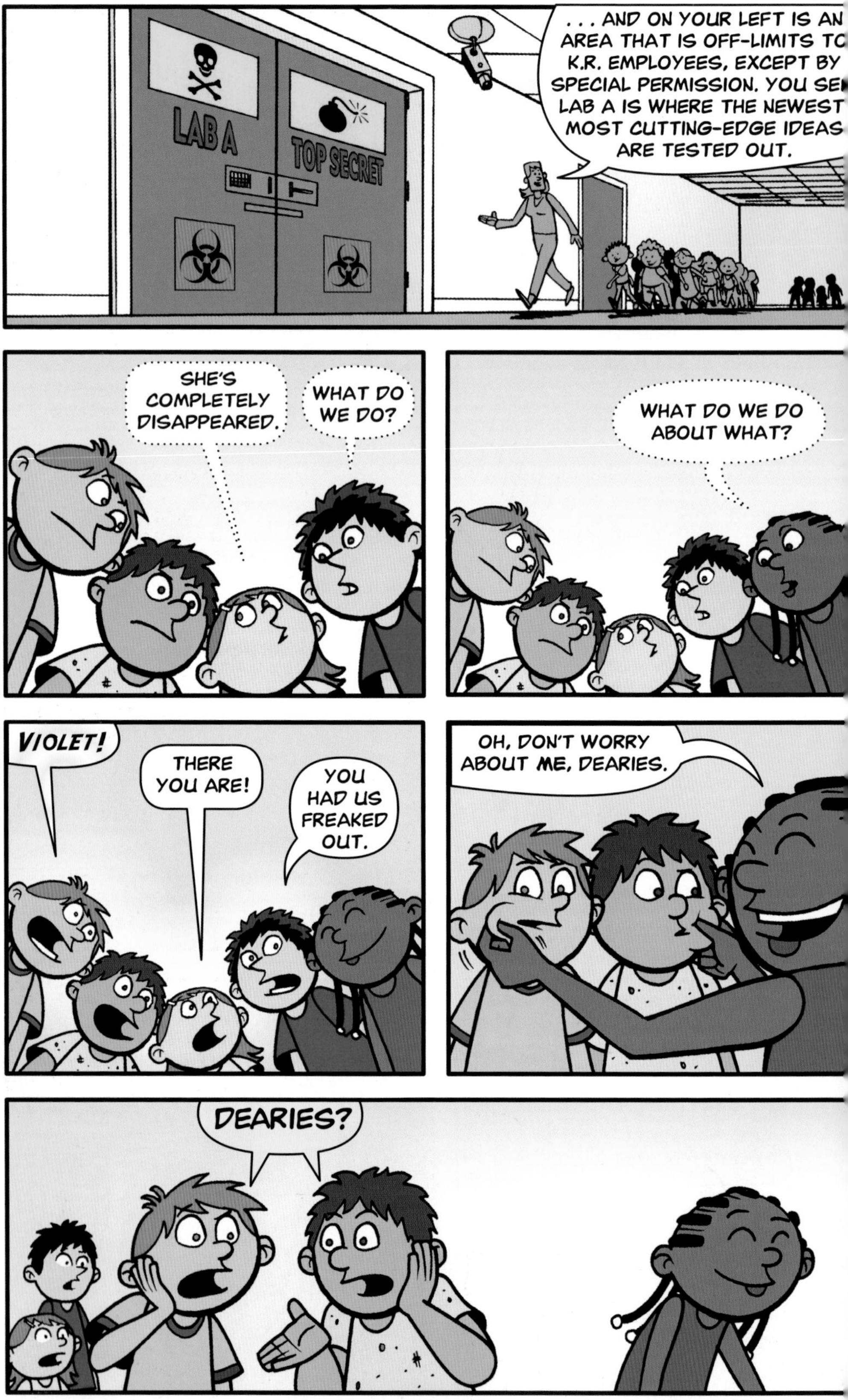
. . . AND ON YOUR LEFT IS AN AREA THAT IS OFF-LIMITS TO K.R. EMPLOYEES, EXCEPT BY SPECIAL PERMISSION. YOU SEE LAB A IS WHERE THE NEWEST MOST CUTTING-EDGE IDEAS ARE TESTED OUT.
LAB A
TOP SECRET
SHE'S COMPLETELY DISAPPEARED.
WHAT DO WE DO?
WHAT DO WE DO ABOUT WHAT?
VIOLET!
THERE YOU ARE!
YOU HAD US FREAKED OUT.
OH, DON'T WORRY ABOUT ME, DEARIES.
DEARIES?

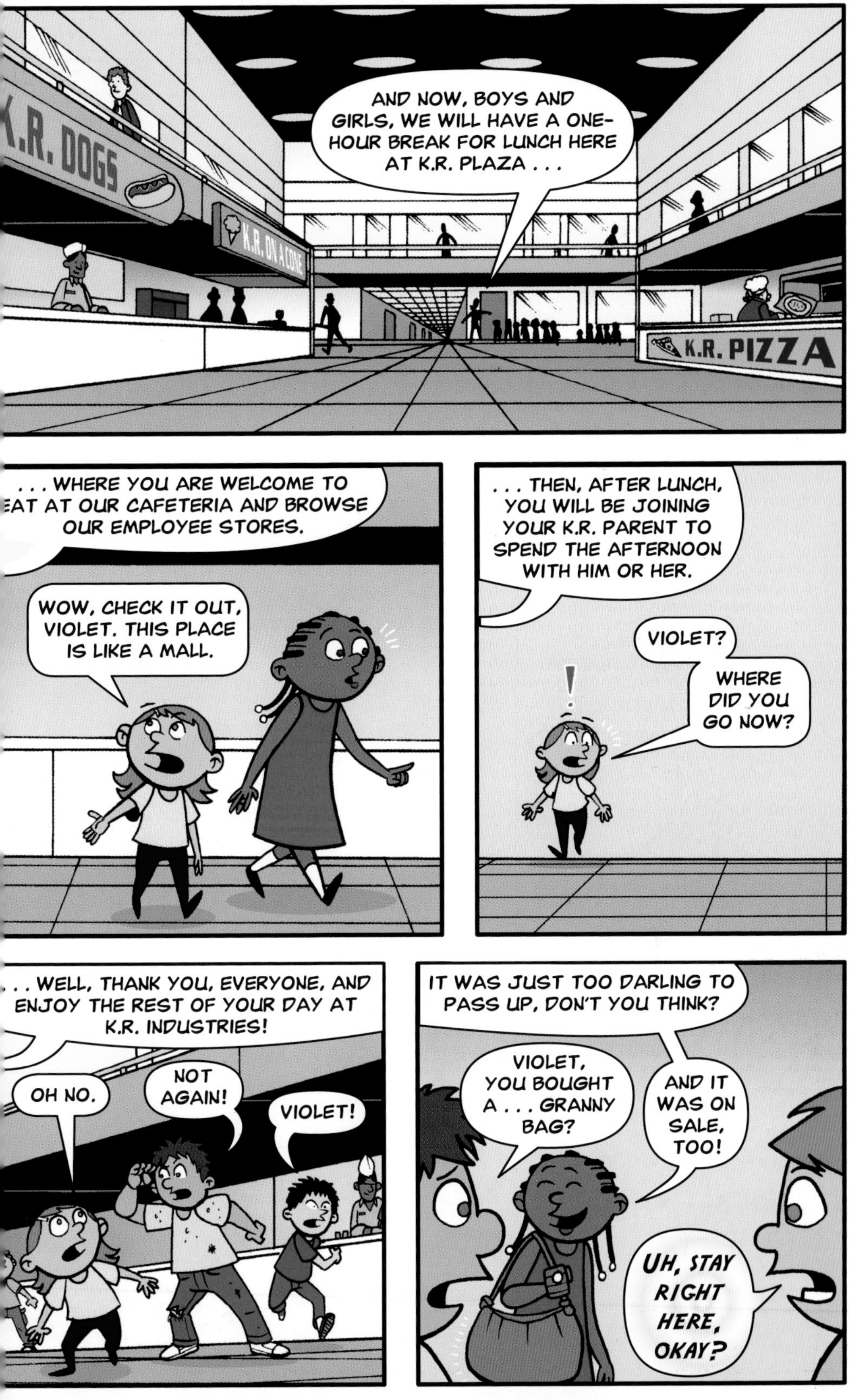
K.R. DOGS
K.R. ON A CONE
AND NOW, BOYS AND GIRLS, WE WILL HAVE A ONE-HOUR BREAK FOR LUNCH HERE AT K.R. PLAZA . . .
K.R. PIZZA
. . . WHERE YOU ARE WELCOME TO EAT AT OUR CAFETERIA AND BROWSE OUR EMPLOYEE STORES.
WOW, CHECK IT OUT, VIOLET. THIS PLACE IS LIKE A MALL.
. . . THEN, AFTER LUNCH, YOU WILL BE JOINING YOUR K.R. PARENT TO SPEND THE AFTERNOON WITH HIM OR HER.
VIOLET?
!
WHERE DID YOU GO NOW?
. . . WELL, THANK YOU, EVERYONE, AND ENJOY THE REST OF YOUR DAY AT K.R. INDUSTRIES!
OH NO.
NOT AGAIN!
VIOLET!
IT WAS JUST TOO DARLING TO PASS UP, DON'T YOU THINK?
VIOLET, YOU BOUGHT A . . . GRANNY BAG?
AND IT WAS ON SALE, TOO!
UH, STAY RIGHT HERE, OKAY?

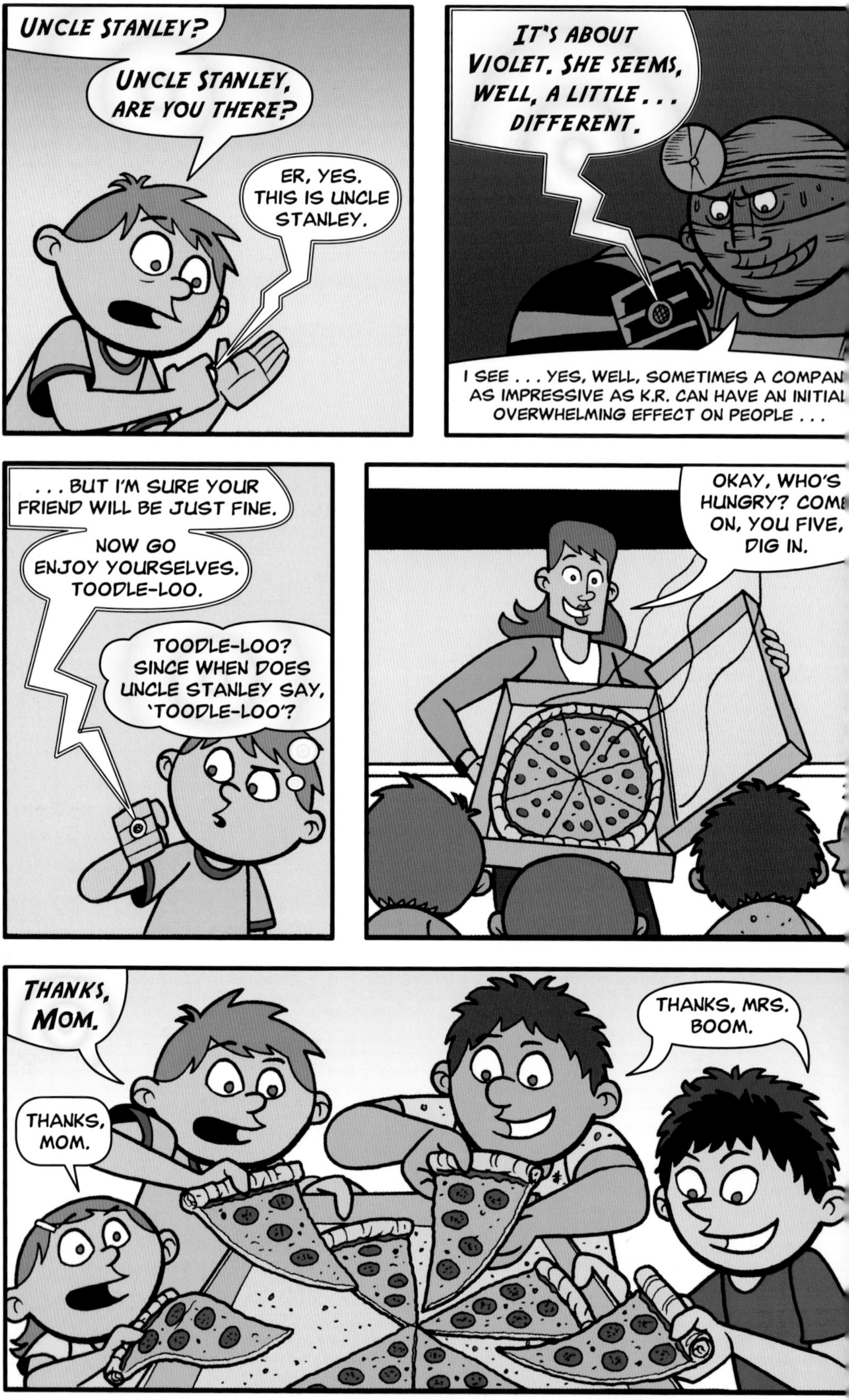
UNCLE STANLEY?
UNCLE STANLEY, ARE YOU THERE?
ER, YES. THIS IS UNCLE STANLEY.
IT'S ABOUT VIOLET. SHE SEEMS, WELL, A LITTLE . . . DIFFERENT.
I SEE . . . YES, WELL, SOMETIMES A COMPAN AS IMPRESSIVE AS K.R. CAN HAVE AN INITIAL OVERWHELMING EFFECT ON PEOPLE . . .
. . . BUT I'M SURE YOUR FRIEND WILL BE JUST FINE.
NOW GO ENJOY YOURSELVES. TOODLE-LOO.
TOODLE-LOO? SINCE WHEN DOES UNCLE STANLEY SAY, 'TOODLE-LOO'?
OKAY, WHO'S HUNGRY? COM ON, YOU FIVE, DIG IN.
THANKS, MOM.
THANKS, MOM.
THANKS, MRS. BOOM.

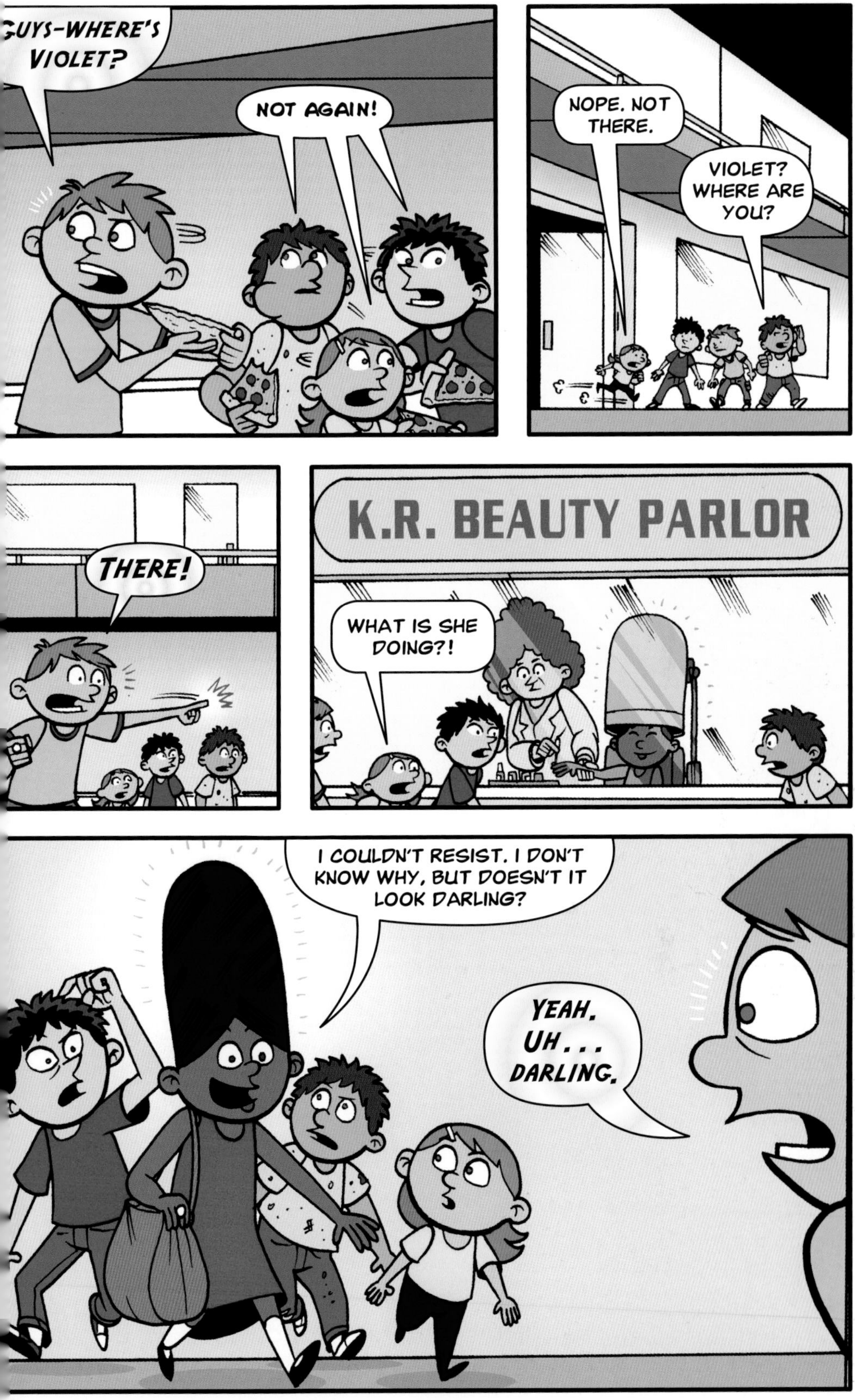
GUYS–WHERE'S VIOLET?
NOT AGAIN!
NOPE. NOT THERE.
VIOLET? WHERE ARE YOU?
THERE!
K.R. BEAUTY PARLOR
WHAT IS SHE DOING?!
I COULDN'T RESIST. I DON'T KNOW WHY, BUT DOESN'T IT LOOK DARLING?
YEAH. UH . . . DARLING.

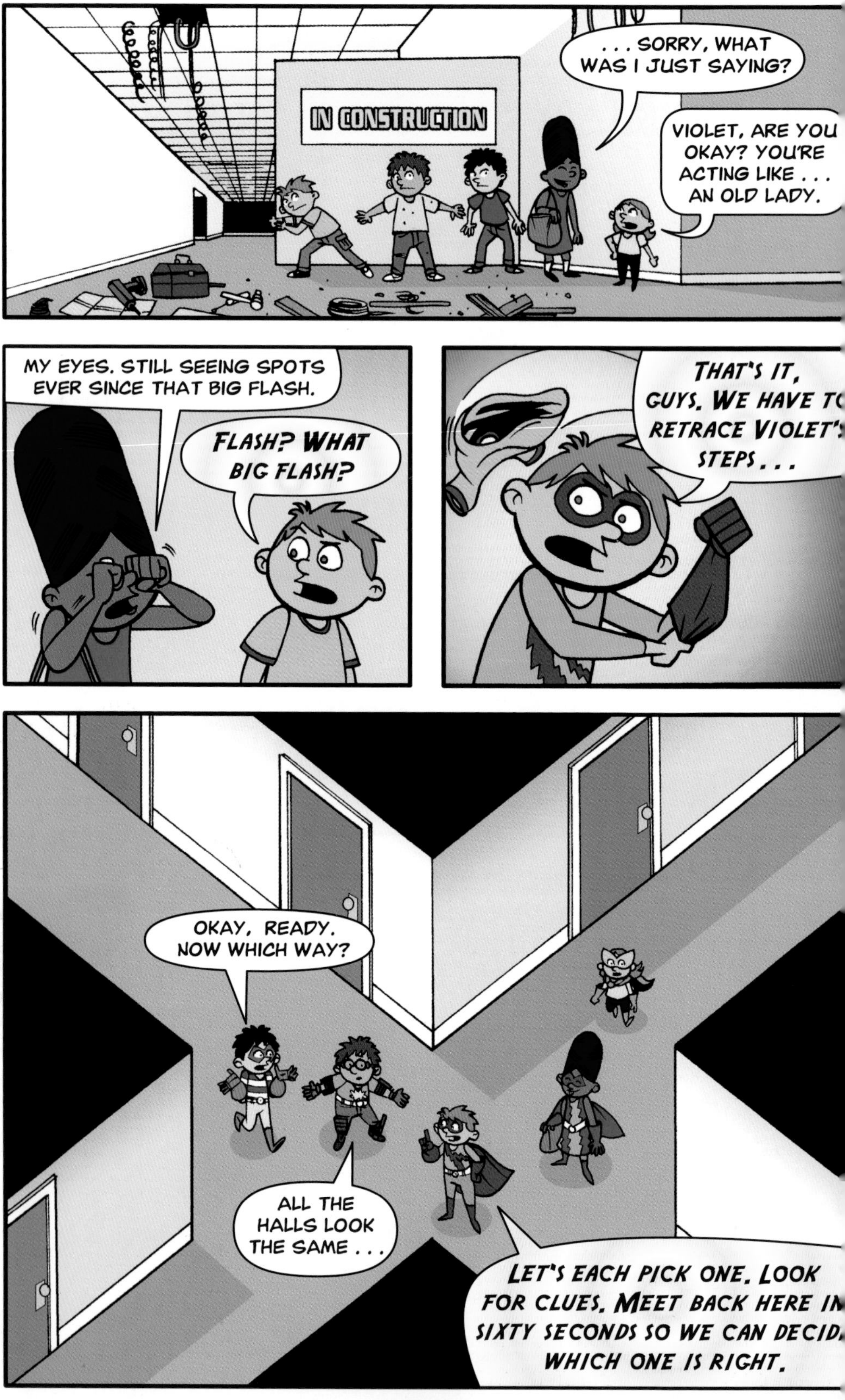
IN CONSTRUCTION
. . . SORRY, WHAT WAS I JUST SAYING?
VIOLET, ARE YOU OKAY? YOU'RE ACTING LIKE . . . AN OLD LADY.
MY EYES. STILL SEEING SPOTS EVER SINCE THAT BIG FLASH.
FLASH? WHAT BIG FLASH?
THAT'S IT, GUYS. WE HAVE T
RETRACE VIOLET'
STEPS . . .
OKAY, READY. NOW WHICH WAY?
ALL THE HALLS LOOK THE SAME . . .
LET'S EACH PICK ONE. LOOK FOR CLUES. MEET BACK HERE I
SIXTY SECONDS SO WE CAN DECID
WHICH ONE IS RIGHT.

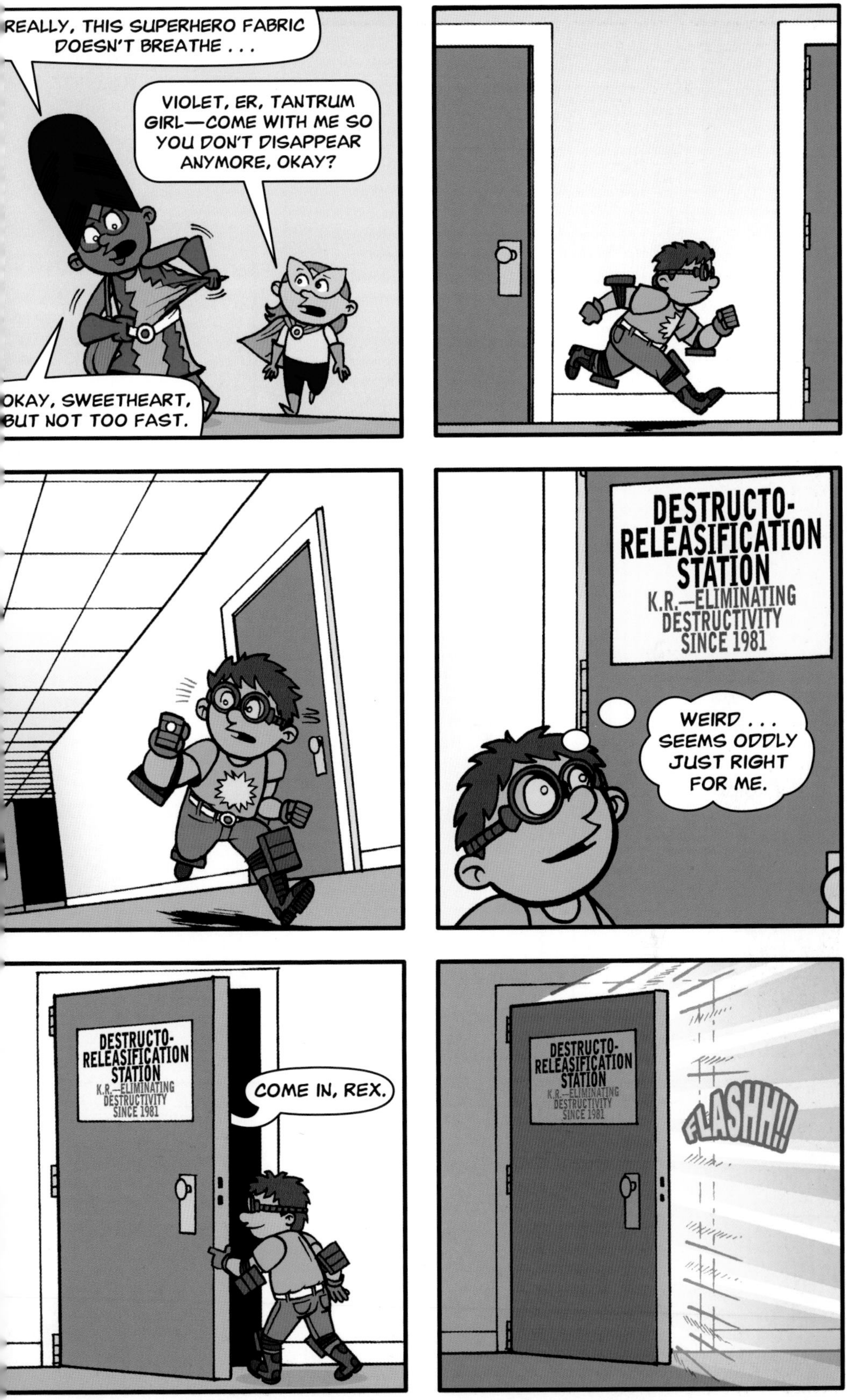
REALLY, THIS SUPERHERO FABRIC DOESN'T BREATHE . . .
VIOLET, ER, TANTRUM GIRL—COME WITH ME SO YOU DON'T DISAPPEAR ANYMORE, OKAY?
OKAY, SWEETHEART, BUT NOT TOO FAST.
DESTRUCTO-RELEASIFICATION STATION
K.R.—ELIMINATING DESTRUCTIVITY SINCE 1981
WEIRD . . . SEEMS ODDLY JUST RIGHT FOR ME.
DESTRUCTO-RELEASIFICATION STATION
K.R.—ELIMINATING DESTRUCTIVITY SINCE 1981
COME IN, REX.
DESTRUCTO-RELEASIFICATION STATION
K.R.—ELIMINATING DESTRUCTIVITY SINCE 1981
FLASHH!!

DE-FIDGETIFICATION WALL
K.R.—KEEPING EMPLOYEES SITTING STILL SINCE 1981
WELCOME, SID
HMMM . . . IMAGINE THAT! SERIOUSLY . . .

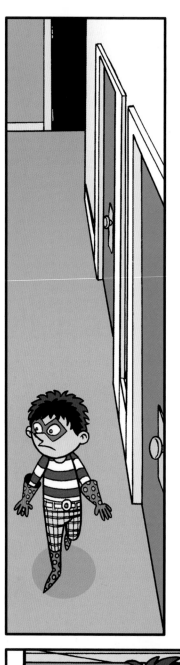

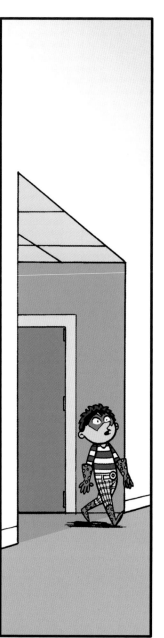

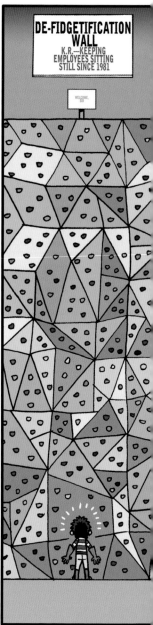

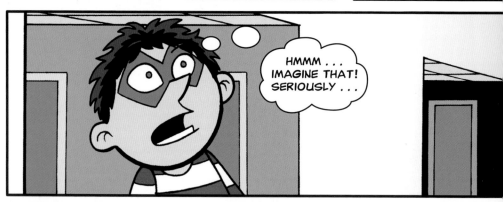

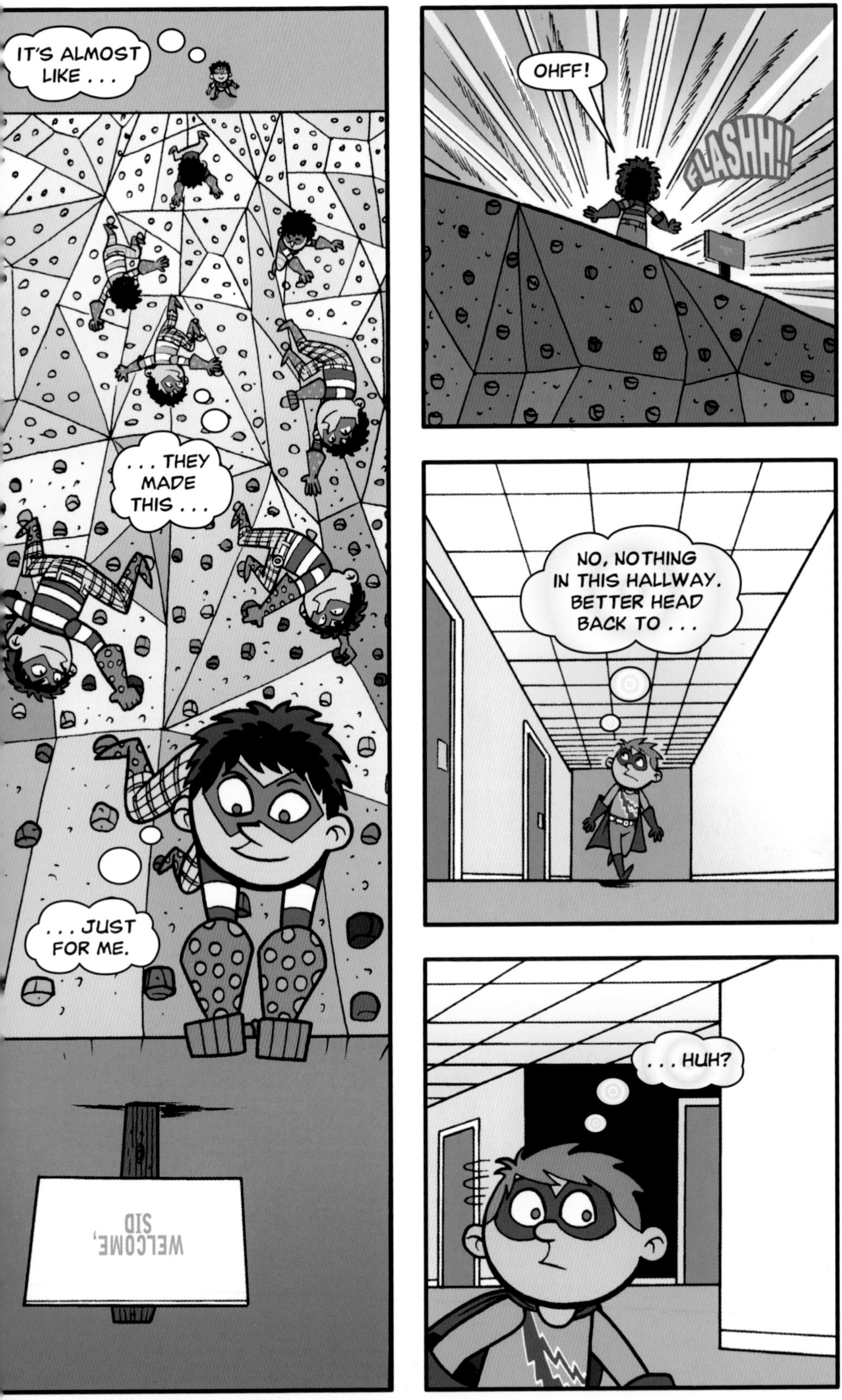
IT'S ALMOST LIKE . . .
. . . THEY MADE THIS . . .
. . . JUST FOR ME.
WELCOME, SID
OHFF!
FLASHH!!
NO, NOTHING IN THIS HALLWAY. BETTER HEAD BACK TO . . .
. . . HUH?

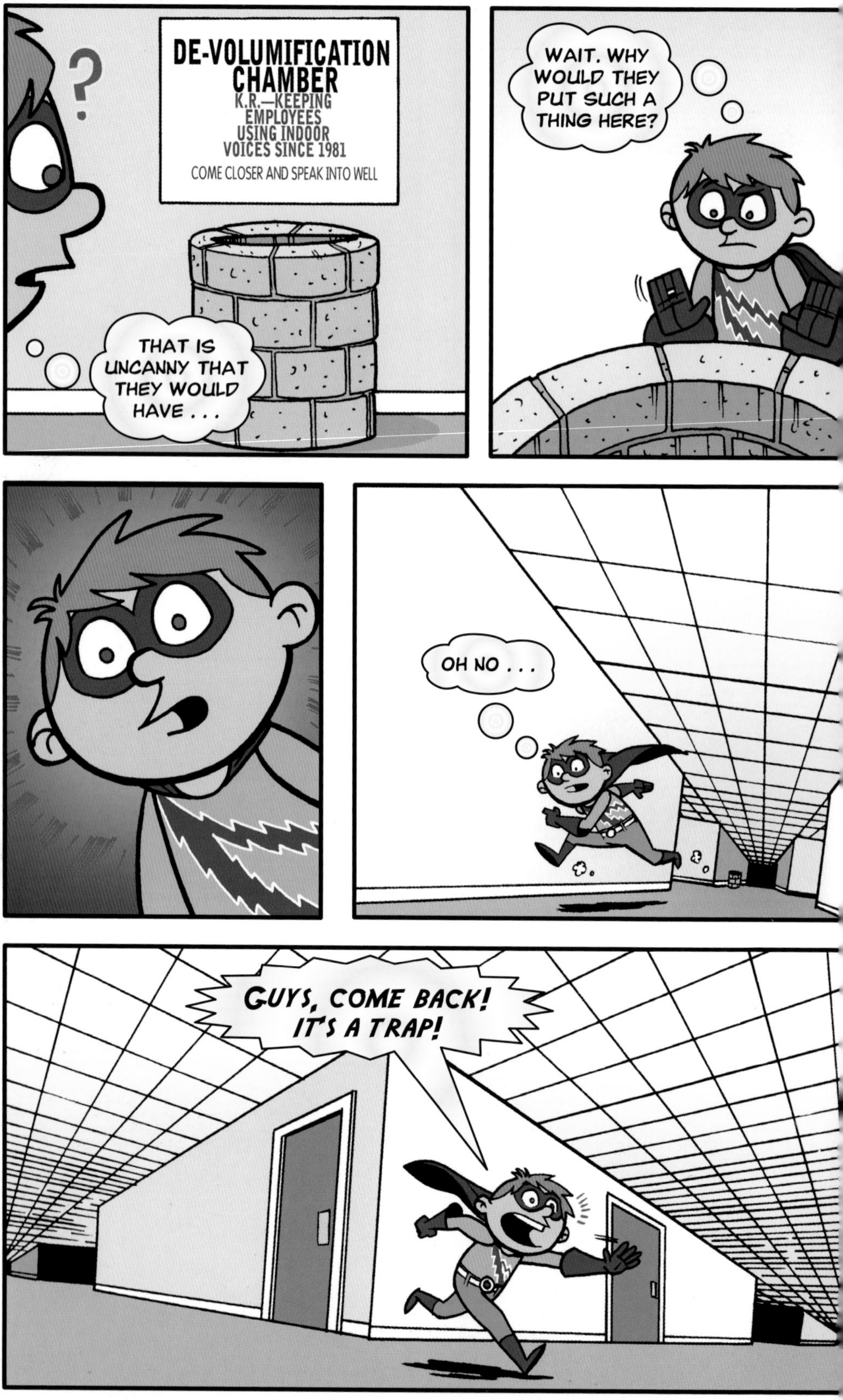
?
DE-VOLUMIFICATION CHAMBER
K.R.—KEEPING EMPLOYEES USING INDOOR VOICES SINCE 1981
COME CLOSER AND SPEAK INTO WELL
THAT IS UNCANNY THAT THEY WOULD HAVE . . .
WAIT. WHY WOULD THEY PUT SUCH A THING HERE?
OH NO . . .
GUYS, COME BACK! IT'S A TRAP!

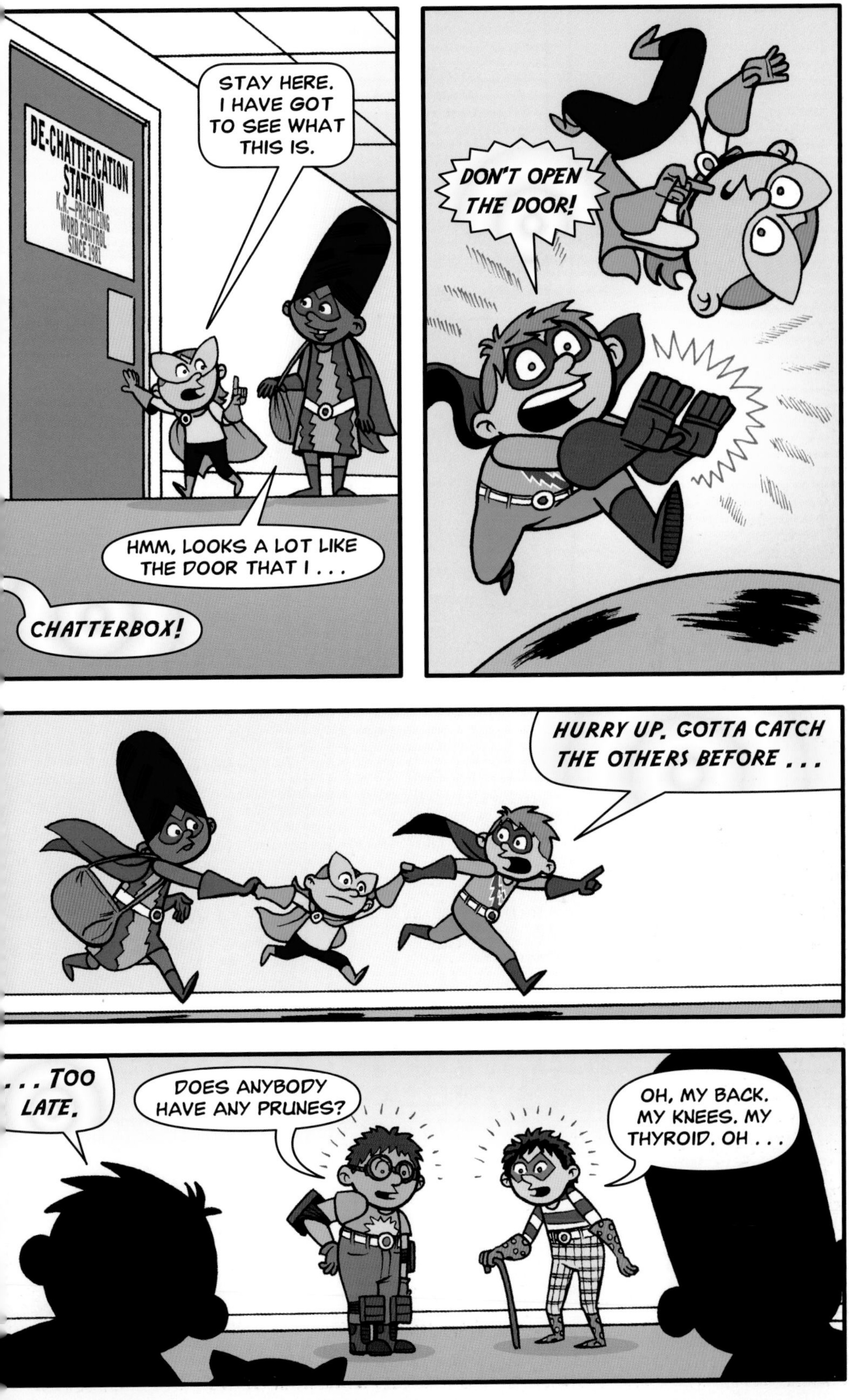
DE-CHATTIFICATION STATION
K.R.—PRACTICING WORD CONTROL SINCE 1901
STAY HERE. I HAVE GOT TO SEE WHAT THIS IS.
HMM, LOOKS A LOT LIKE THE DOOR THAT I . . .
CHATTERBOX!
DON'T OPEN THE DOOR!
HURRY UP, GOTTA CATCH THE OTHERS BEFORE . . .
. . . TOO LATE.
DOES ANYBODY HAVE ANY PRUNES?
OH, MY BACK. MY KNEES. MY THYROID. OH . . .

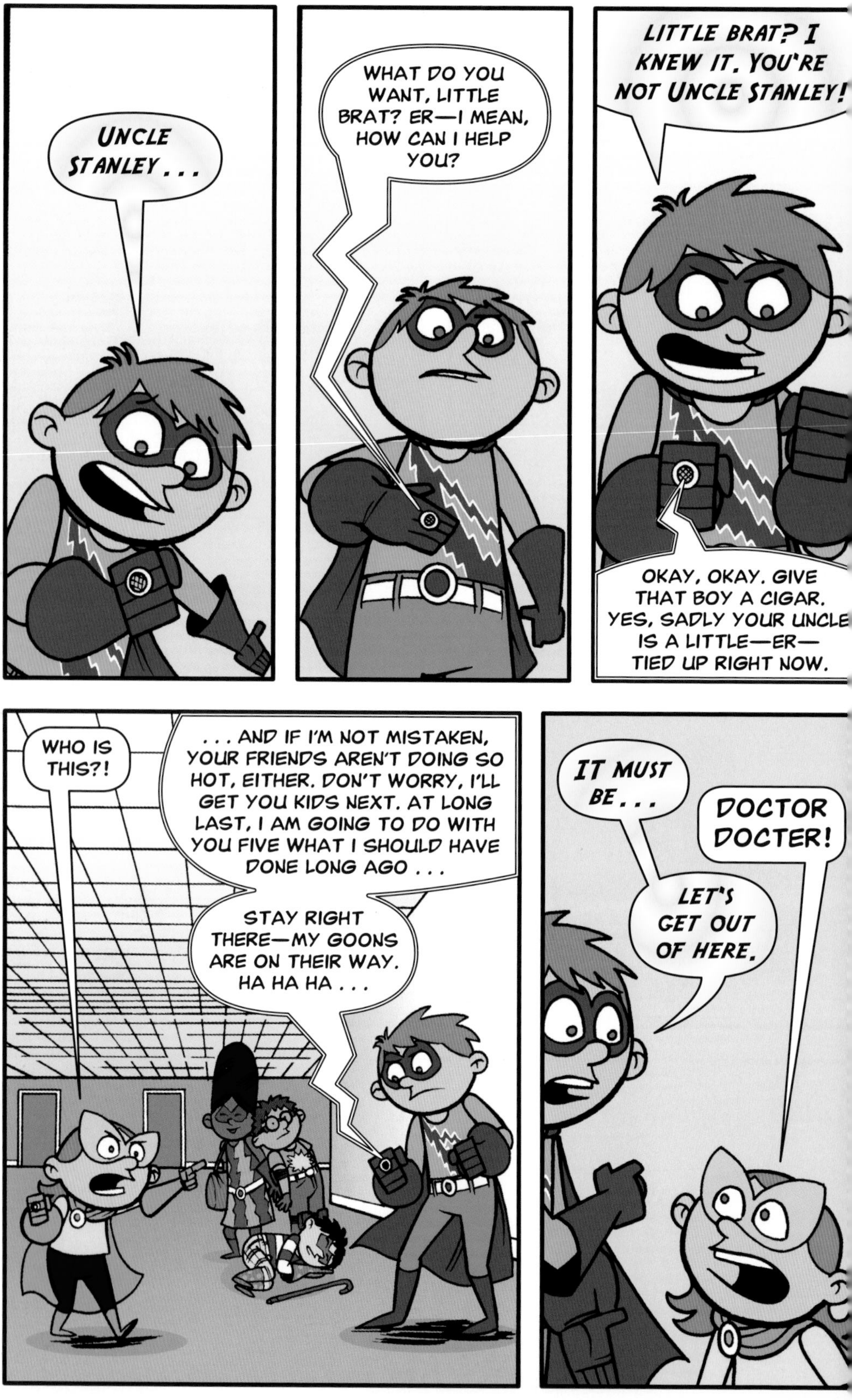
UNCLE STANLEY . . .
WHAT DO YOU WANT, LITTLE BRAT? ER—I MEAN, HOW CAN I HELP YOU?
LITTLE BRAT? I KNEW IT. YOU'RE NOT UNCLE STANLEY!
OKAY, OKAY. GIVE THAT BOY A CIGAR. YES, SADLY YOUR UNCLE IS A LITTLE—ER—TIED UP RIGHT NOW.
WHO IS THIS?!
. . . AND IF I'M NOT MISTAKEN, YOUR FRIENDS AREN'T DOING SO HOT, EITHER. DON'T WORRY, I'LL GET YOU KIDS NEXT. AT LONG LAST, I AM GOING TO DO WITH YOU FIVE WHAT I SHOULD HAVE DONE LONG AGO . . .
STAY RIGHT THERE—MY GOONS ARE ON THEIR WAY. HA HA HA . . .
IT MUST BE . . .
DOCTOR DOCTER!
LET'S GET OUT OF HERE.

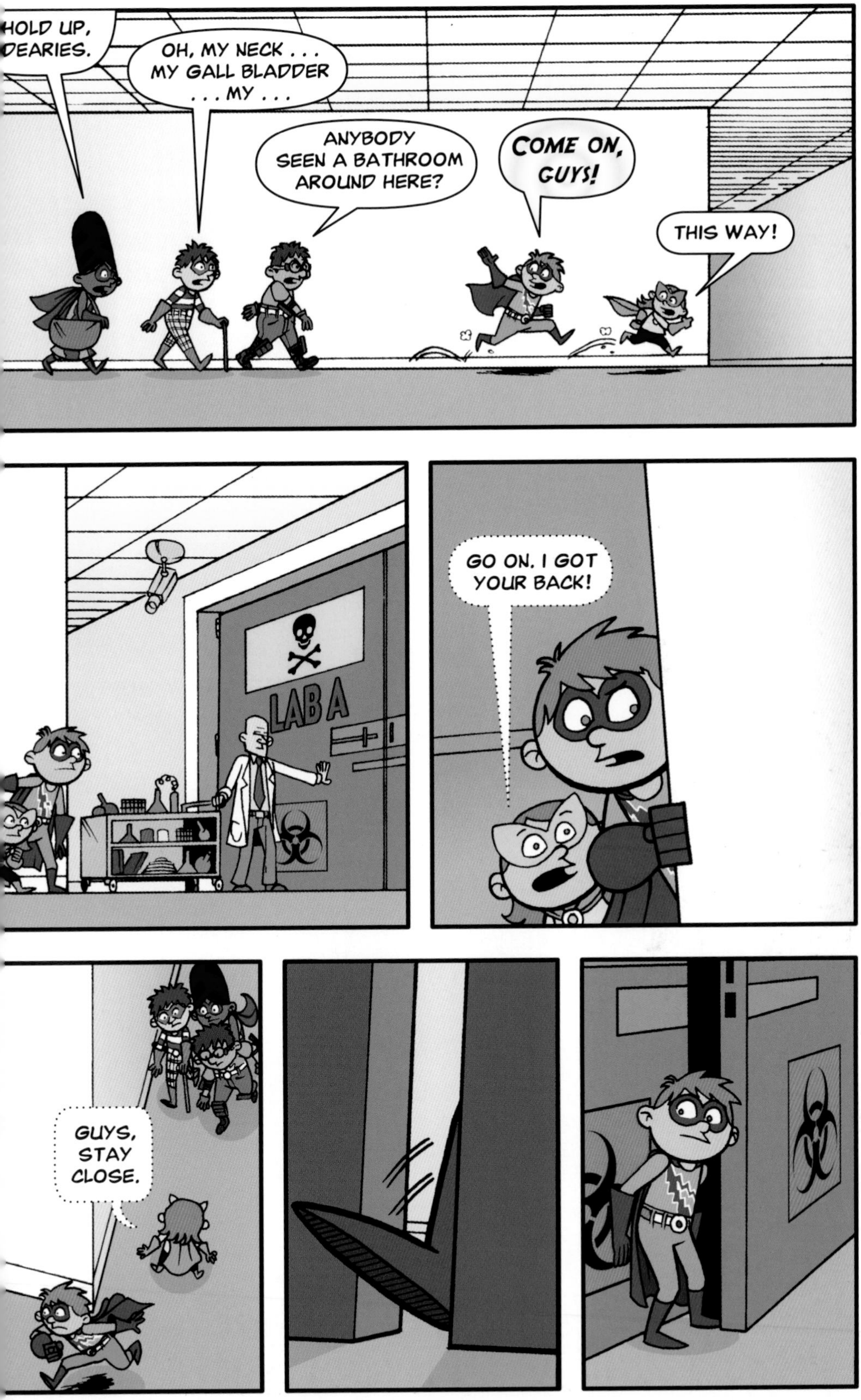
HOLD UP, DEARIES.
OH, MY NECK . . . MY GALL BLADDER . . . MY . . .
ANYBODY SEEN A BATHROOM AROUND HERE?
COME ON, GUYS!
THIS WAY!
LAB A
GO ON. I GOT YOUR BACK!
GUYS, STAY CLOSE.

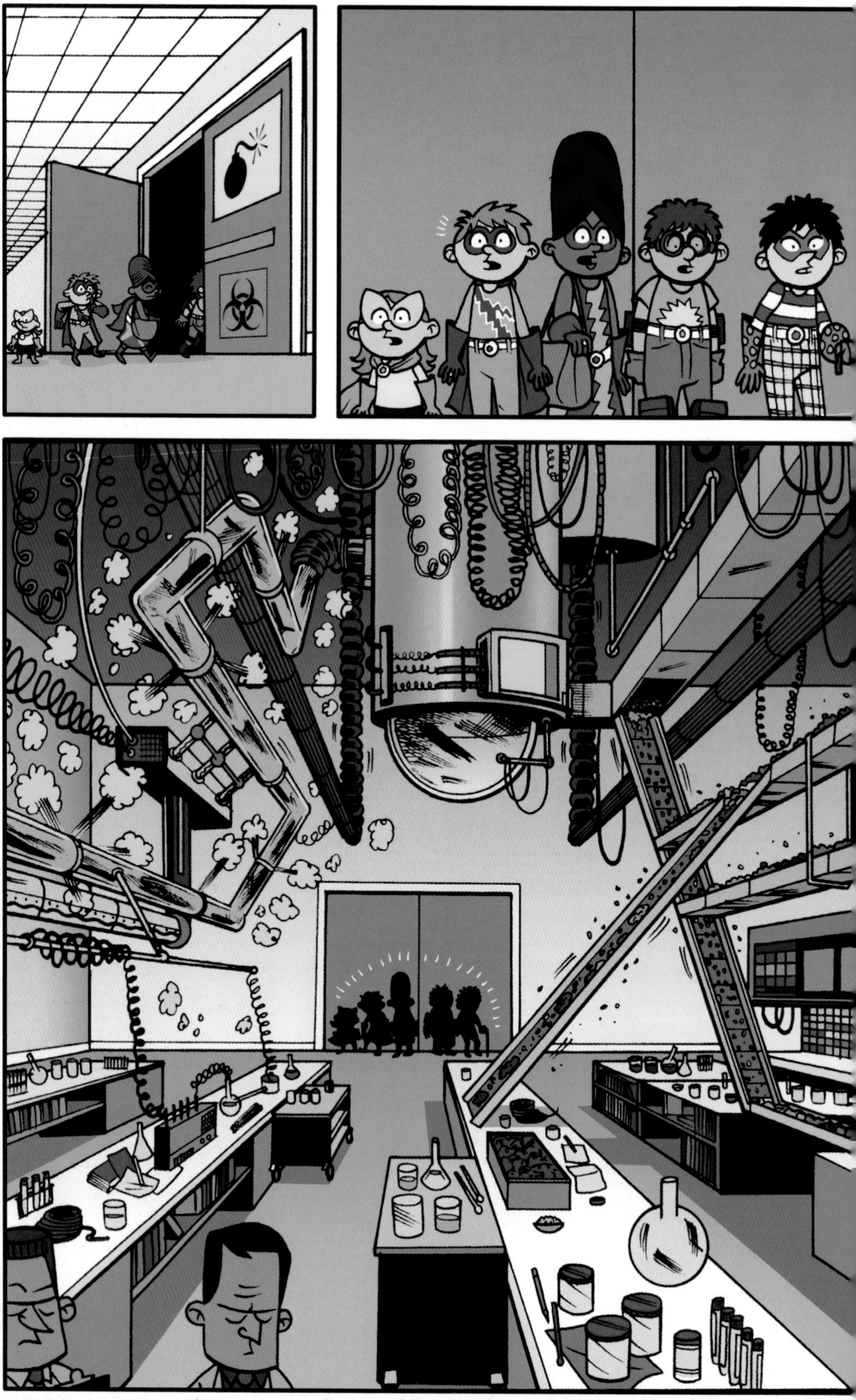

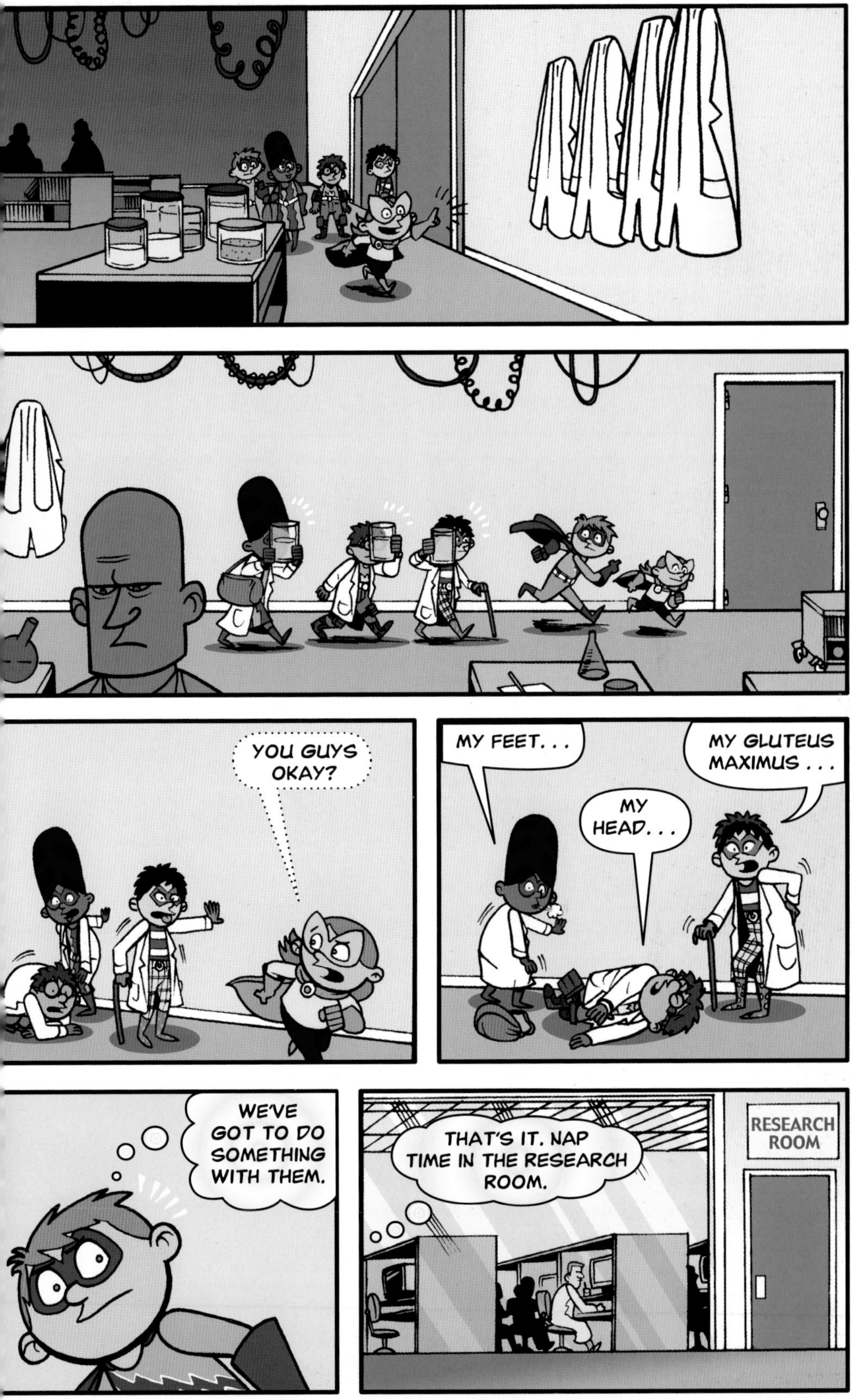
YOU GUYS OKAY?
MY FEET. . .
MY HEAD. . .
MY GLUTEUS MAXIMUS . . .
WE'VE GOT TO DO SOMETHING WITH THEM.
THAT'S IT. NAP TIME IN THE RESEARCH ROOM.
RESEARCH ROOM

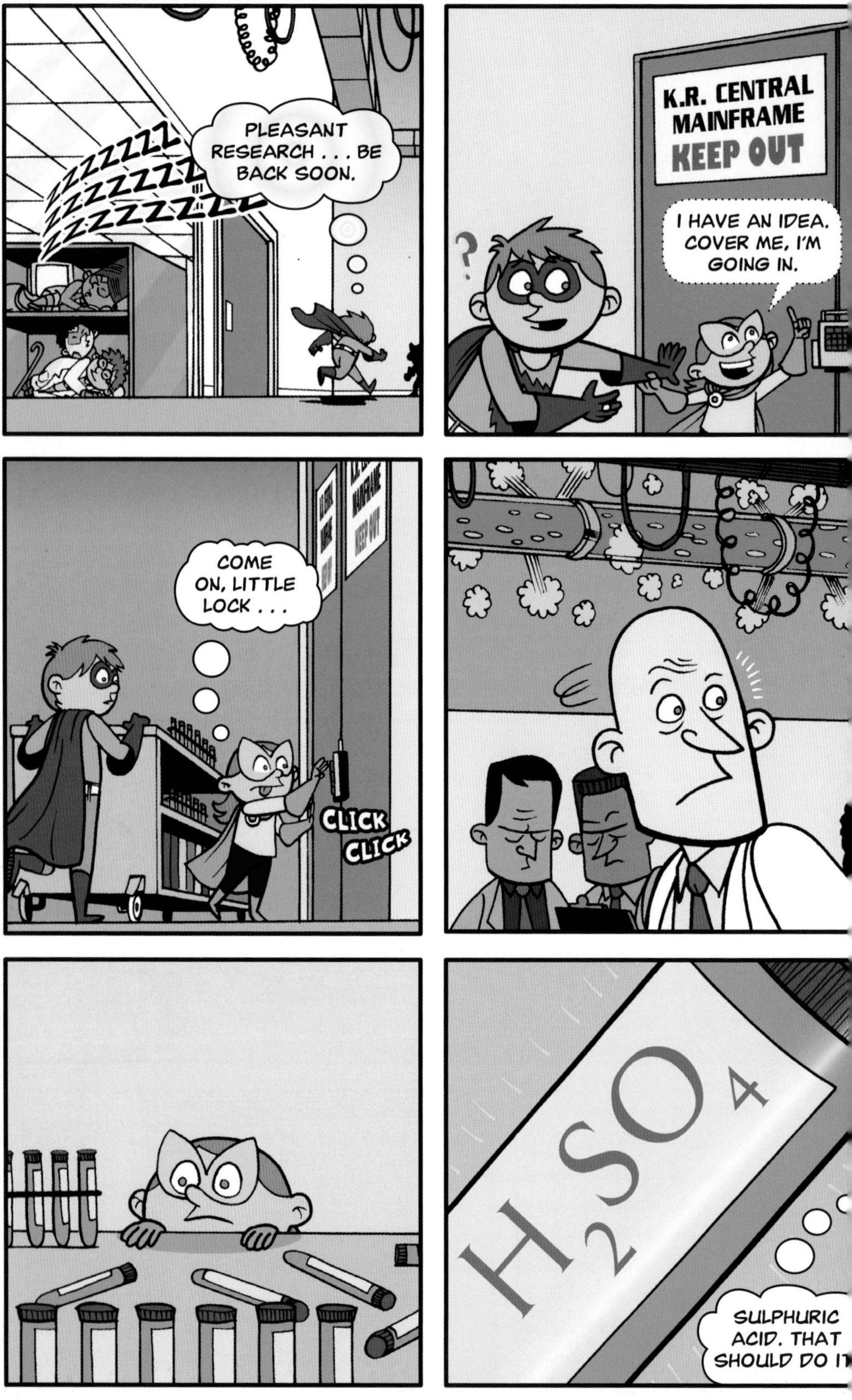
ZZZZZZZ
ZZZZZZZZ
ZZZZZZZZZ
PLEASANT RESEARCH . . . BE BACK SOON.
K.R. CENTRAL MAINFRAME
KEEP OUT
I HAVE AN IDEA. COVER ME, I'M GOING IN.
COME ON, LITTLE LOCK . . .
CLICK
CLICK
$H_2SO_4$
SULPHURIC ACID. THAT SHOULD DO I

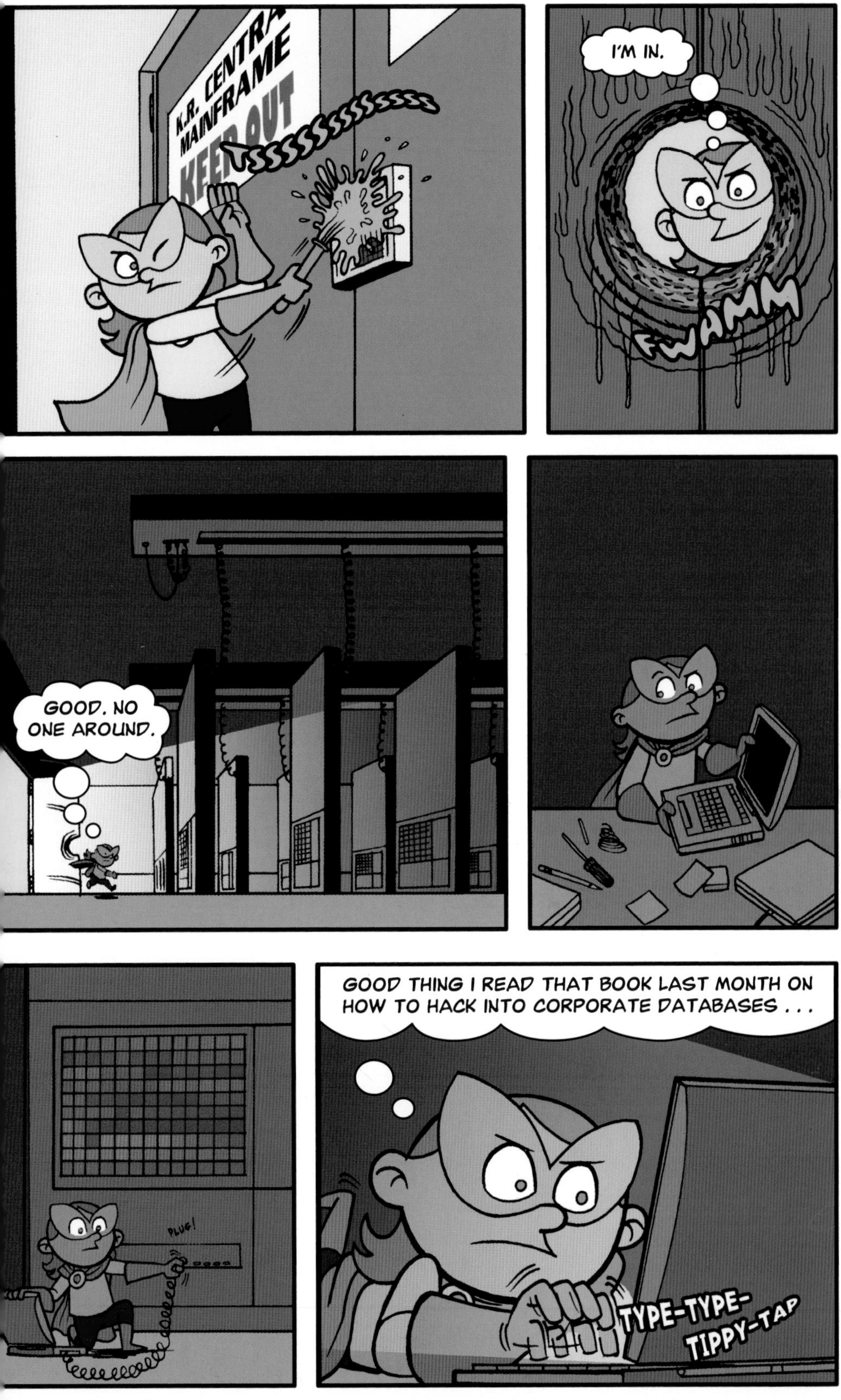
K.R. CENTRA
MAINFRAME
KEEP OUT
TSSSSSSSSSSSSSSSS
I'M IN.
FWAMM
GOOD. NO ONE AROUND.
PLUG!
GOOD THING I READ THAT BOOK LAST MONTH ON HOW TO HACK INTO CORPORATE DATABASES . . .
TYPE-TYPE-TIPPY-TAP

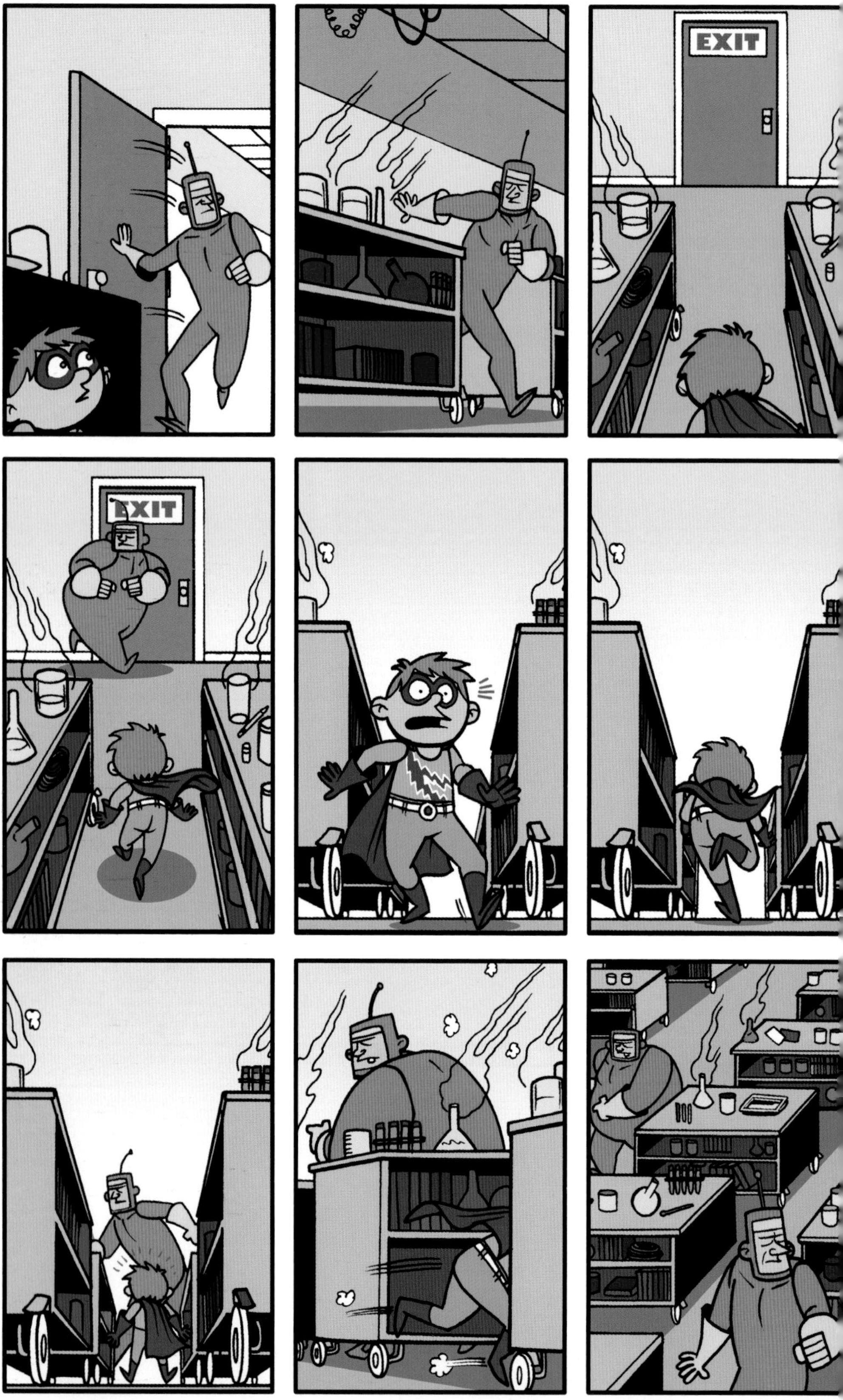
EXIT
EXIT

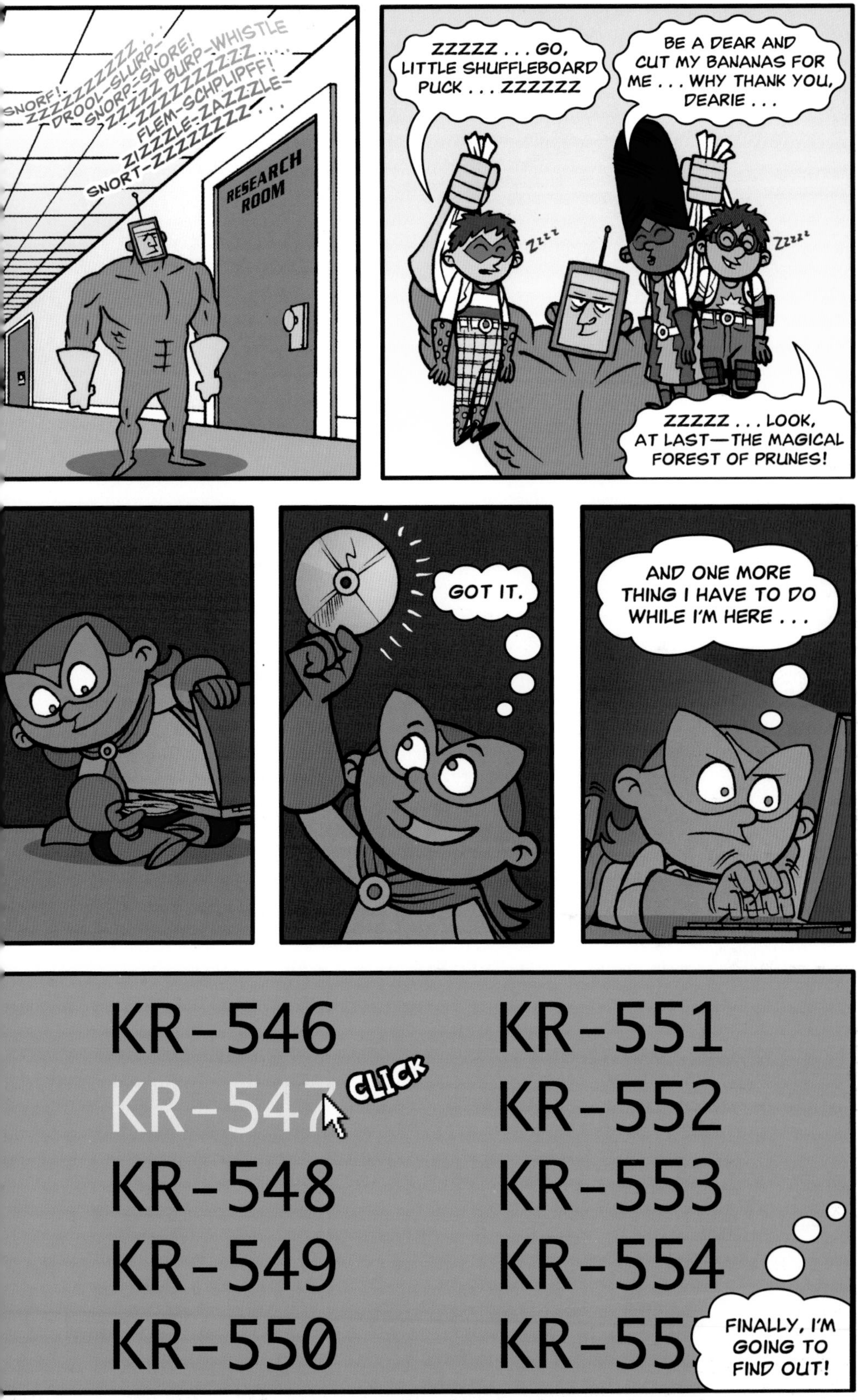
SNORF!
ZZZZZZZZZZ . . .
DROOL-SLURP-
SNORP-SNORE!
ZZZZZZ BURP-WHISTLE
-ZZZZZZZZZZ . . .
FLEM-SCHPLIPFF!
ZIZZZZLE-ZAZZZZLE-
SNORT-ZZZZZZZZ . . .
RESEARCH ROOM
ZZZZZ . . . GO, LITTLE SHUFFLEBOARD PUCK . . . ZZZZZZ
BE A DEAR AND CUT MY BANANAS FOR ME . . . WHY THANK YOU, DEARIE . . .
Zzzz
Zzzzz
ZZZZZ . . . LOOK, AT LAST—THE MAGICAL FOREST OF PRUNES!
GOT IT.
AND ONE MORE THING I HAVE TO DO WHILE I'M HERE . . .
KR-546
KR-547
CLICK
KR-548
KR-549
KR-550
KR-551
KR-552
KR-553
KR-554
FINALLY, I'M GOING TO FIND OUT!

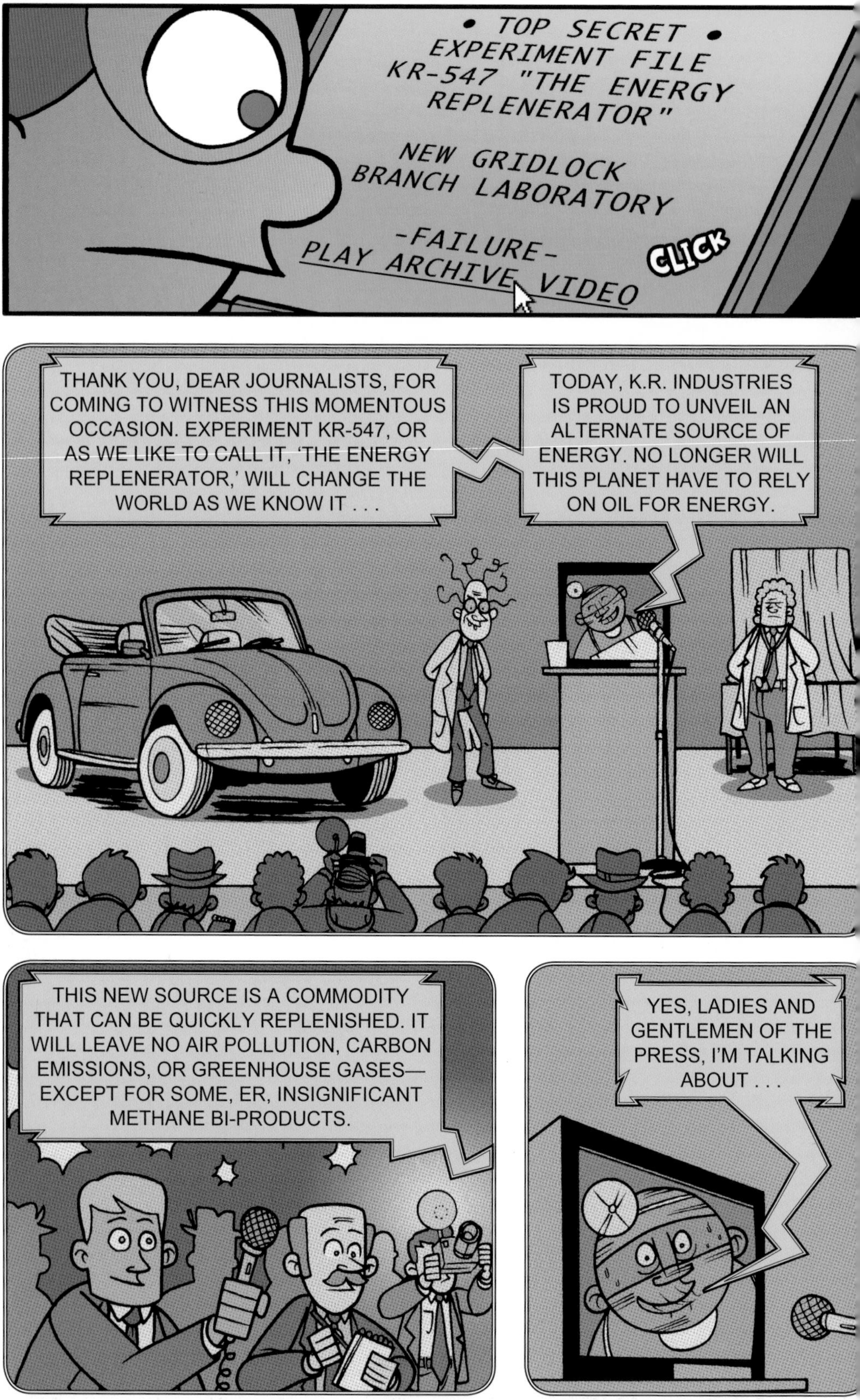
• TOP SECRET •
EXPERIMENT FILE
KR-547 "THE ENERGY REPLENERATOR"
NEW GRIDLOCK BRANCH LABORATORY
-FAILURE-
PLAY ARCHIVE VIDEO
CLICK
THANK YOU, DEAR JOURNALISTS, FOR COMING TO WITNESS THIS MOMENTOUS OCCASION. EXPERIMENT KR-547, OR AS WE LIKE TO CALL IT, 'THE ENERGY REPLENERATOR,' WILL CHANGE THE WORLD AS WE KNOW IT . . .
TODAY, K.R. INDUSTRIES IS PROUD TO UNVEIL AN ALTERNATE SOURCE OF ENERGY. NO LONGER WILL THIS PLANET HAVE TO RELY ON OIL FOR ENERGY.
THIS NEW SOURCE IS A COMMODITY THAT CAN BE QUICKLY REPLENISHED. IT WILL LEAVE NO AIR POLLUTION, CARBON EMISSIONS, OR GREENHOUSE GASES— EXCEPT FOR SOME, ER, INSIGNIFICANT METHANE BI-PRODUCTS.
YES, LADIES AND GENTLEMEN OF THE PRESS, I'M TALKING ABOUT . . .

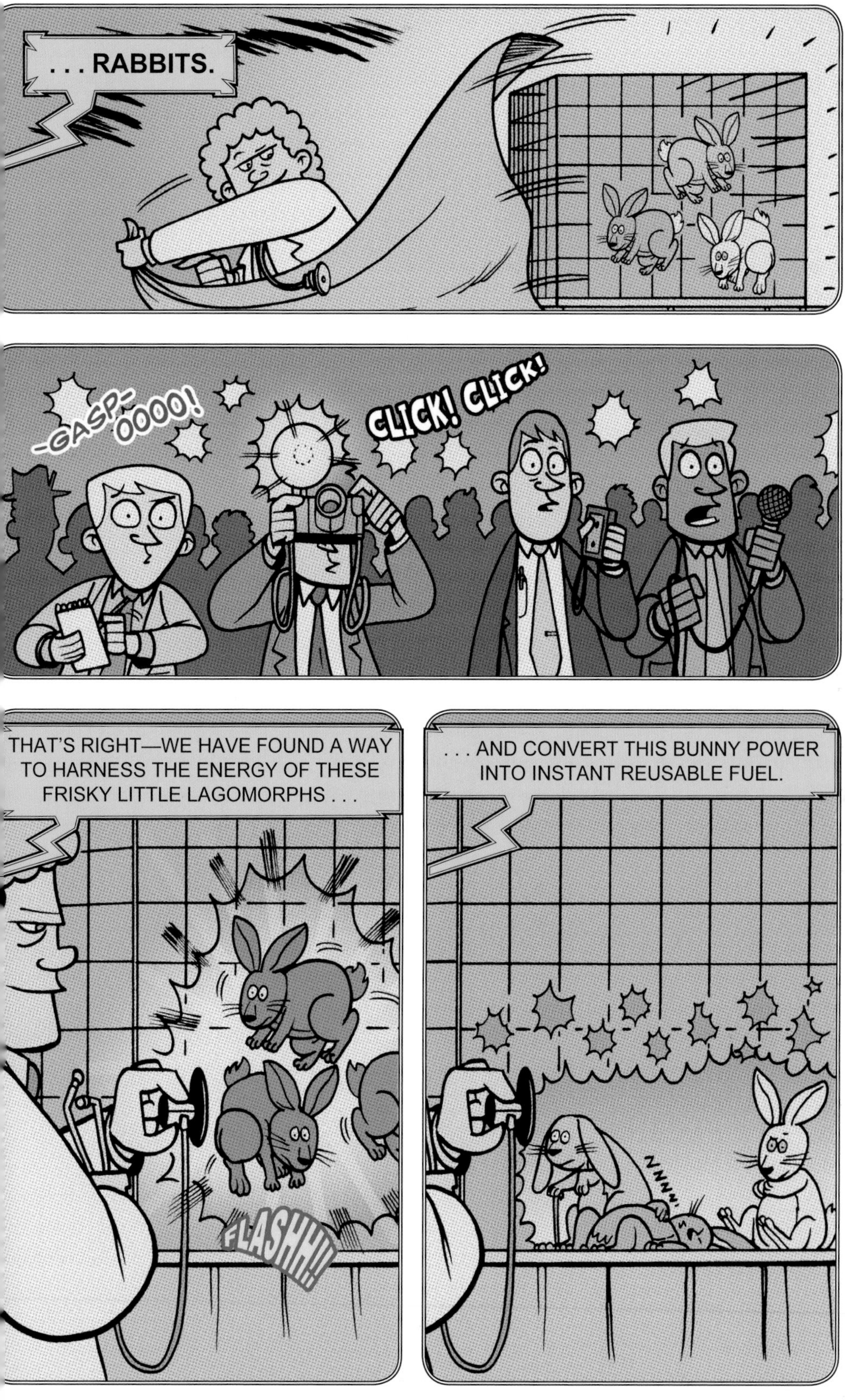
. . . RABBITS.
-GASP- OOOO!
CLICK! CLICK!
THAT'S RIGHT—WE HAVE FOUND A WAY TO HARNESS THE ENERGY OF THESE FRISKY LITTLE LAGOMORPHS . . .
FLASHH!!
. . . AND CONVERT THIS BUNNY POWER INTO INSTANT REUSABLE FUEL.
ZZZZ

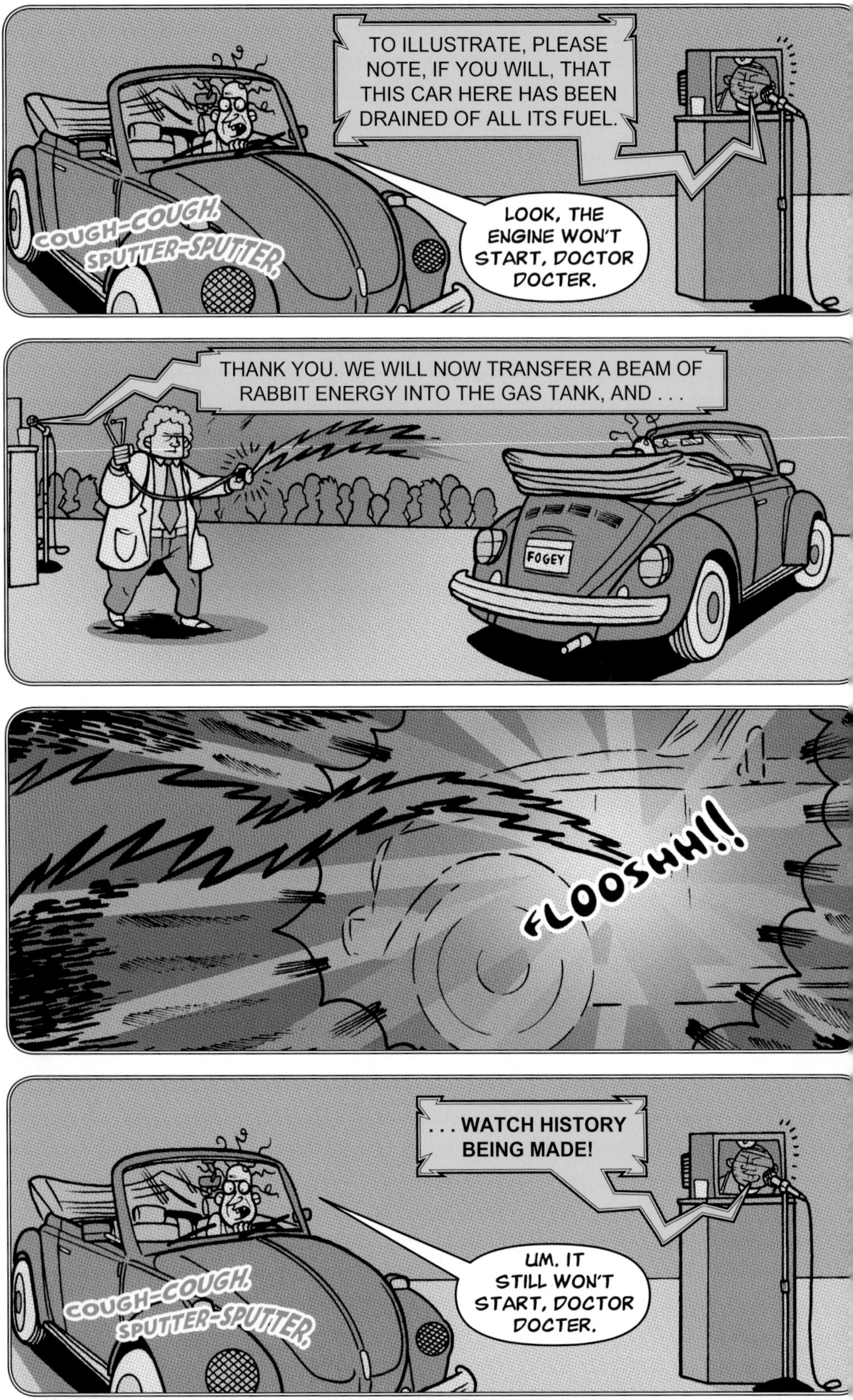
TO ILLUSTRATE, PLEASE NOTE, IF YOU WILL, THAT THIS CAR HERE HAS BEEN DRAINED OF ALL ITS FUEL.
COUGH-COUGH. SPUTTER-SPUTTER.
LOOK, THE ENGINE WON'T START, DOCTOR DOCTER.
THANK YOU. WE WILL NOW TRANSFER A BEAM OF RABBIT ENERGY INTO THE GAS TANK, AND . . .
FOGEY
FLOOSHH!!
. . . WATCH HISTORY BEING MADE!
COUGH-COUGH. SPUTTER-SPUTTER.
UM. IT STILL WON'T START, DOCTOR DOCTER.

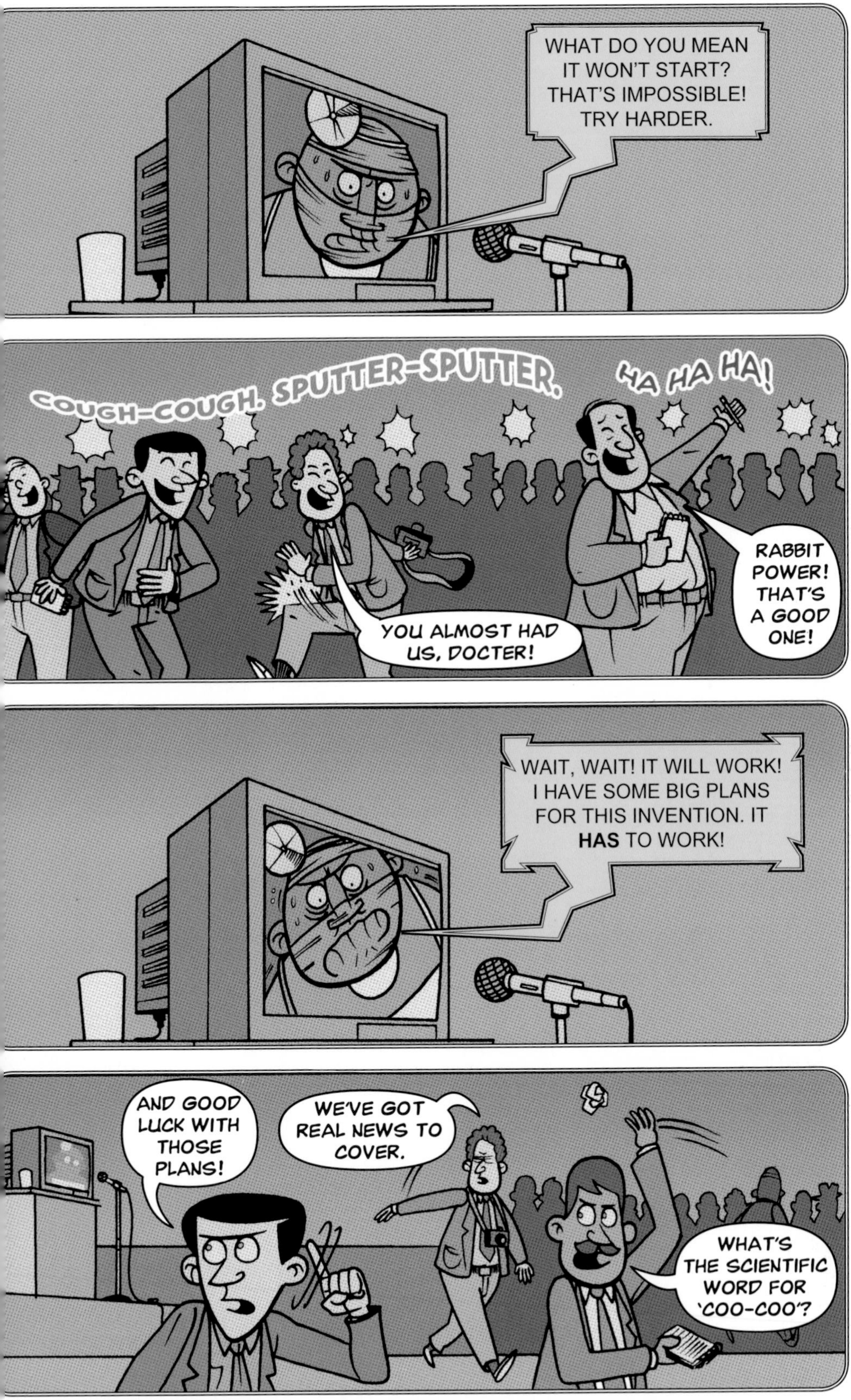
WHAT DO YOU MEAN IT WON'T START? THAT'S IMPOSSIBLE! TRY HARDER.
COUGH-COUGH. SPUTTER-SPUTTER.
HA HA HA!
YOU ALMOST HAD US, DOCTER!
RABBIT POWER! THAT'S A GOOD ONE!
WAIT, WAIT! IT WILL WORK! I HAVE SOME BIG PLANS FOR THIS INVENTION. IT **HAS** TO WORK!
AND GOOD LUCK WITH THOSE PLANS!
WE'VE GOT REAL NEWS TO COVER.
WHAT'S THE SCIENTIFIC WORD FOR 'COO-COO'?

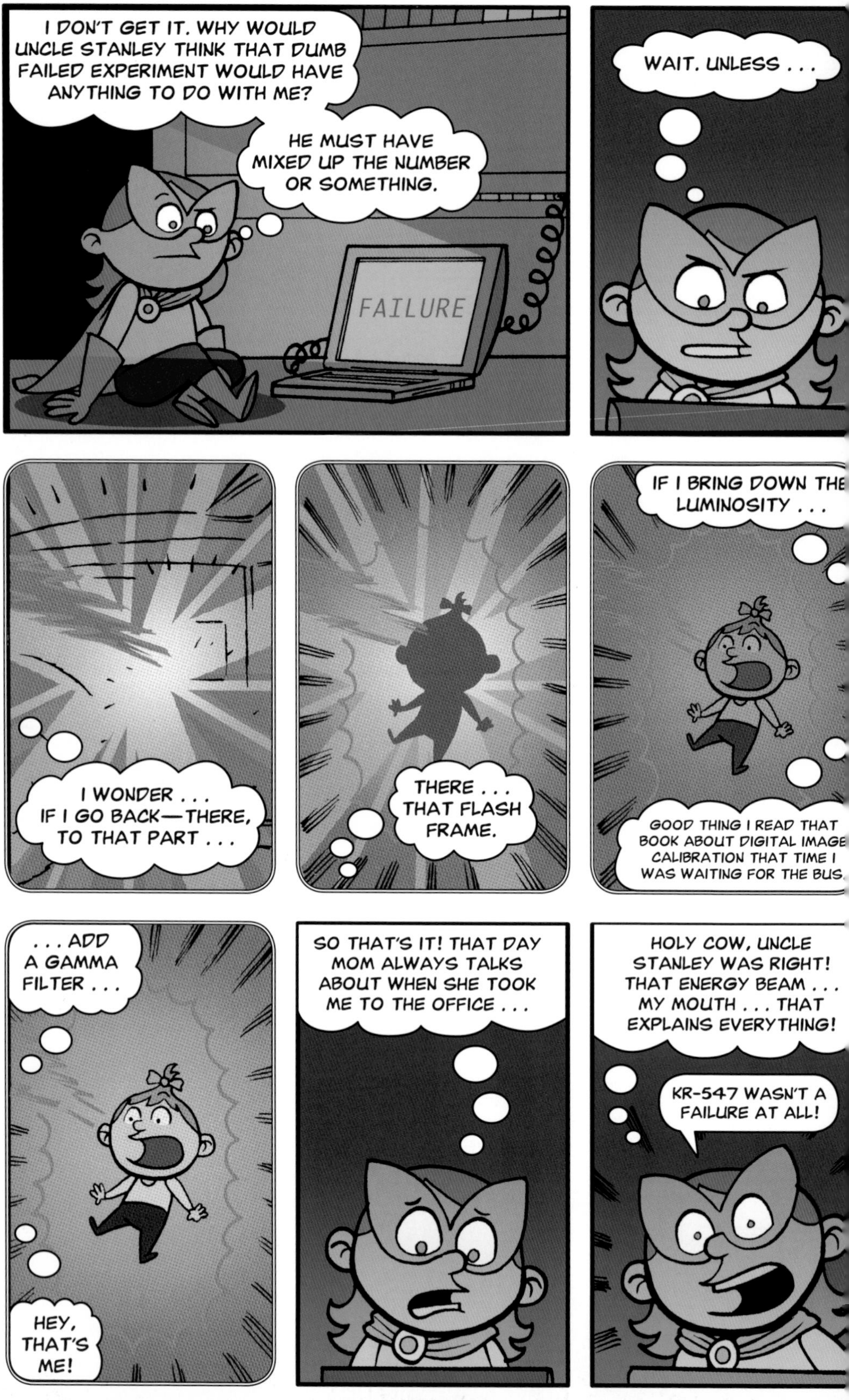
I DON'T GET IT. WHY WOULD UNCLE STANLEY THINK THAT DUMB FAILED EXPERIMENT WOULD HAVE ANYTHING TO DO WITH ME?
HE MUST HAVE MIXED UP THE NUMBER OR SOMETHING.
FAILURE
WAIT. UNLESS . . .
I WONDER . . . IF I GO BACK—THERE, TO THAT PART . . .
THERE . . . THAT FLASH FRAME.
IF I BRING DOWN THE LUMINOSITY . . .
GOOD THING I READ THAT BOOK ABOUT DIGITAL IMAGE CALIBRATION THAT TIME I WAS WAITING FOR THE BUS.
. . . ADD A GAMMA FILTER . . .
HEY, THAT'S ME!
SO THAT'S IT! THAT DAY MOM ALWAYS TALKS ABOUT WHEN SHE TOOK ME TO THE OFFICE . . .
HOLY COW, UNCLE STANLEY WAS RIGHT! THAT ENERGY BEAM . . . MY MOUTH . . . THAT EXPLAINS EVERYTHING!
KR-547 WASN'T A FAILURE AT ALL!

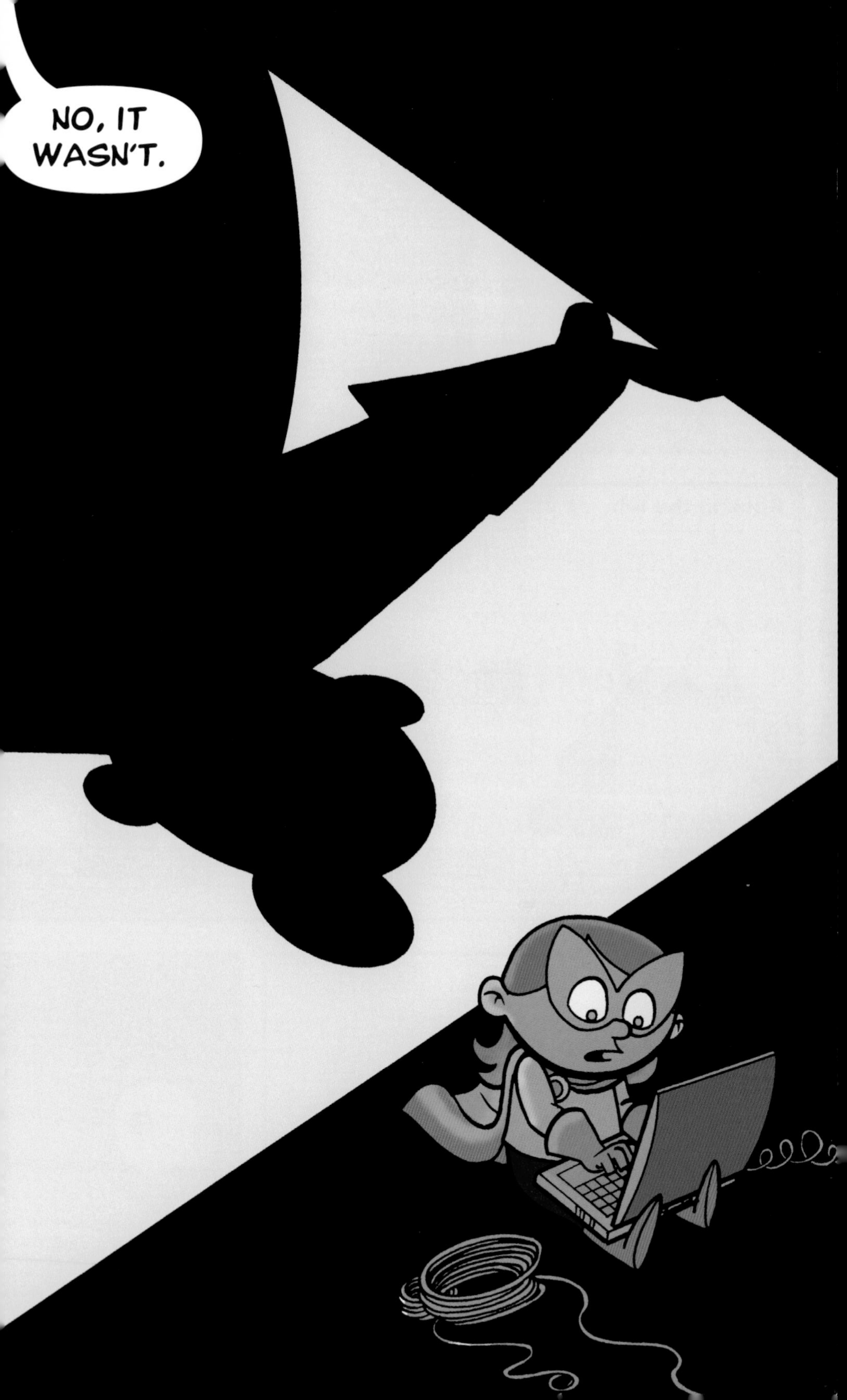
NO, IT WASN'T.

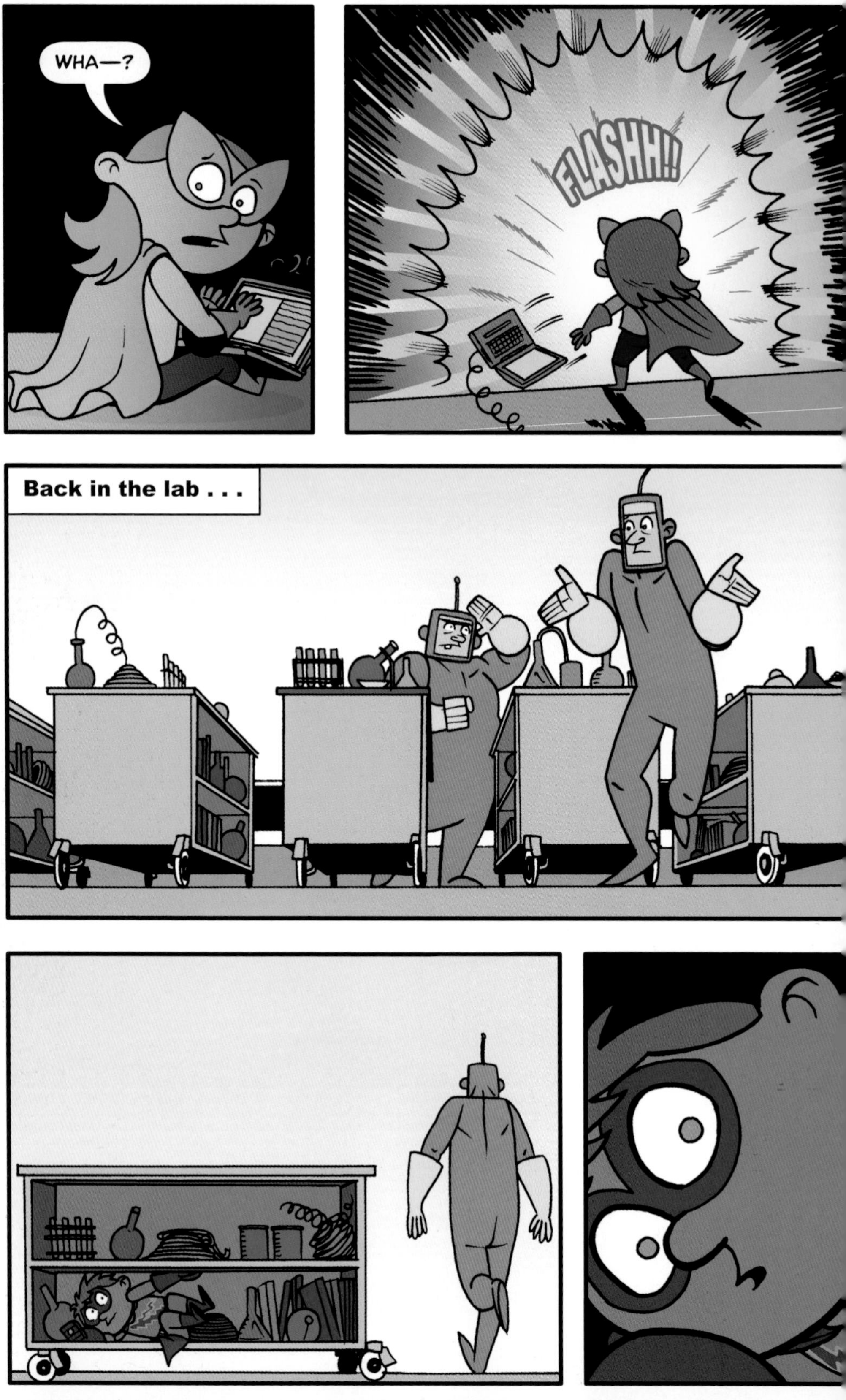
WHA—?
FLASHH!!
Back in the lab . . .

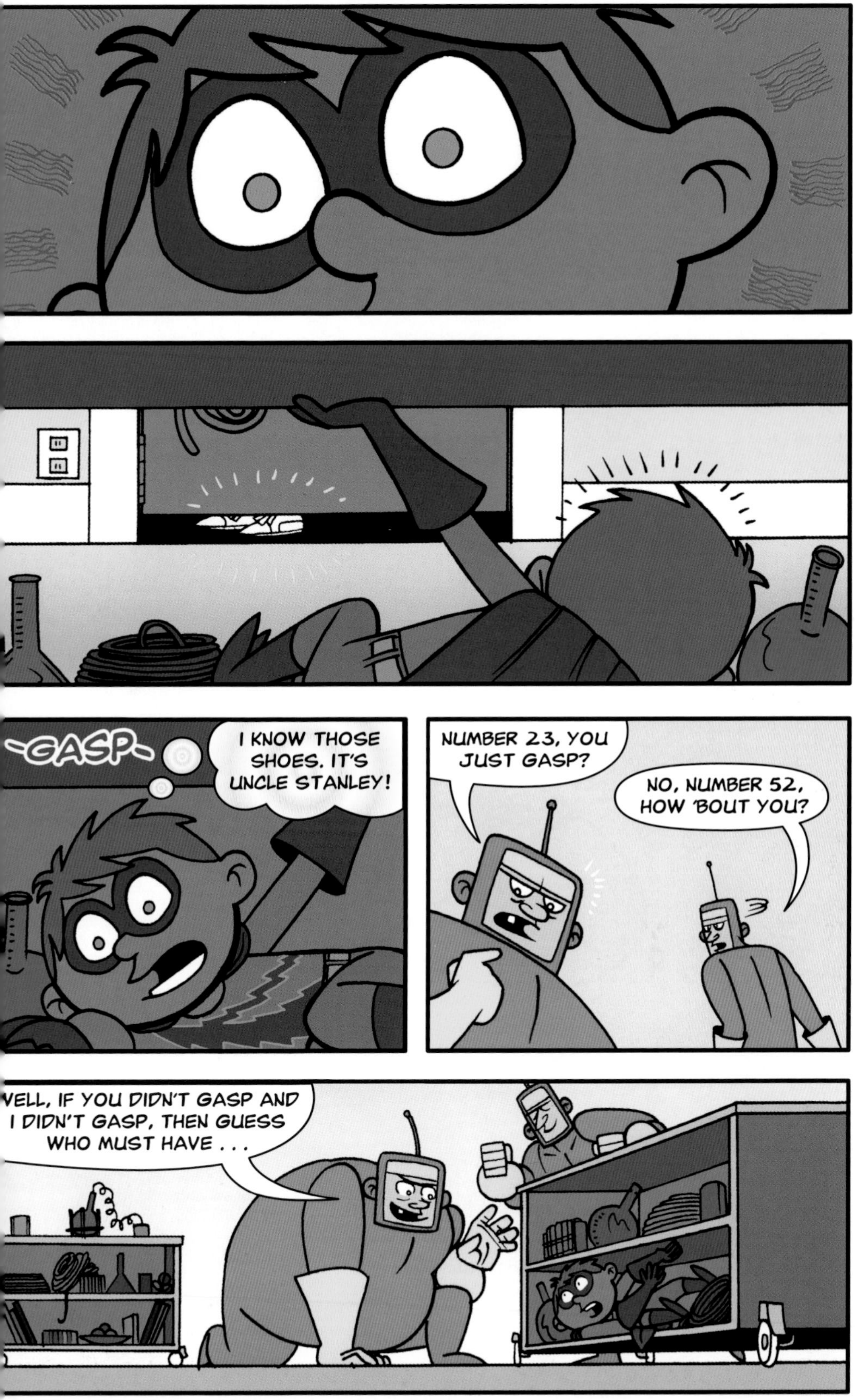
-GASP-
I KNOW THOSE SHOES. IT'S UNCLE STANLEY!
NUMBER 23, YOU JUST GASP?
NO, NUMBER 52, HOW 'BOUT YOU?
WELL, IF YOU DIDN'T GASP AND I DIDN'T GASP, THEN GUESS WHO MUST HAVE . . .

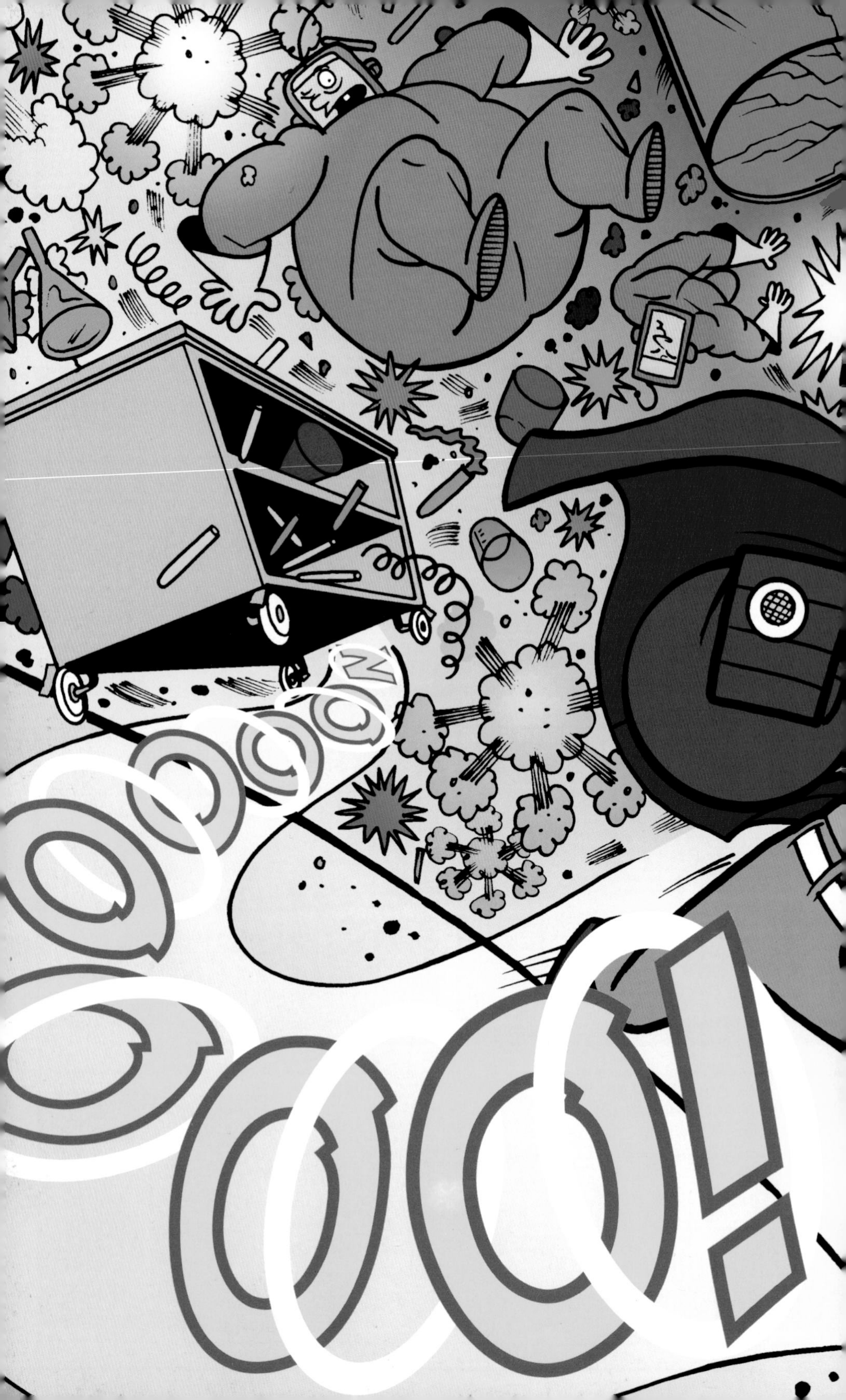
NOOOOOOO!

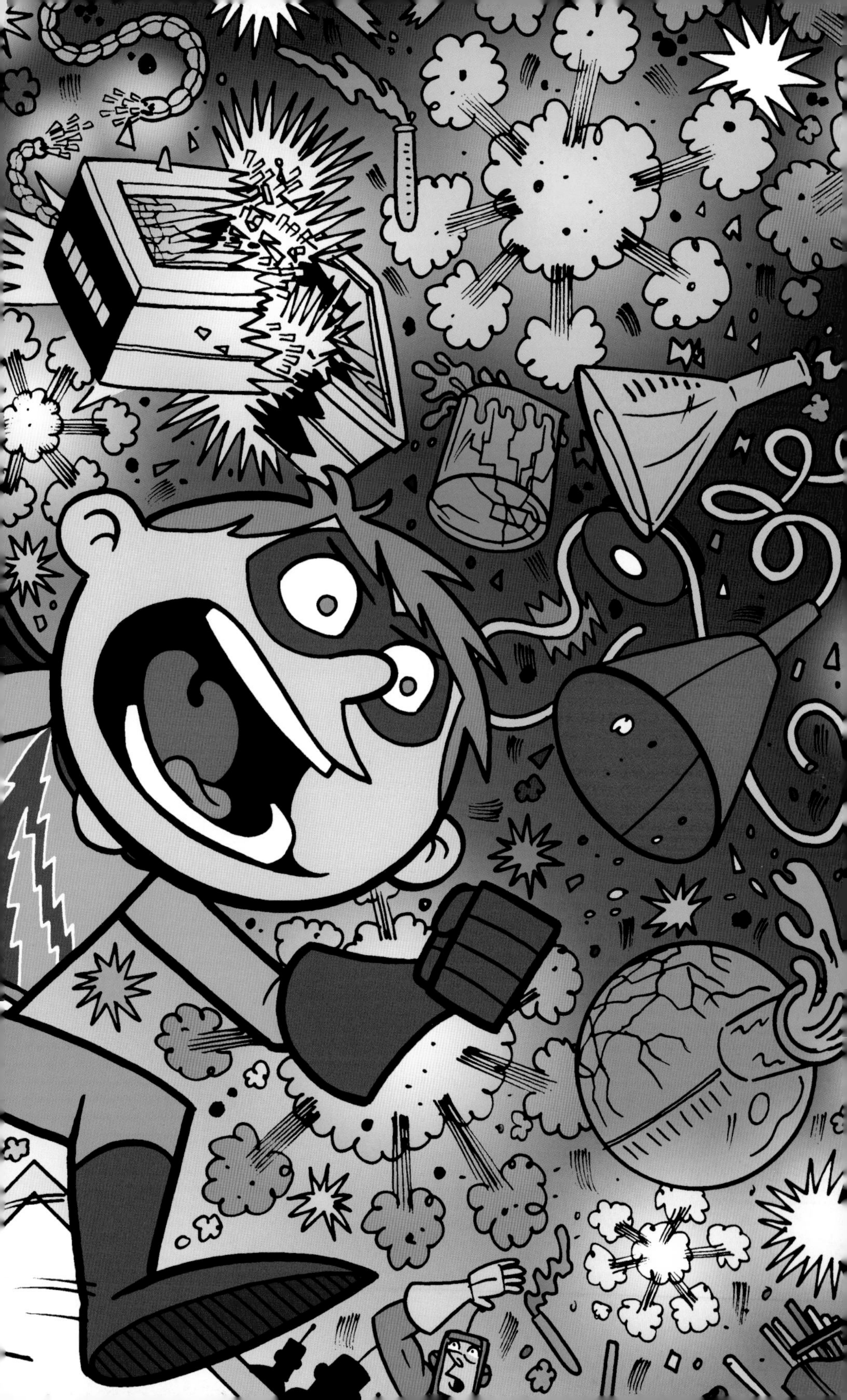

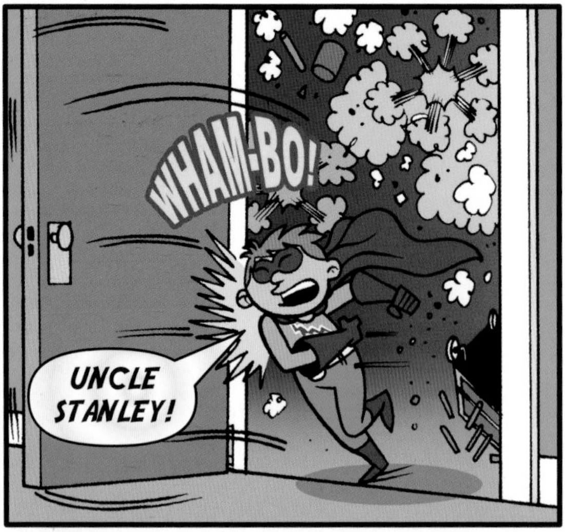
WHAM-BO!
UNCLE STANLEY!

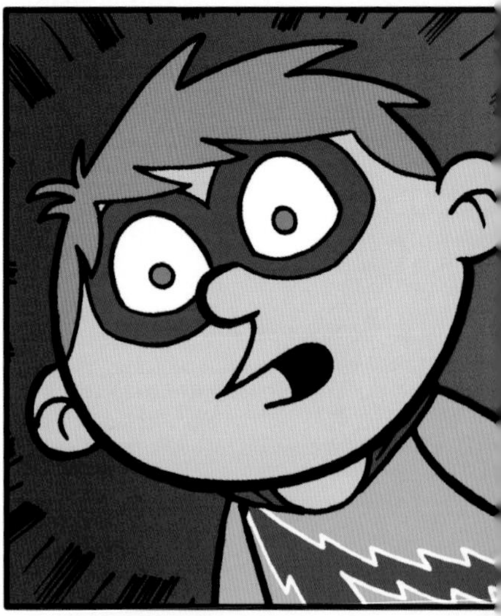

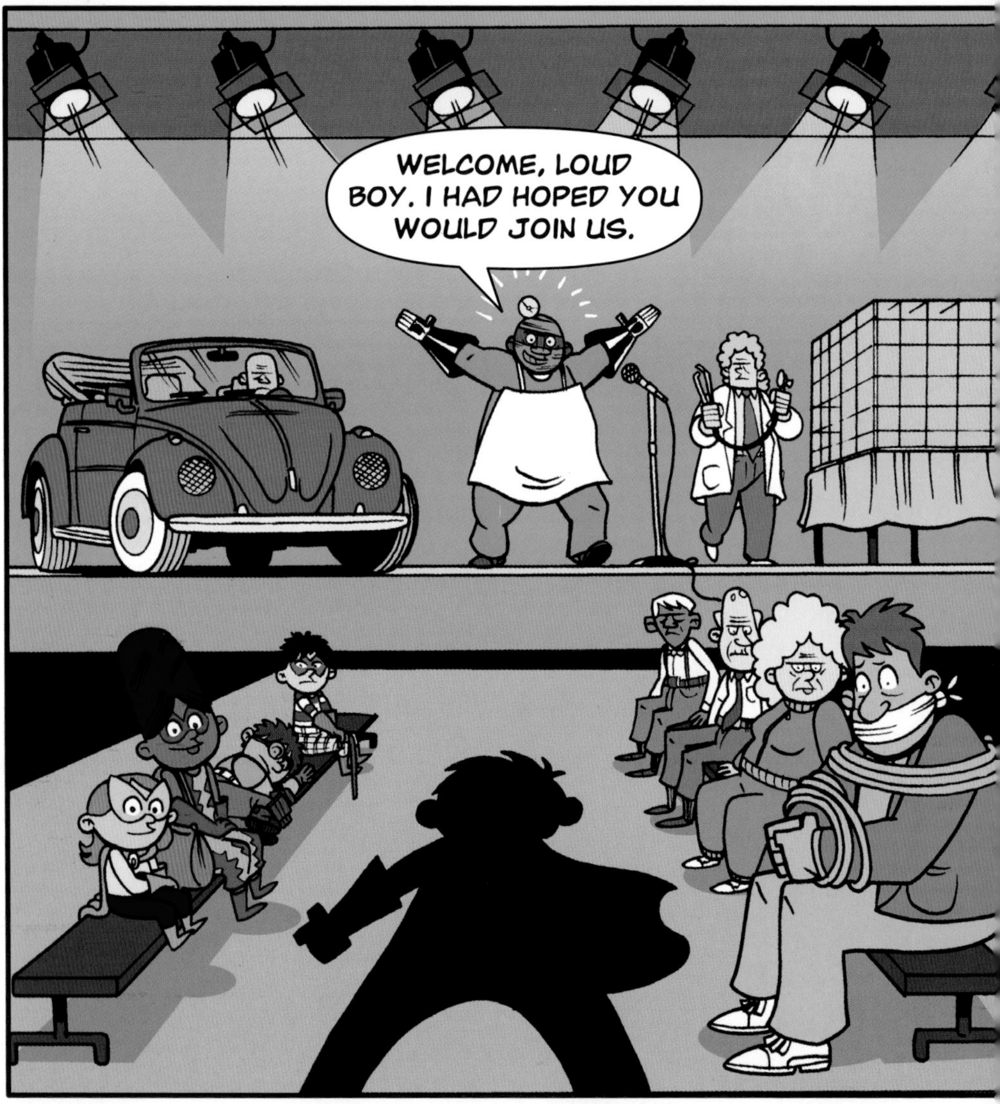
WELCOME, LOUD BOY. I HAD HOPED YOU WOULD JOIN US.

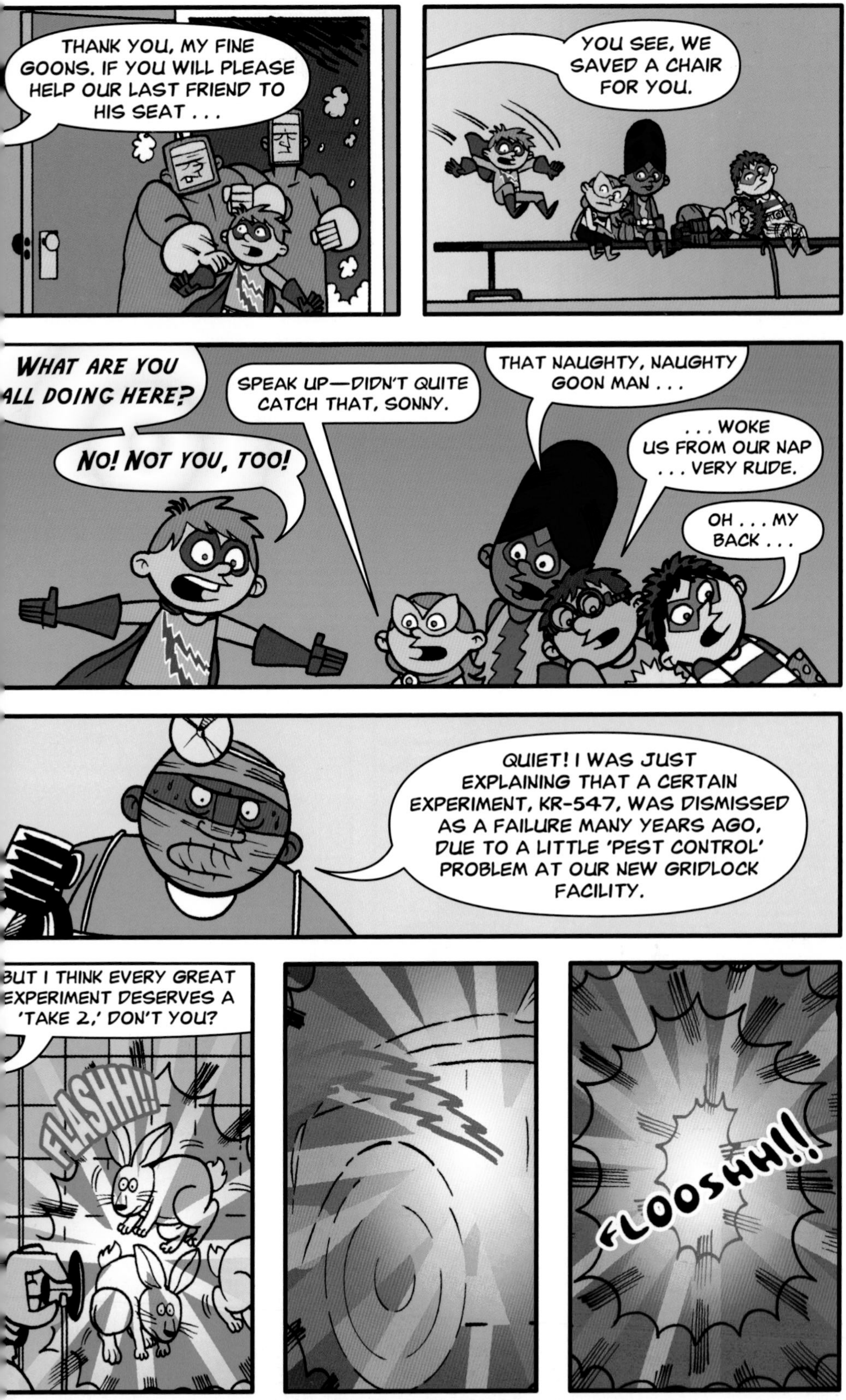
THANK YOU, MY FINE GOONS. IF YOU WILL PLEASE HELP OUR LAST FRIEND TO HIS SEAT . . .
YOU SEE, WE SAVED A CHAIR FOR YOU.
WHAT ARE YOU ALL DOING HERE?
NO! NOT YOU, TOO!
SPEAK UP—DIDN'T QUITE CATCH THAT, SONNY.
THAT NAUGHTY, NAUGHTY GOON MAN . . .
. . . WOKE US FROM OUR NAP . . . VERY RUDE.
OH . . . MY BACK . . .
QUIET! I WAS JUST EXPLAINING THAT A CERTAIN EXPERIMENT, KR-547, WAS DISMISSED AS A FAILURE MANY YEARS AGO, DUE TO A LITTLE 'PEST CONTROL' PROBLEM AT OUR NEW GRIDLOCK FACILITY.
BUT I THINK EVERY GREAT EXPERIMENT DESERVES A 'TAKE 2,' DON'T YOU?
FLASHH!!
FLOOSHH!!

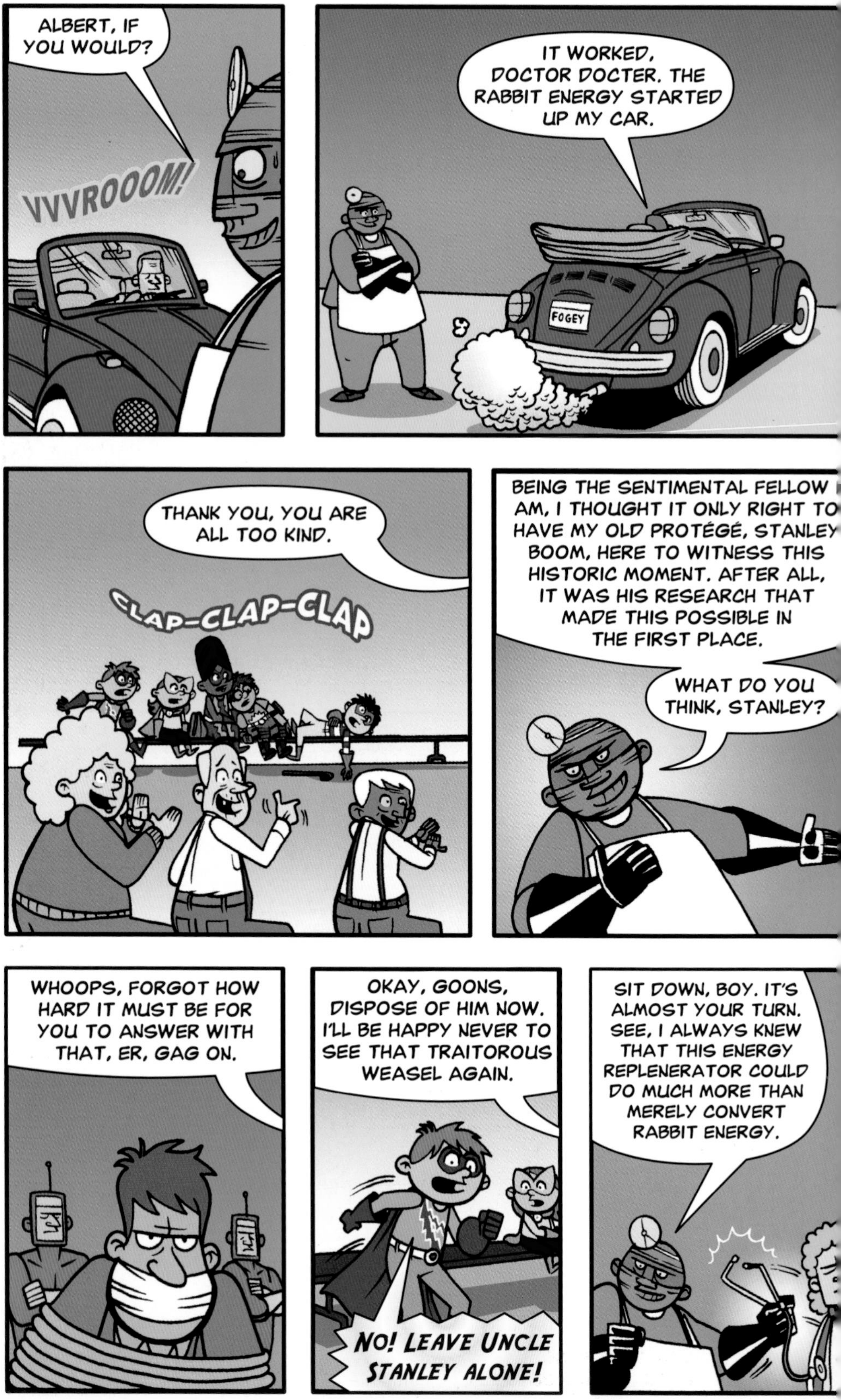
ALBERT, IF YOU WOULD?
VVVROOOM!
IT WORKED, DOCTOR DOCTER. THE RABBIT ENERGY STARTED UP MY CAR.
FOGEY
THANK YOU, YOU ARE ALL TOO KIND.
CLAP-CLAP-CLAP
BEING THE SENTIMENTAL FELLOW I AM, I THOUGHT IT ONLY RIGHT TO HAVE MY OLD PROTÉGÉ, STANLEY BOOM, HERE TO WITNESS THIS HISTORIC MOMENT. AFTER ALL, IT WAS HIS RESEARCH THAT MADE THIS POSSIBLE IN THE FIRST PLACE.
WHAT DO YOU THINK, STANLEY?
WHOOPS, FORGOT HOW HARD IT MUST BE FOR YOU TO ANSWER WITH THAT, ER, GAG ON.
OKAY, GOONS, DISPOSE OF HIM NOW. I'LL BE HAPPY NEVER TO SEE THAT TRAITOROUS WEASEL AGAIN.
NO! LEAVE UNCLE STANLEY ALONE!
SIT DOWN, BOY. IT'S ALMOST YOUR TURN. SEE, I ALWAYS KNEW THAT THIS ENERGY REPLENERATOR COULD DO MUCH MORE THAN MERELY CONVERT RABBIT ENERGY.

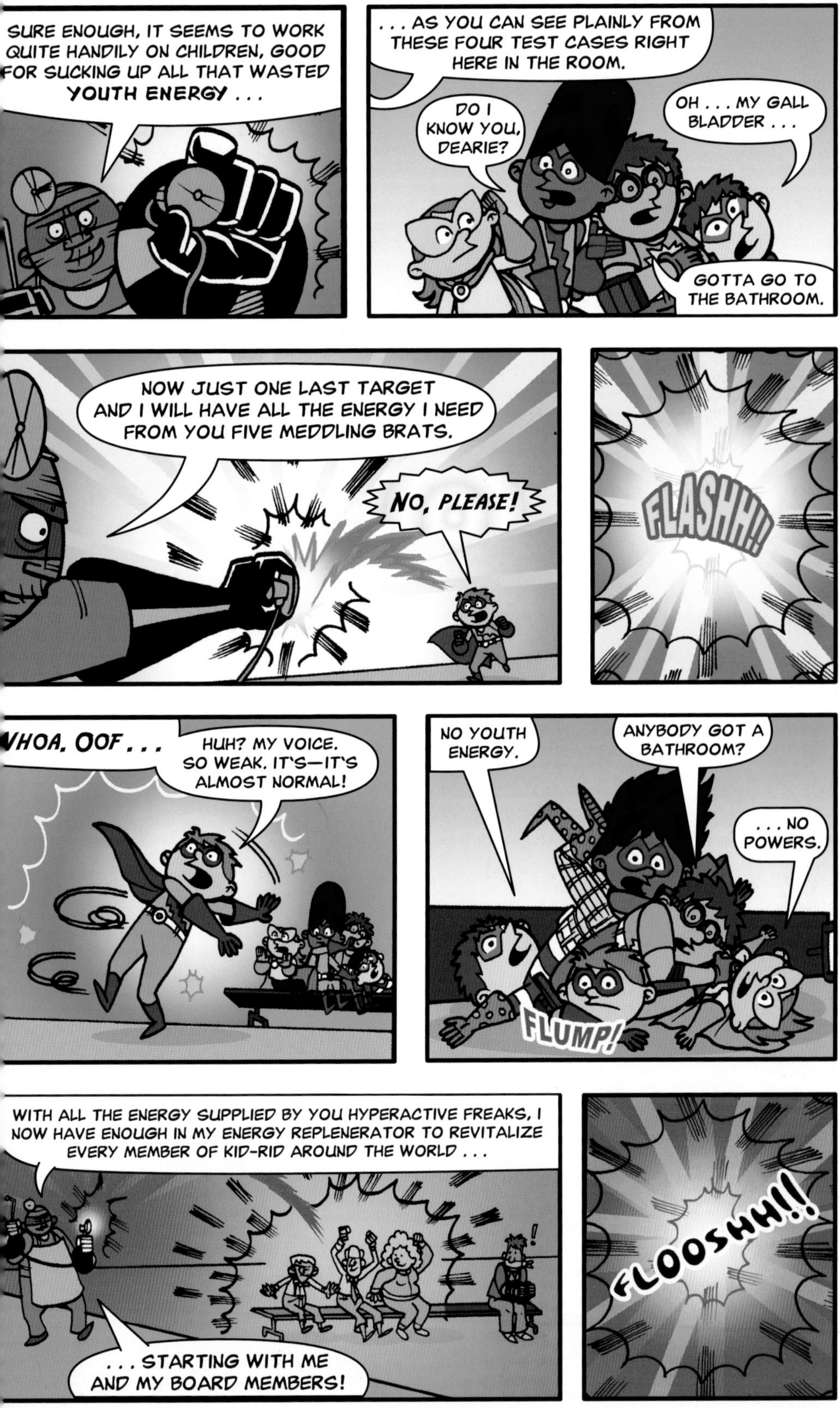
SURE ENOUGH, IT SEEMS TO WORK QUITE HANDILY ON CHILDREN, GOOD FOR SUCKING UP ALL THAT WASTED YOUTH ENERGY . . .
. . . AS YOU CAN SEE PLAINLY FROM THESE FOUR TEST CASES RIGHT HERE IN THE ROOM.
DO I KNOW YOU, DEARIE?
OH . . . MY GALL BLADDER . . .
GOTTA GO TO THE BATHROOM.
NOW JUST ONE LAST TARGET AND I WILL HAVE ALL THE ENERGY I NEED FROM YOU FIVE MEDDLING BRATS.
NO, PLEASE!
FLASHH!!
WHOA. OOF . . .
HUH? MY VOICE. SO WEAK. IT'S—IT'S ALMOST NORMAL!
NO YOUTH ENERGY.
ANYBODY GOT A BATHROOM?
. . . NO POWERS.
FLUMP!
WITH ALL THE ENERGY SUPPLIED BY YOU HYPERACTIVE FREAKS, I NOW HAVE ENOUGH IN MY ENERGY REPLENERATOR TO REVITALIZE EVERY MEMBER OF KID-RID AROUND THE WORLD . . .
. . . STARTING WITH ME AND MY BOARD MEMBERS!
FLOOSHH!!

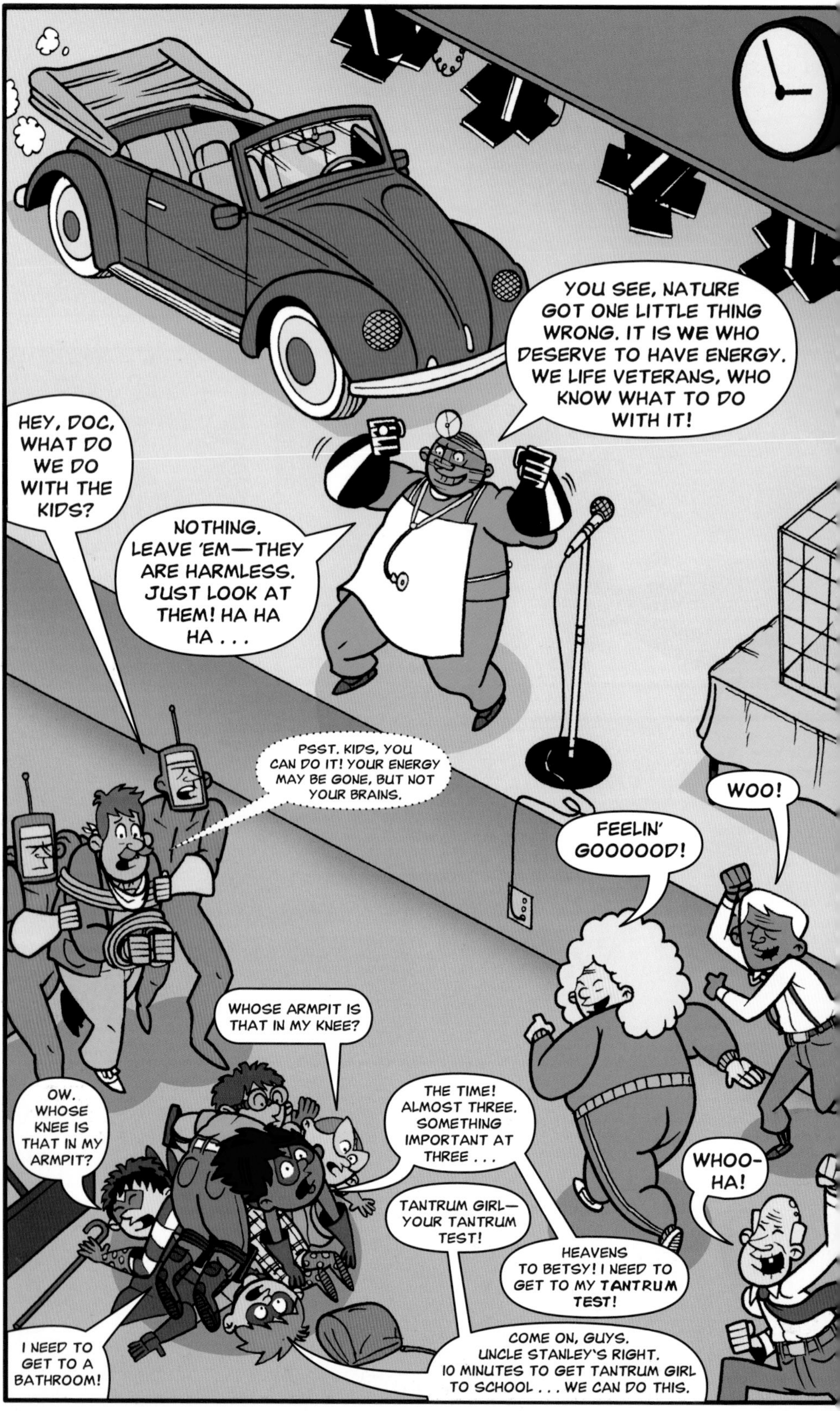
YOU SEE, NATURE GOT ONE LITTLE THING WRONG. IT IS WE WHO DESERVE TO HAVE ENERGY. WE LIFE VETERANS, WHO KNOW WHAT TO DO WITH IT!
HEY, DOC, WHAT DO WE DO WITH THE KIDS?
NOTHING. LEAVE 'EM—THEY ARE HARMLESS. JUST LOOK AT THEM! HA HA HA . . .
PSST. KIDS, YOU CAN DO IT! YOUR ENERGY MAY BE GONE, BUT NOT YOUR BRAINS.
WOO!
FEELIN' GOOOOOD!
WHOSE ARMPIT IS THAT IN MY KNEE?
OW. WHOSE KNEE IS THAT IN MY ARMPIT?
THE TIME! ALMOST THREE. SOMETHING IMPORTANT AT THREE . . .
WHOO-HA!
TANTRUM GIRL—YOUR TANTRUM TEST!
HEAVENS TO BETSY! I NEED TO GET TO MY TANTRUM TEST!
I NEED TO GET TO A BATHROOM!
COME ON, GUYS. UNCLE STANLEY'S RIGHT. 10 MINUTES TO GET TANTRUM GIRL TO SCHOOL . . . WE CAN DO THIS.

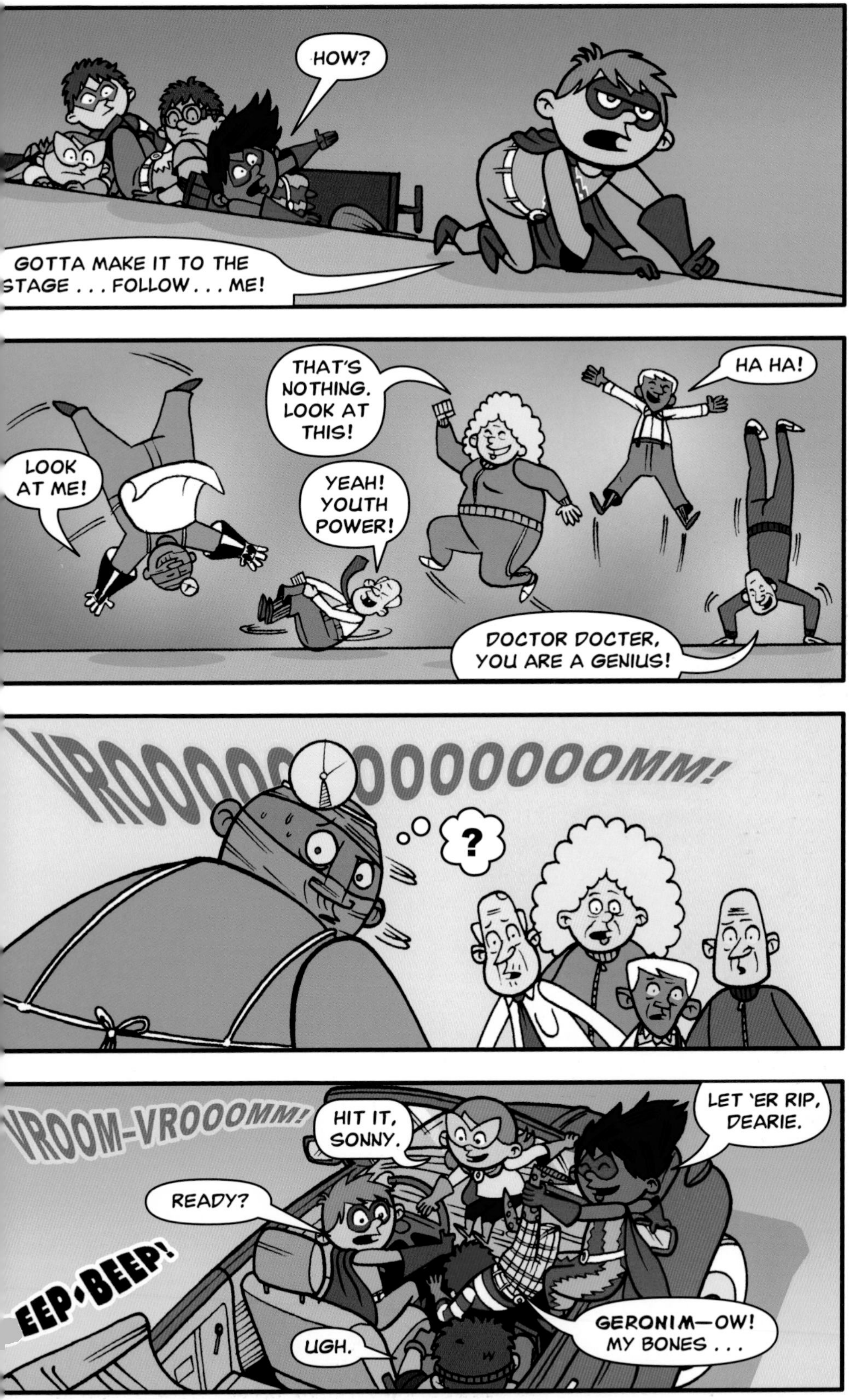
HOW?
GOTTA MAKE IT TO THE STAGE . . . FOLLOW . . . ME!
LOOK AT ME!
THAT'S NOTHING. LOOK AT THIS!
YEAH! YOUTH POWER!
HA HA!
DOCTOR DOCTER, YOU ARE A GENIUS!
VROOOOOOOOOOOOOMM!
?
VROOM-VROOOMM!
HIT IT, SONNY.
LET 'ER RIP, DEARIE.
READY?
EEP-BEEP!
UGH.
GERONIM—OW! MY BONES . . .

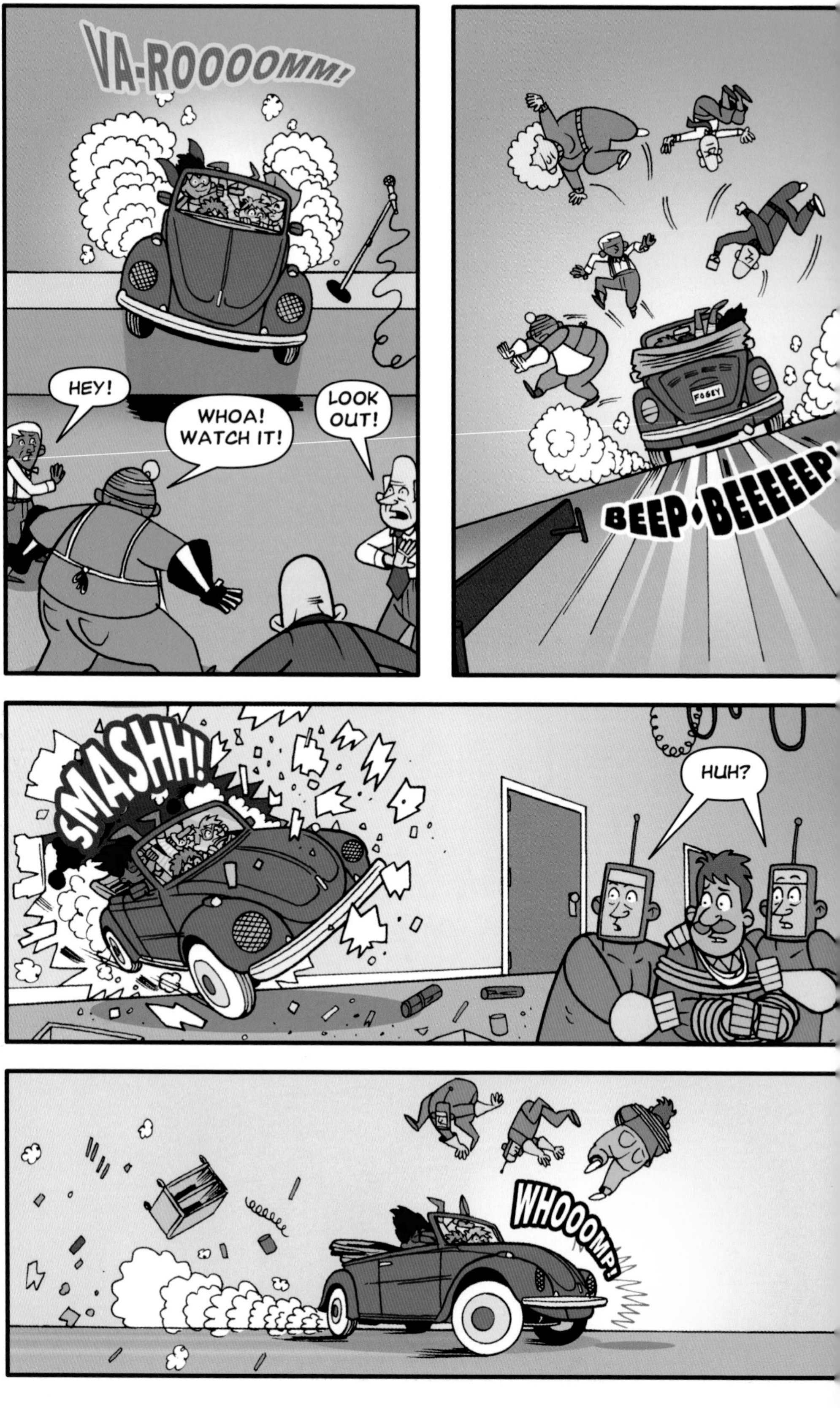
VA-ROOOOOMM!
HEY!
WHOA! WATCH IT!
LOOK OUT!
FOGEY
BEEP-BEEEEEP!
SMASHH!
HUH?
WHOOOMP!

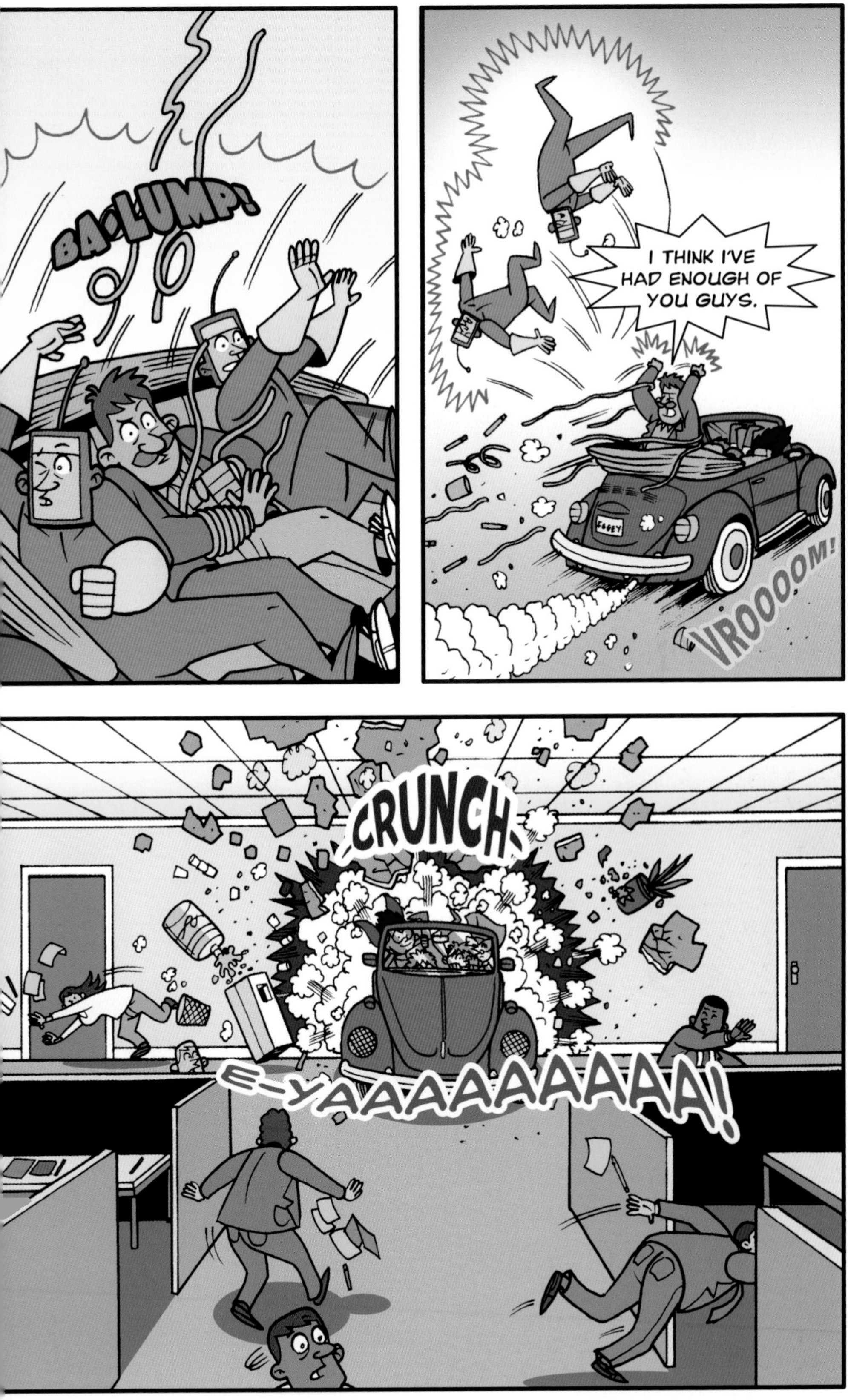
BA-LUMP!
I THINK I'VE HAD ENOUGH OF YOU GUYS.
VROOOOOM!
CRUNCH
E-YAAAAAAAAAA!

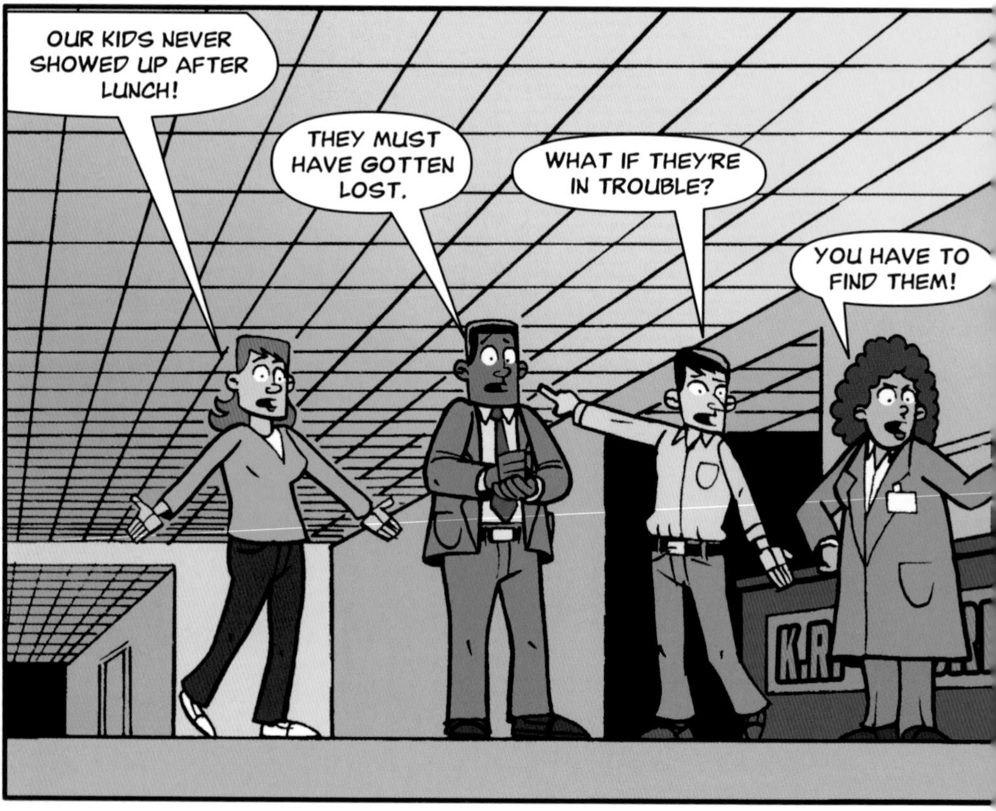
OUR KIDS NEVER SHOWED UP AFTER LUNCH!
THEY MUST HAVE GOTTEN LOST.
WHAT IF THEY'RE IN TROUBLE?
YOU HAVE TO FIND THEM!

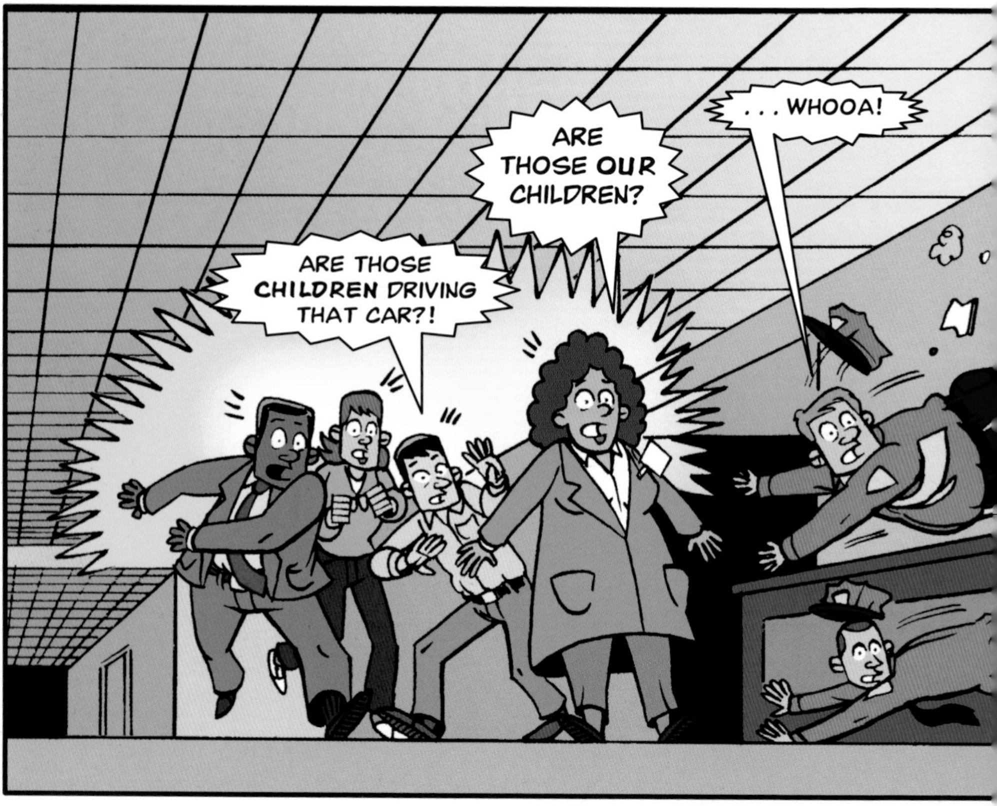
ARE THOSE **CHILDREN** DRIVING THAT CAR?!
ARE THOSE **OUR** CHILDREN?
. . . WHOOA!

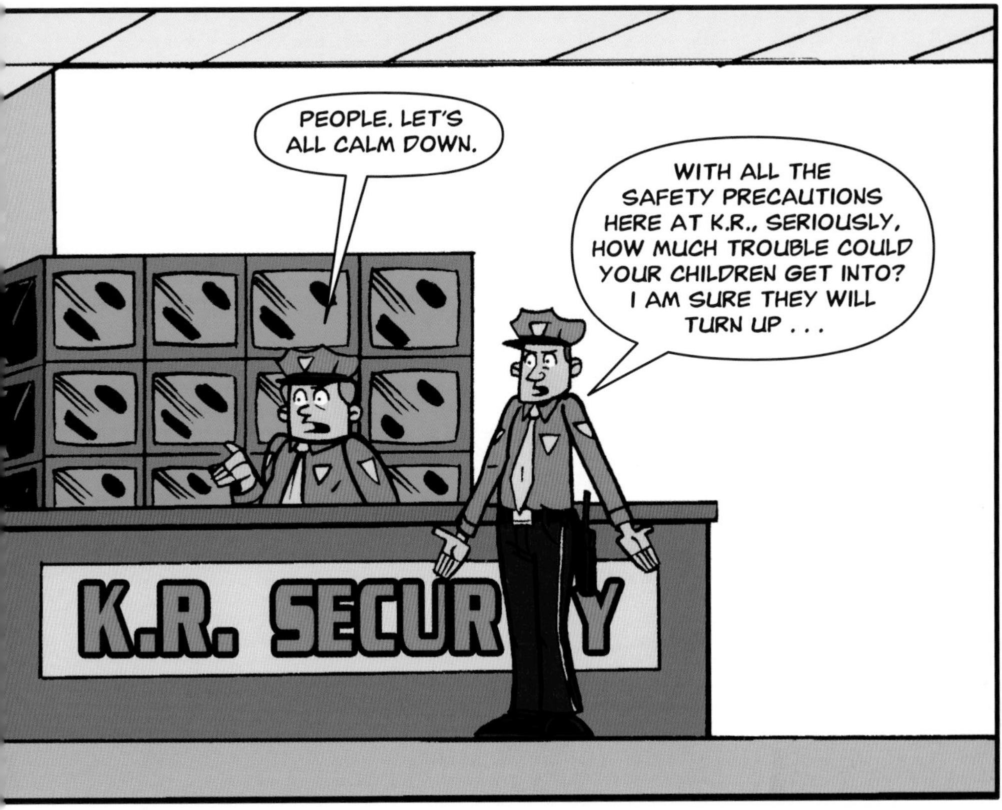
PEOPLE. LET'S ALL CALM DOWN.
WITH ALL THE SAFETY PRECAUTIONS HERE AT K.R., SERIOUSLY, HOW MUCH TROUBLE COULD YOUR CHILDREN GET INTO? I AM SURE THEY WILL TURN UP . . .
K.R. SECUR Y

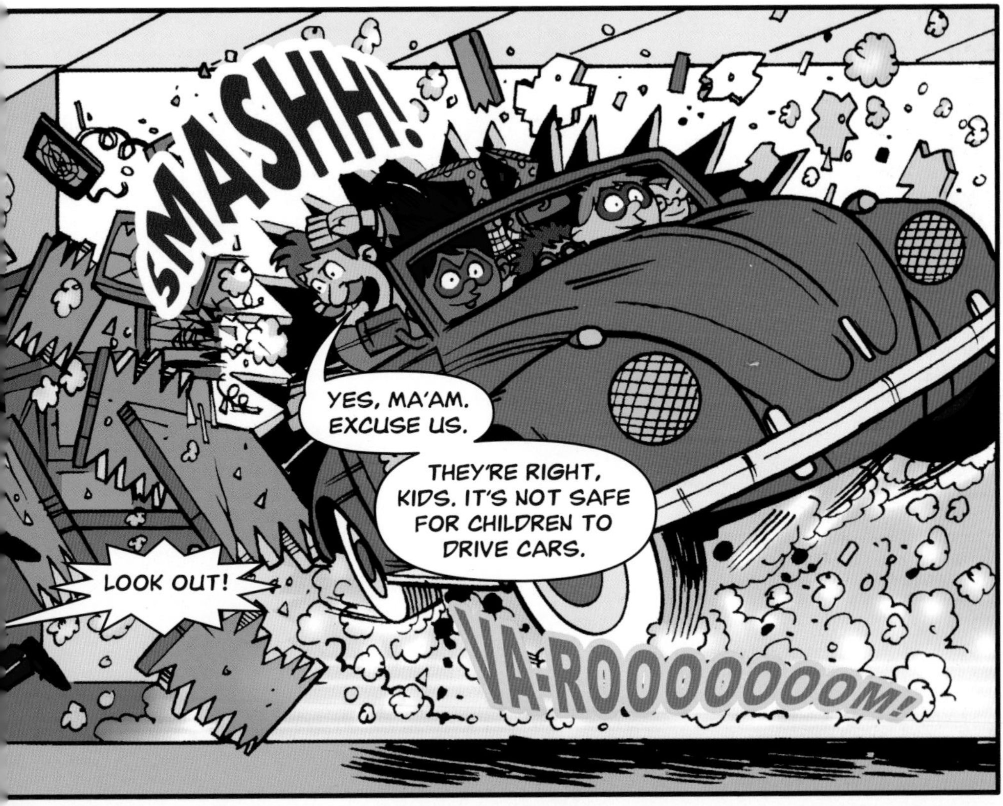
SMASHH!
YES, MA'AM. EXCUSE US.
THEY'RE RIGHT, KIDS. IT'S NOT SAFE FOR CHILDREN TO DRIVE CARS.
LOOK OUT!
VA-ROOOOOOOM!

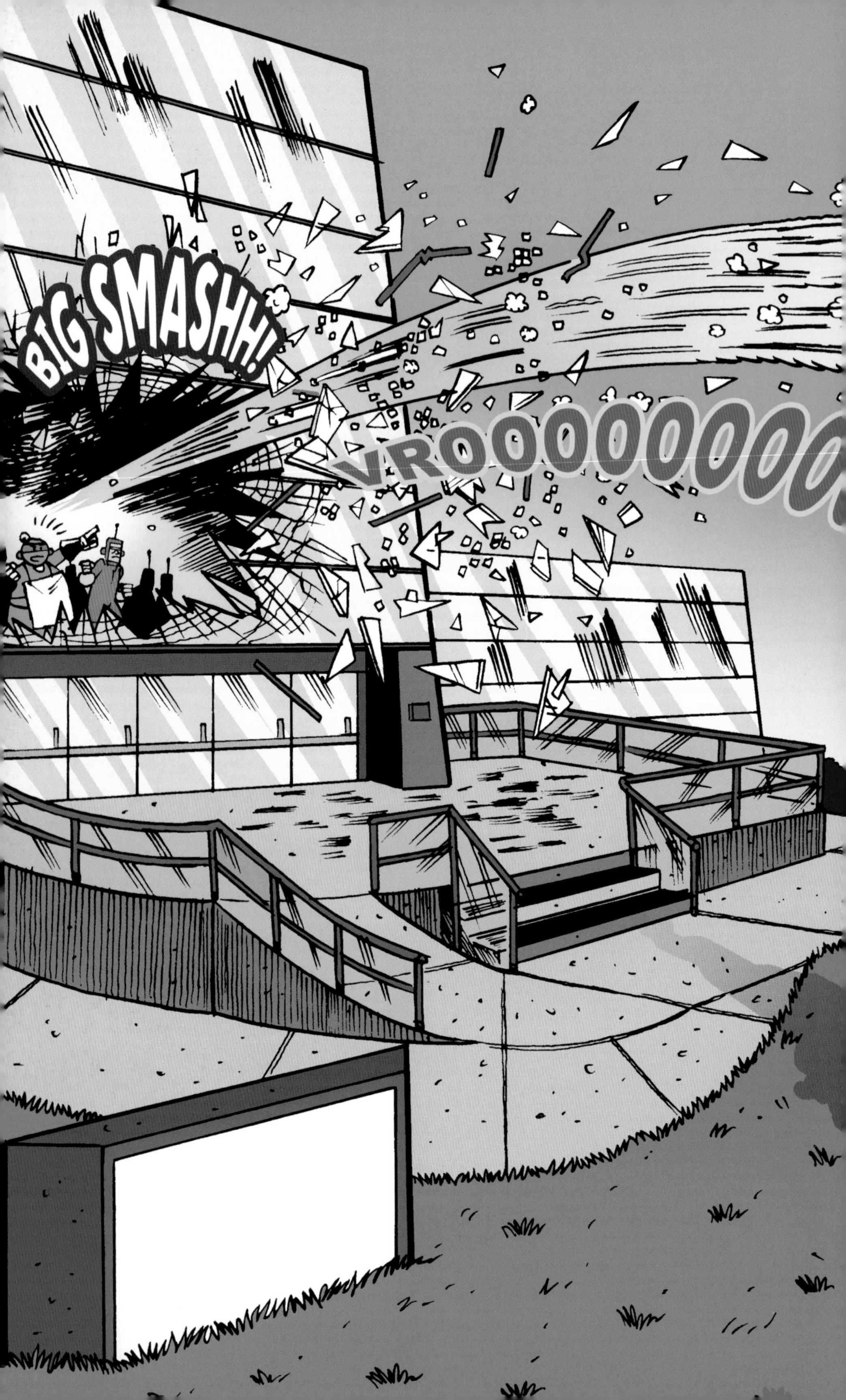
BIG SMASHH!
VROOOOOOOOO

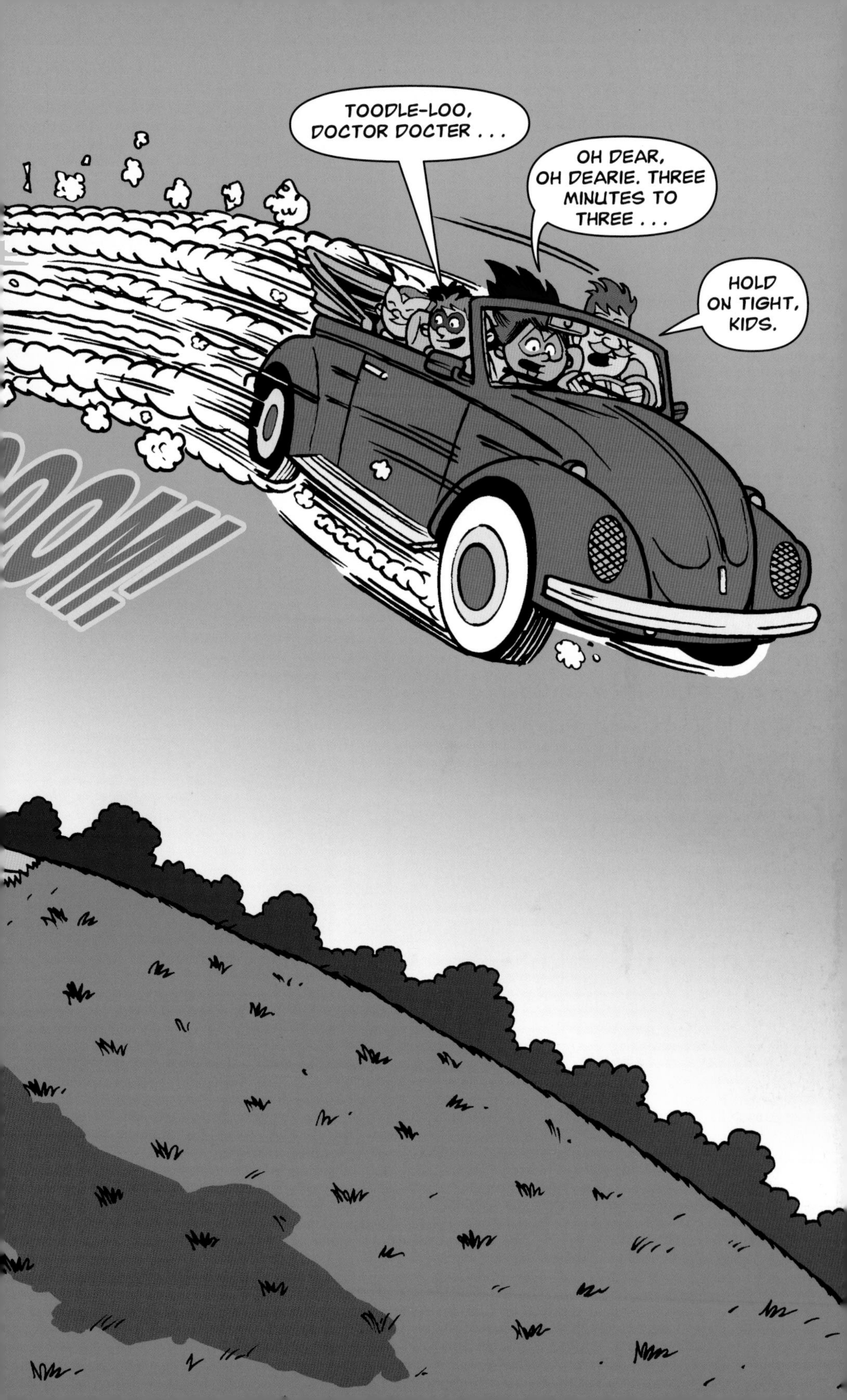
TOODLE-LOO, DOCTOR DOCTER . . .
OH DEAR, OH DEARIE. THREE MINUTES TO THREE . . .
HOLD ON TIGHT, KIDS.

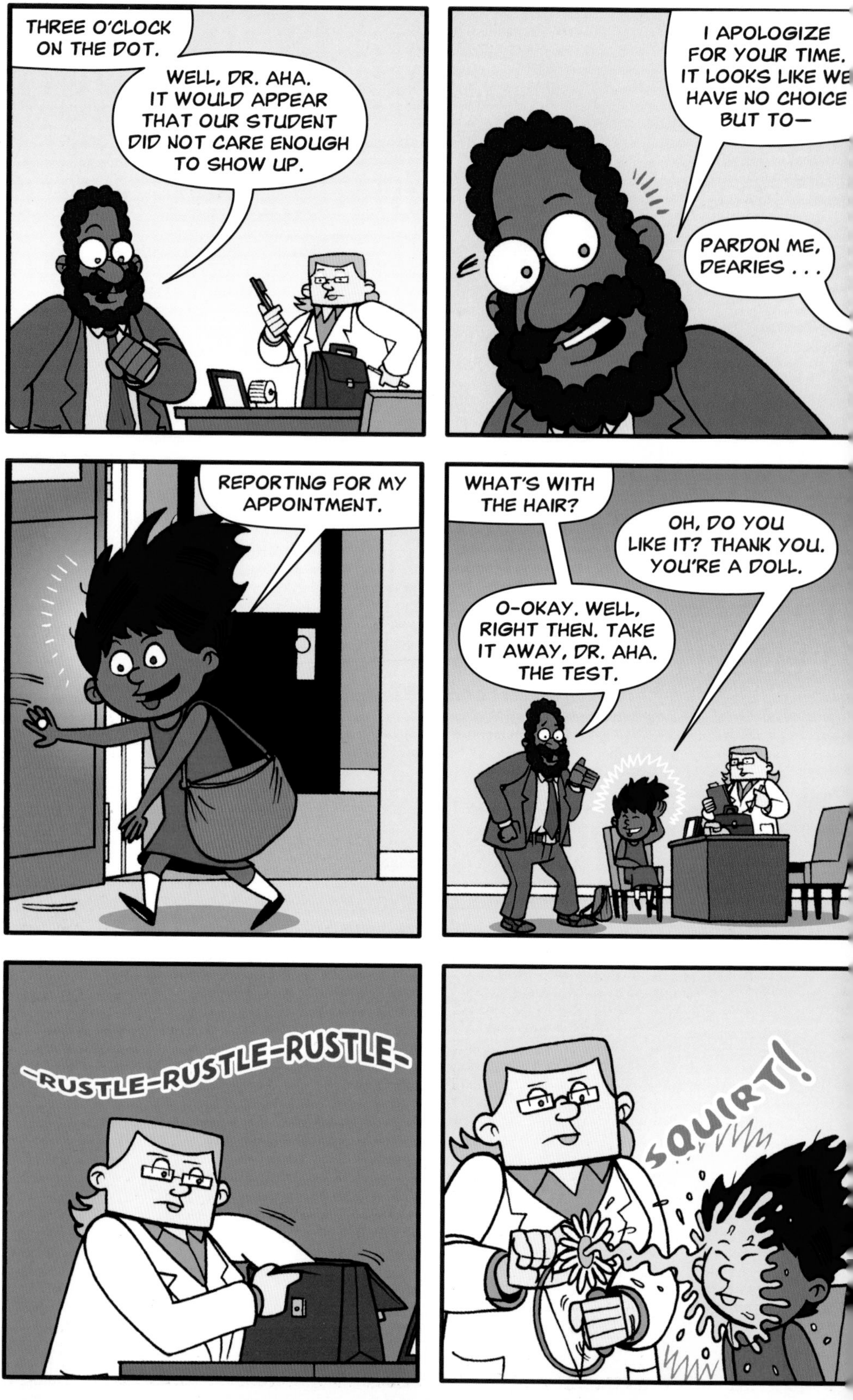
THREE O'CLOCK ON THE DOT.
WELL, DR. AHA. IT WOULD APPEAR THAT OUR STUDENT DID NOT CARE ENOUGH TO SHOW UP.
I APOLOGIZE FOR YOUR TIME. IT LOOKS LIKE WE HAVE NO CHOICE BUT TO—
PARDON ME, DEARIES . . .
REPORTING FOR MY APPOINTMENT.
WHAT'S WITH THE HAIR?
OH, DO YOU LIKE IT? THANK YOU. YOU'RE A DOLL.
O-OKAY. WELL, RIGHT THEN. TAKE IT AWAY, DR. AHA. THE TEST.
-RUSTLE-RUSTLE-RUSTLE-
SQUIRT!

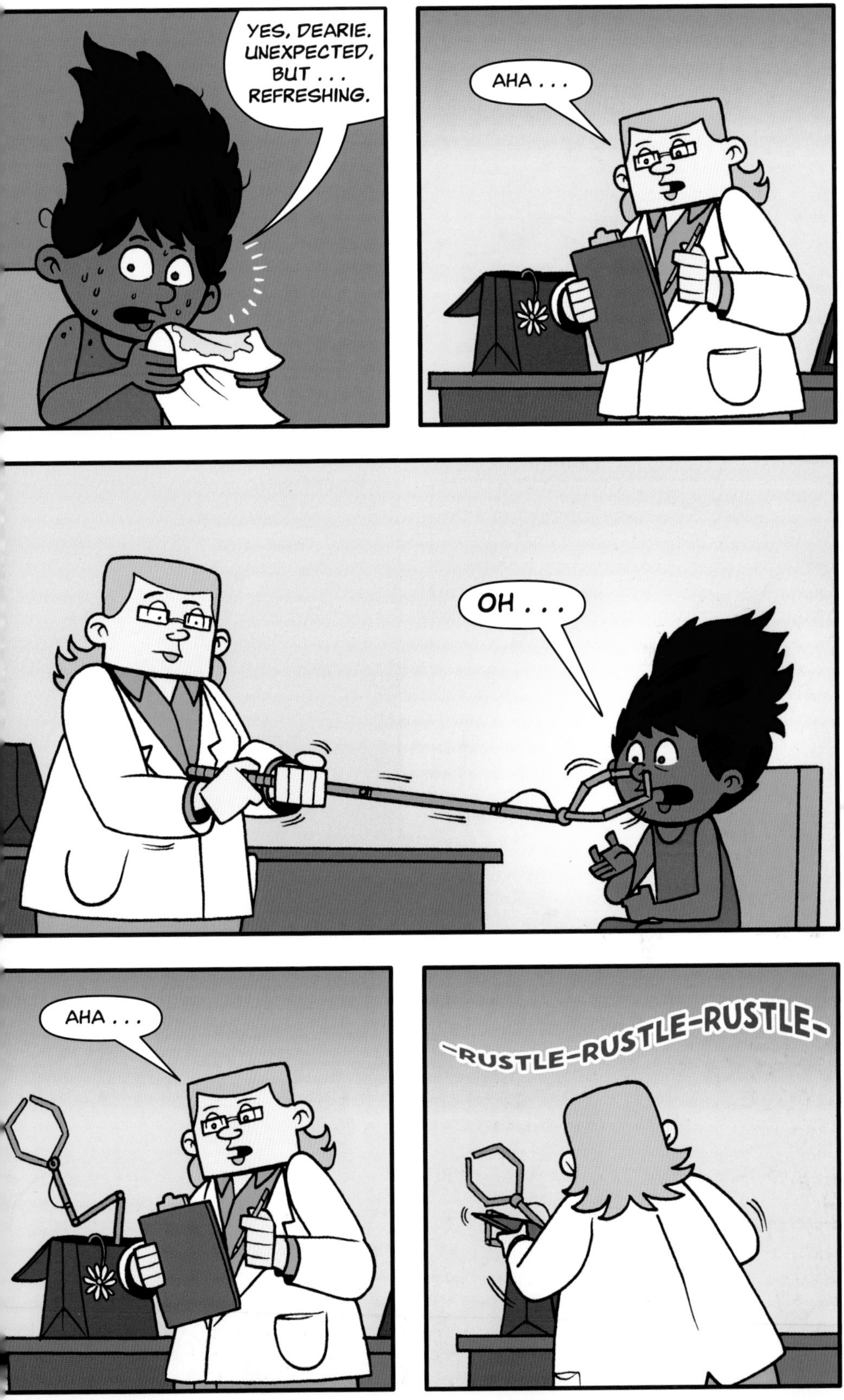
YES, DEARIE. UNEXPECTED, BUT . . . REFRESHING.
AHA . . .
OH . . .
AHA . . .
-RUSTLE-RUSTLE-RUSTLE-

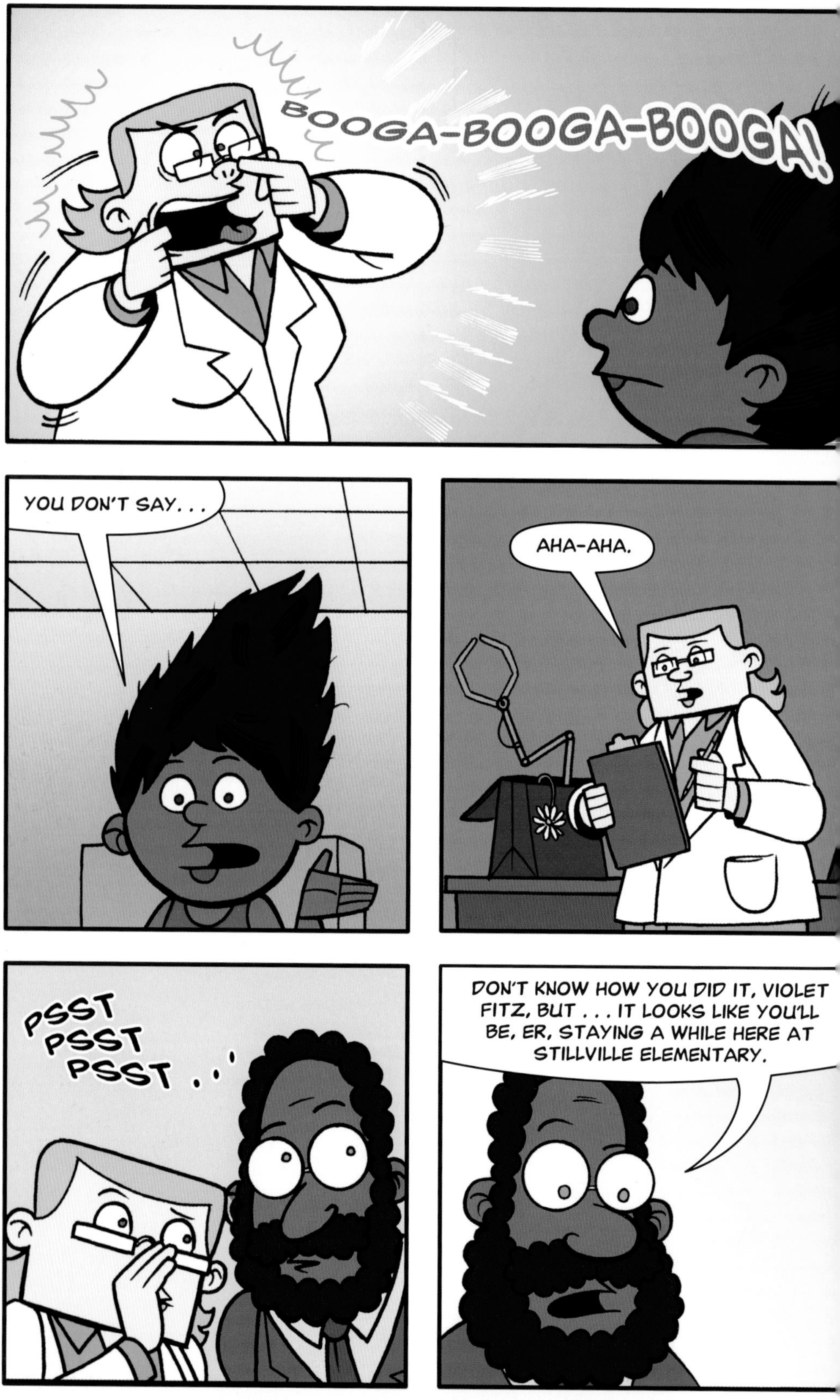

BOOGA-BOOGA-BOOGA!
YOU DON'T SAY. . .
AHA-AHA.
PSST
PSST
PSST . . .
DON'T KNOW HOW YOU DID IT, VIOLET FITZ, BUT . . . IT LOOKS LIKE YOU'LL BE, ER, STAYING A WHILE HERE AT STILLVILLE ELEMENTARY.

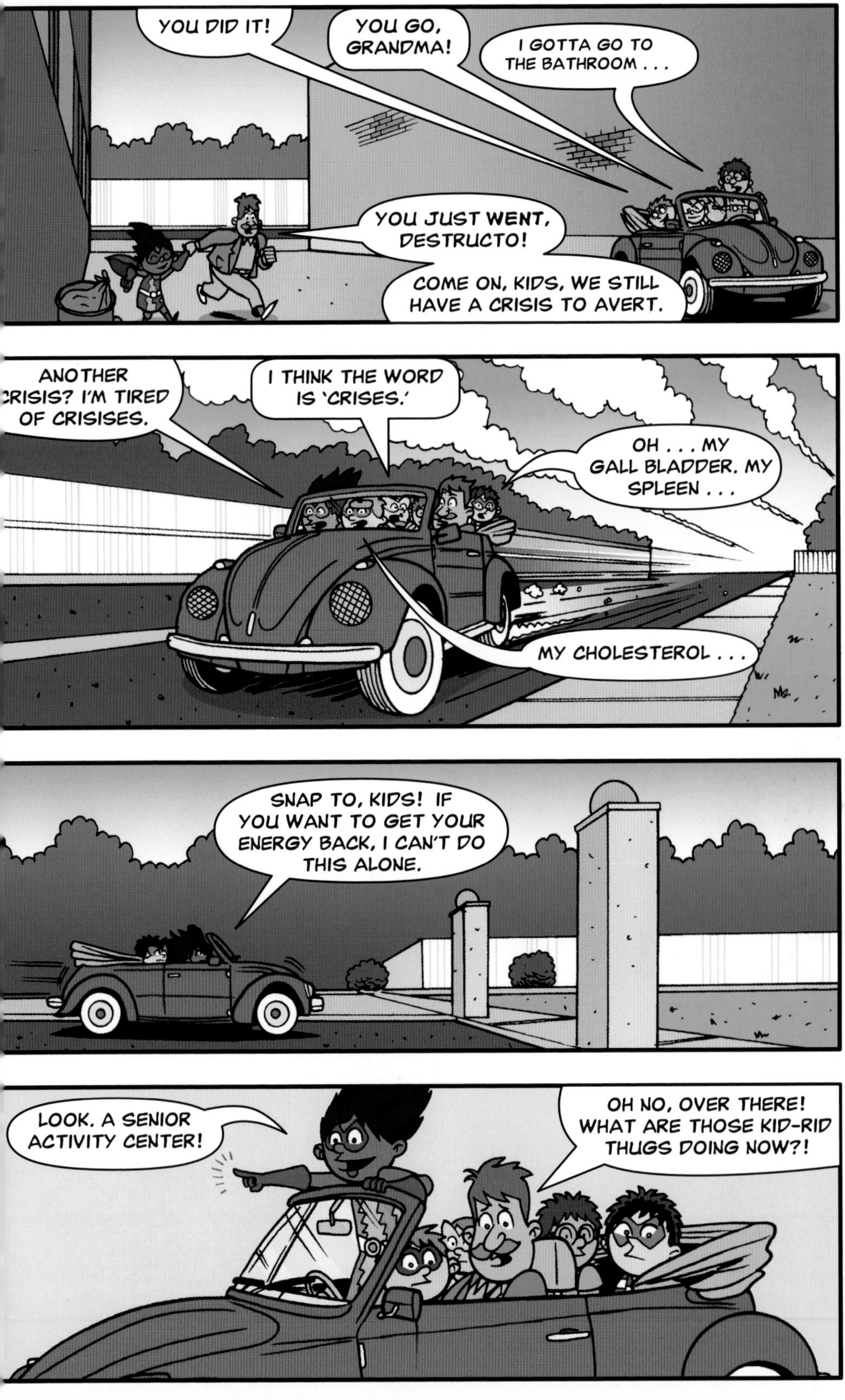

YOU DID IT!
YOU GO, GRANDMA!
I GOTTA GO TO THE BATHROOM . . .
YOU JUST WENT, DESTRUCTO!
COME ON, KIDS, WE STILL HAVE A CRISIS TO AVERT.
ANOTHER CRISIS? I'M TIRED OF CRISISES.
I THINK THE WORD IS 'CRISES.'
OH . . . MY GALL BLADDER. MY SPLEEN . . .
MY CHOLESTEROL . . .
SNAP TO, KIDS! IF YOU WANT TO GET YOUR ENERGY BACK, I CAN'T DO THIS ALONE.
LOOK. A SENIOR ACTIVITY CENTER!
OH NO, OVER THERE! WHAT ARE THOSE KID-RID THUGS DOING NOW?!

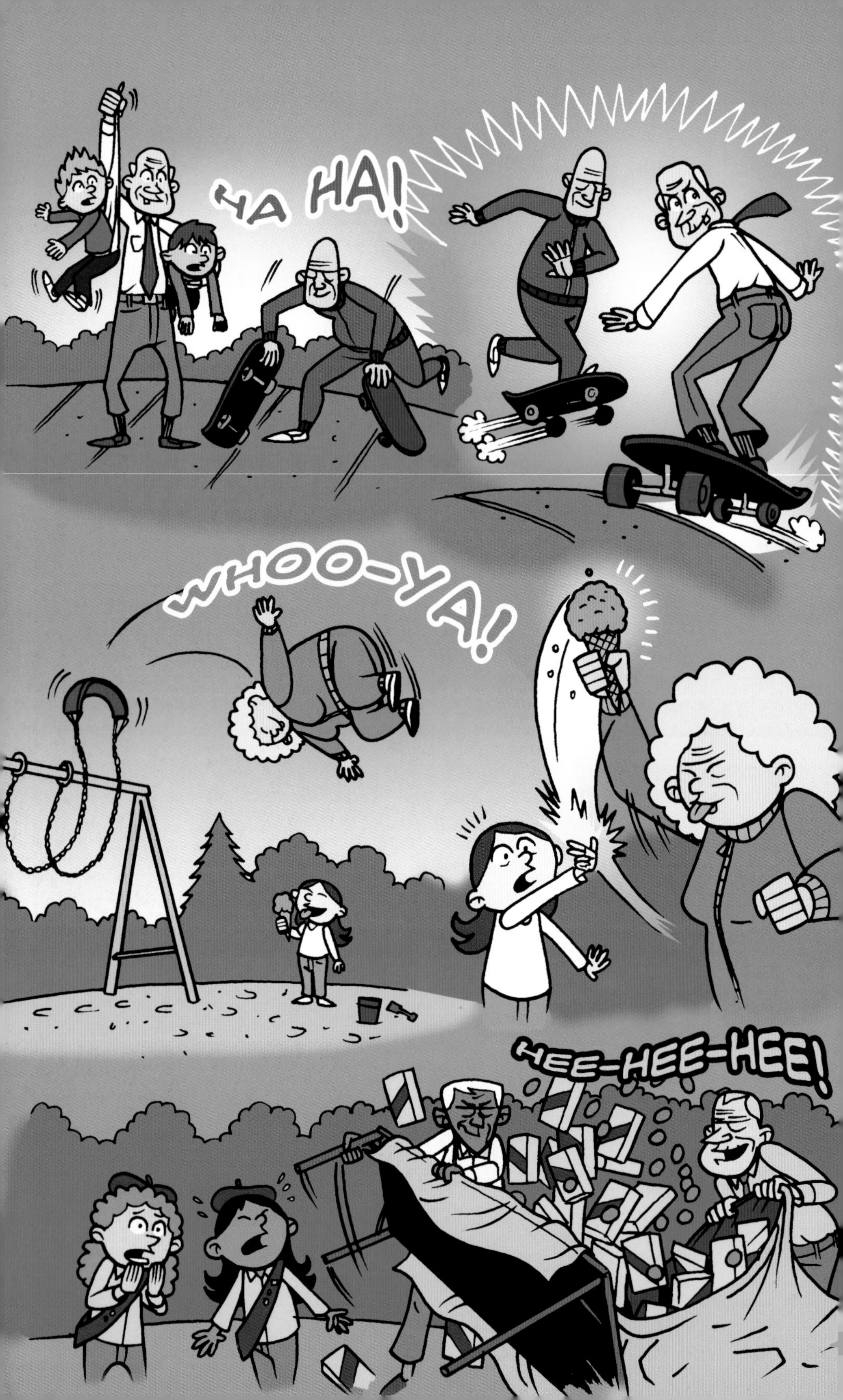
HA HA!
WHOO-YA!
HEE-HEE-HEE!

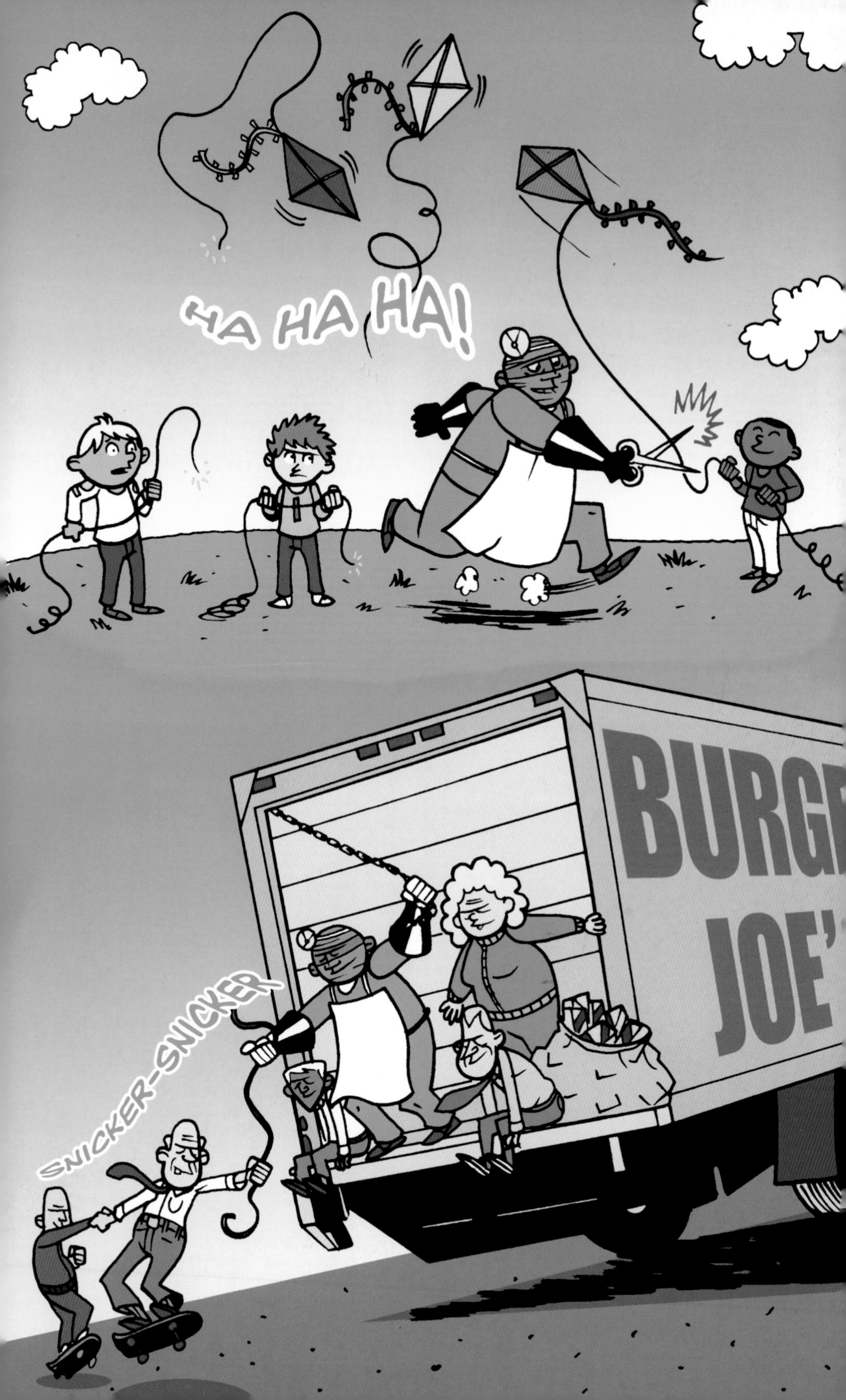
HA HA HA!
SNICKER-SNICKER
BURG
JOE'

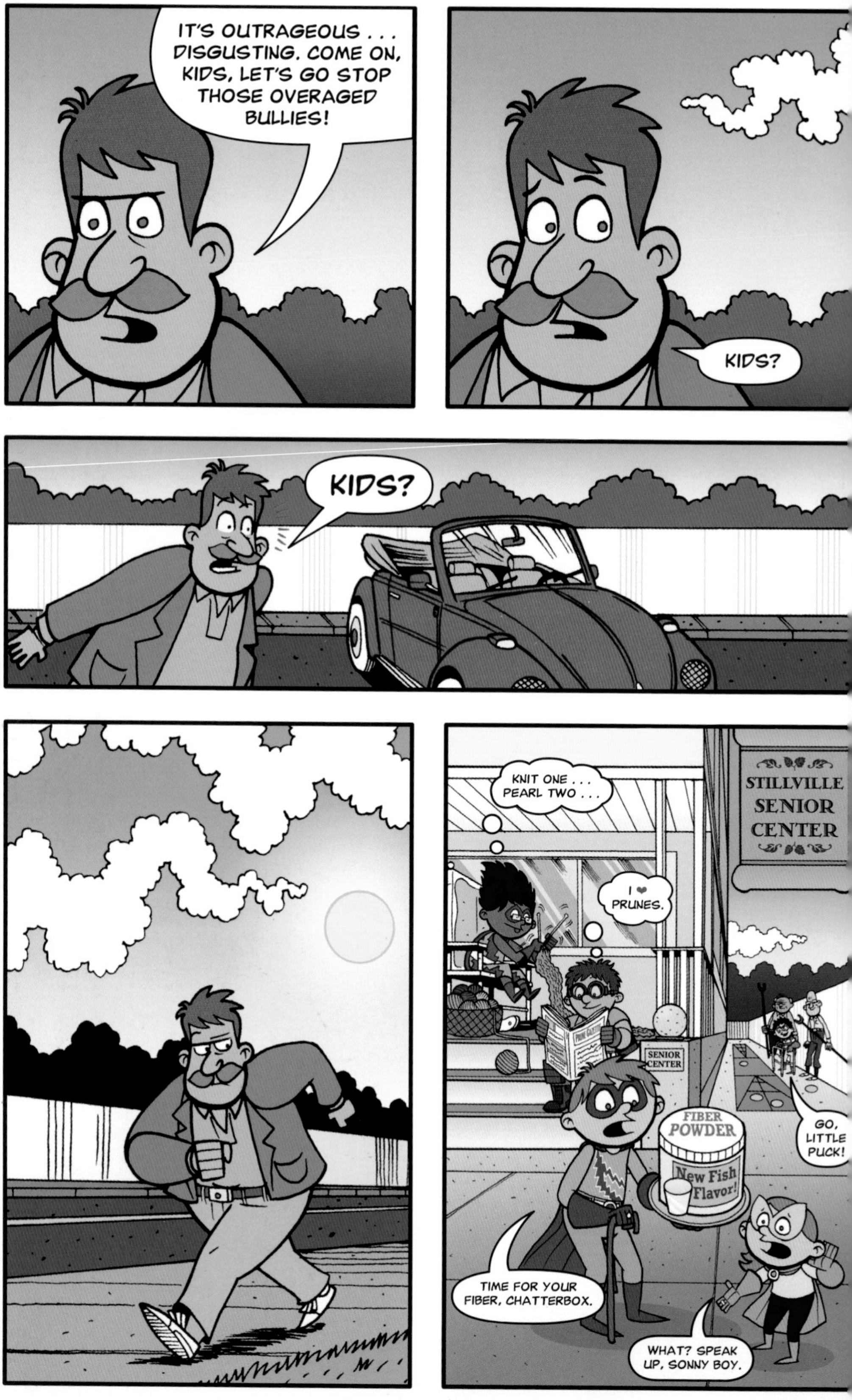
IT'S OUTRAGEOUS . . . DISGUSTING. COME ON, KIDS, LET'S GO STOP THOSE OVERAGED BULLIES!
KIDS?
KIDS?
KNIT ONE . . . PEARL TWO . . .
STILLVILLE SENIOR CENTER
I ❤ PRUNES.
SENIOR CENTER
FIBER POWDER
New Fish Flavor!
GO, LITTLE PUCK!
TIME FOR YOUR FIBER, CHATTERBOX.
WHAT? SPEAK UP, SONNY BOY.

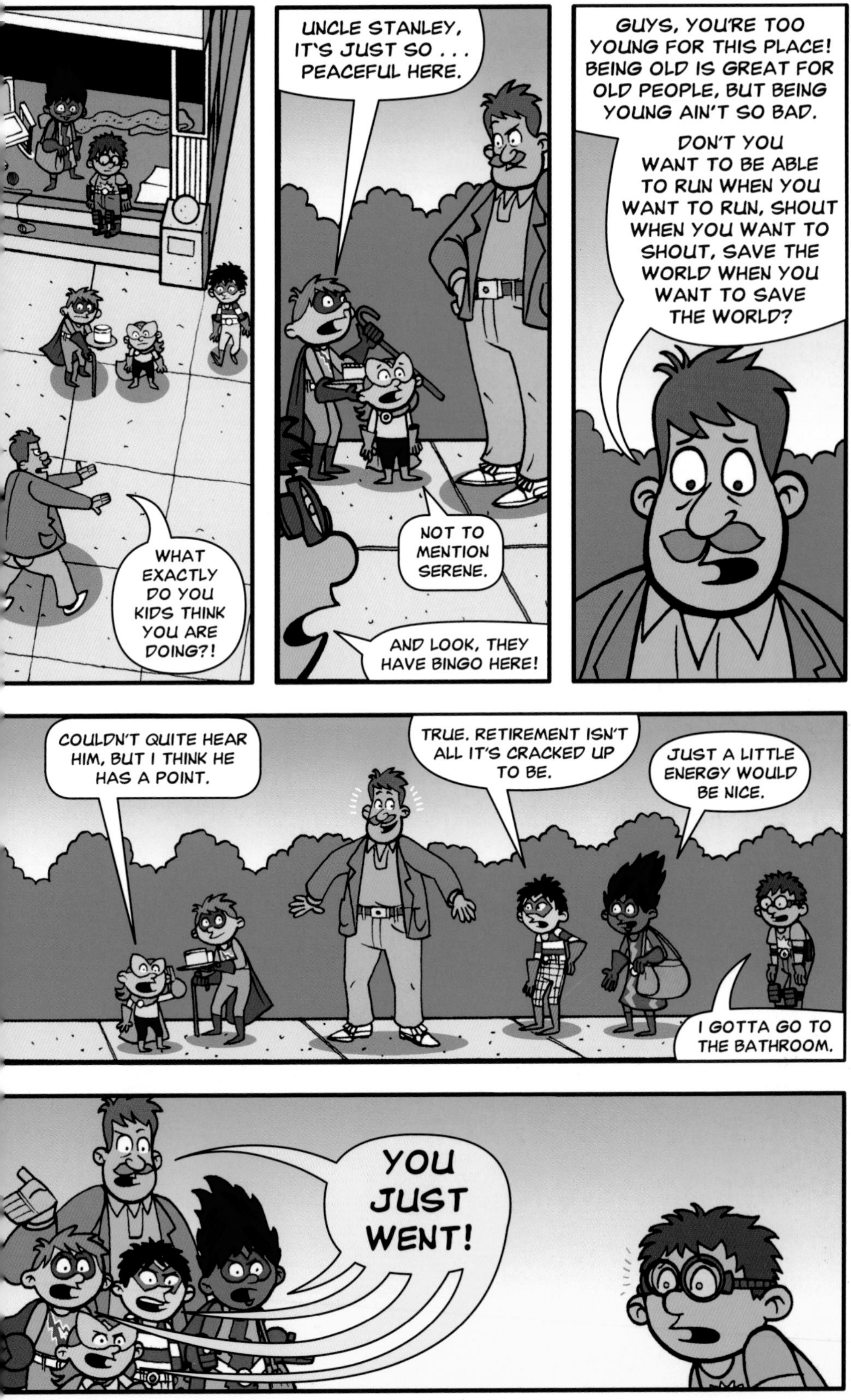
WHAT EXACTLY DO YOU KIDS THINK YOU ARE DOING?!
UNCLE STANLEY, IT'S JUST SO . . . PEACEFUL HERE.
NOT TO MENTION SERENE.
AND LOOK, THEY HAVE BINGO HERE!
GUYS, YOU'RE TOO YOUNG FOR THIS PLACE! BEING OLD IS GREAT FOR OLD PEOPLE, BUT BEING YOUNG AIN'T SO BAD.
DON'T YOU WANT TO BE ABLE TO RUN WHEN YOU WANT TO RUN, SHOUT WHEN YOU WANT TO SHOUT, SAVE THE WORLD WHEN YOU WANT TO SAVE THE WORLD?
COULDN'T QUITE HEAR HIM, BUT I THINK HE HAS A POINT.
TRUE. RETIREMENT ISN'T ALL IT'S CRACKED UP TO BE.
JUST A LITTLE ENERGY WOULD BE NICE.
I GOTTA GO TO THE BATHROOM.
YOU JUST WENT!

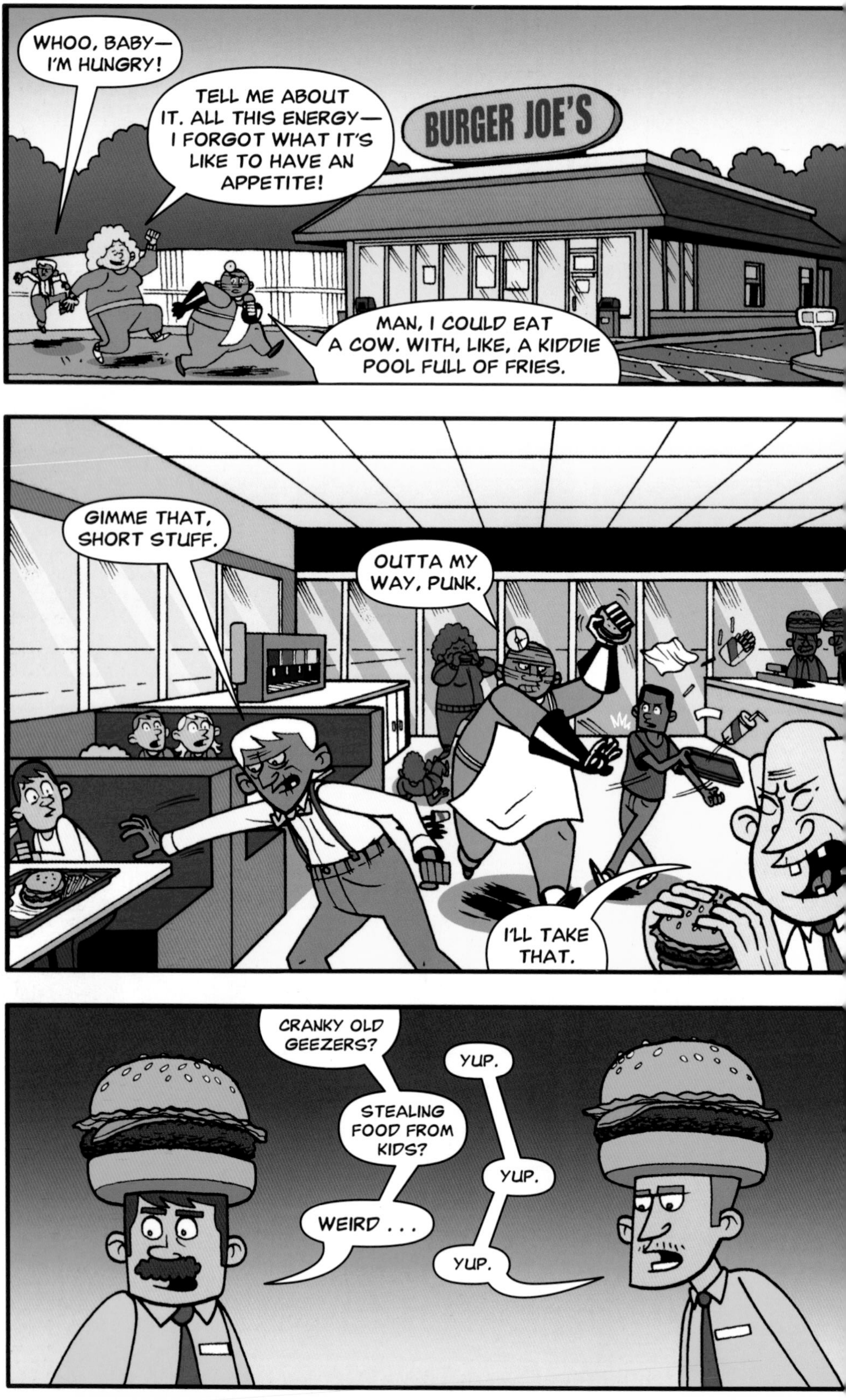
WHOO, BABY—
I'M HUNGRY!
TELL ME ABOUT IT. ALL THIS ENERGY—I FORGOT WHAT IT'S LIKE TO HAVE AN APPETITE!
BURGER JOE'S
MAN, I COULD EAT A COW. WITH, LIKE, A KIDDIE POOL FULL OF FRIES.
GIMME THAT, SHORT STUFF.
OUTTA MY WAY, PUNK.
I'LL TAKE THAT.
CRANKY OLD GEEZERS?
YUP.
STEALING FOOD FROM KIDS?
YUP.
WEIRD . . .
YUP.

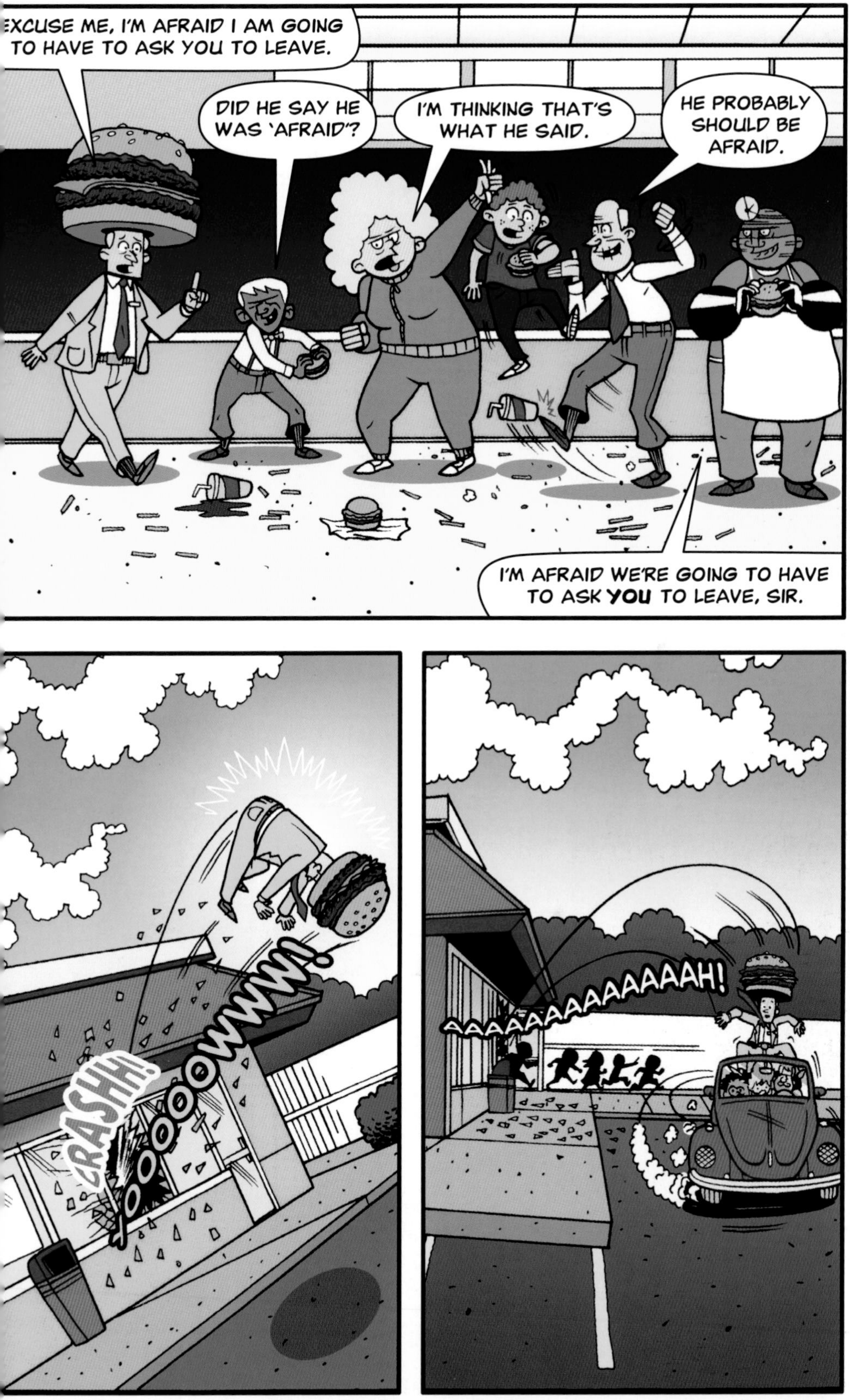
EXCUSE ME, I'M AFRAID I AM GOING TO HAVE TO ASK YOU TO LEAVE.
DID HE SAY HE WAS 'AFRAID'?
I'M THINKING THAT'S WHAT HE SAID.
HE PROBABLY SHOULD BE AFRAID.
I'M AFRAID WE'RE GOING TO HAVE TO ASK **YOU** TO LEAVE, SIR.
CRASHH!
YOOOOOWWWW!
AAAAAAAAAAAAAAH!

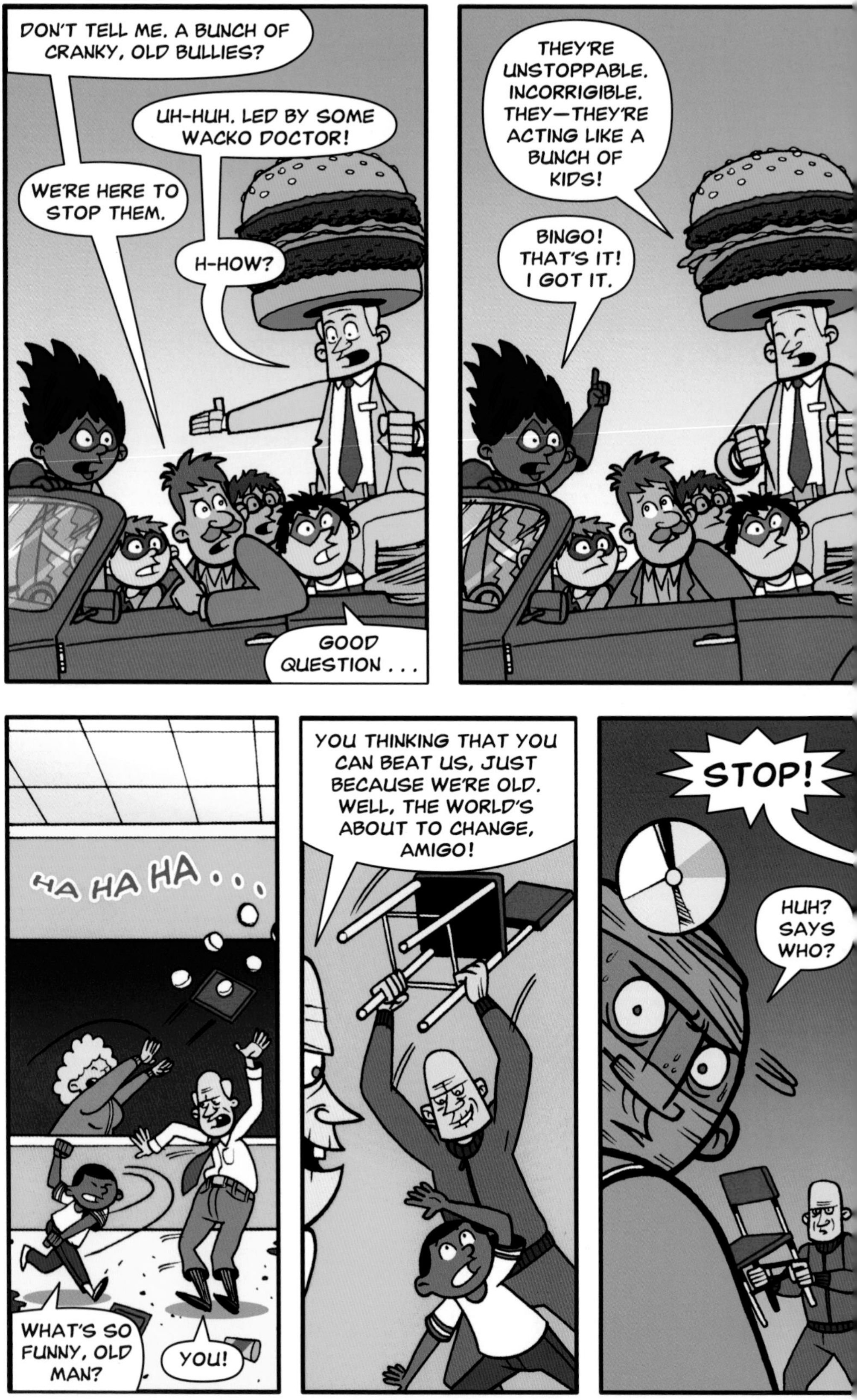
DON'T TELL ME. A BUNCH OF CRANKY, OLD BULLIES?
UH-HUH. LED BY SOME WACKO DOCTOR!
WE'RE HERE TO STOP THEM.
H-HOW?
GOOD QUESTION . . .
THEY'RE UNSTOPPABLE. INCORRIGIBLE. THEY—THEY'RE ACTING LIKE A BUNCH OF KIDS!
BINGO! THAT'S IT! I GOT IT.
HA HA HA . . .
WHAT'S SO FUNNY, OLD MAN?
YOU!
YOU THINKING THAT YOU CAN BEAT US, JUST BECAUSE WE'RE OLD. WELL, THE WORLD'S ABOUT TO CHANGE, AMIGO!
STOP!
HUH? SAYS WHO?

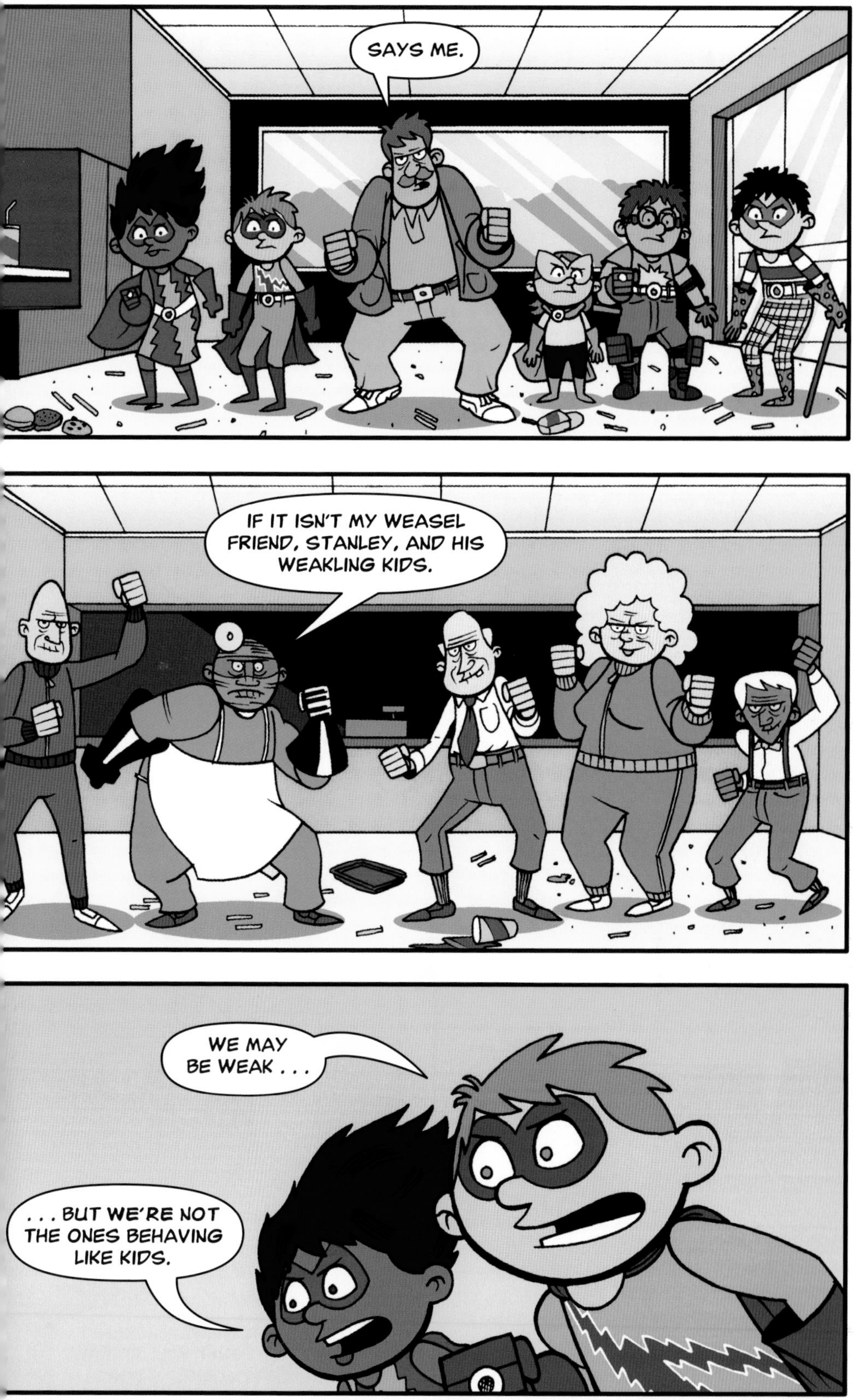
SAYS ME.
IF IT ISN'T MY WEASEL FRIEND, STANLEY, AND HIS WEAKLING KIDS.
WE MAY BE WEAK . . .
. . . BUT WE'RE NOT THE ONES BEHAVING LIKE KIDS.

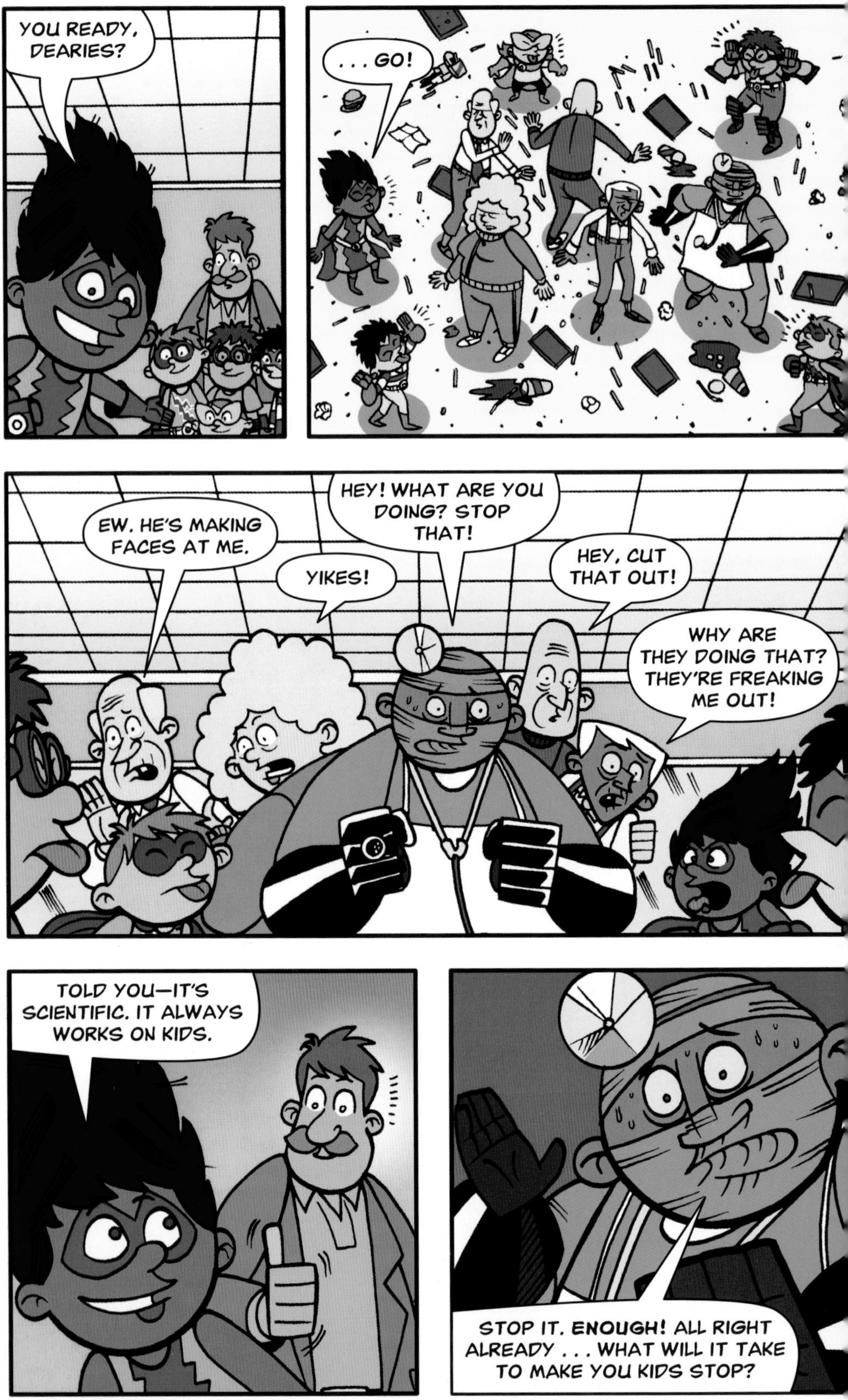
YOU READY, DEARIES?
. . . GO!
EW. HE'S MAKING FACES AT ME.
YIKES!
HEY! WHAT ARE YOU DOING? STOP THAT!
HEY, CUT THAT OUT!
WHY ARE THEY DOING THAT? THEY'RE FREAKING ME OUT!
TOLD YOU—IT'S SCIENTIFIC. IT ALWAYS WORKS ON KIDS.
STOP IT. ENOUGH! ALL RIGHT ALREADY . . . WHAT WILL IT TAKE TO MAKE YOU KIDS STOP?

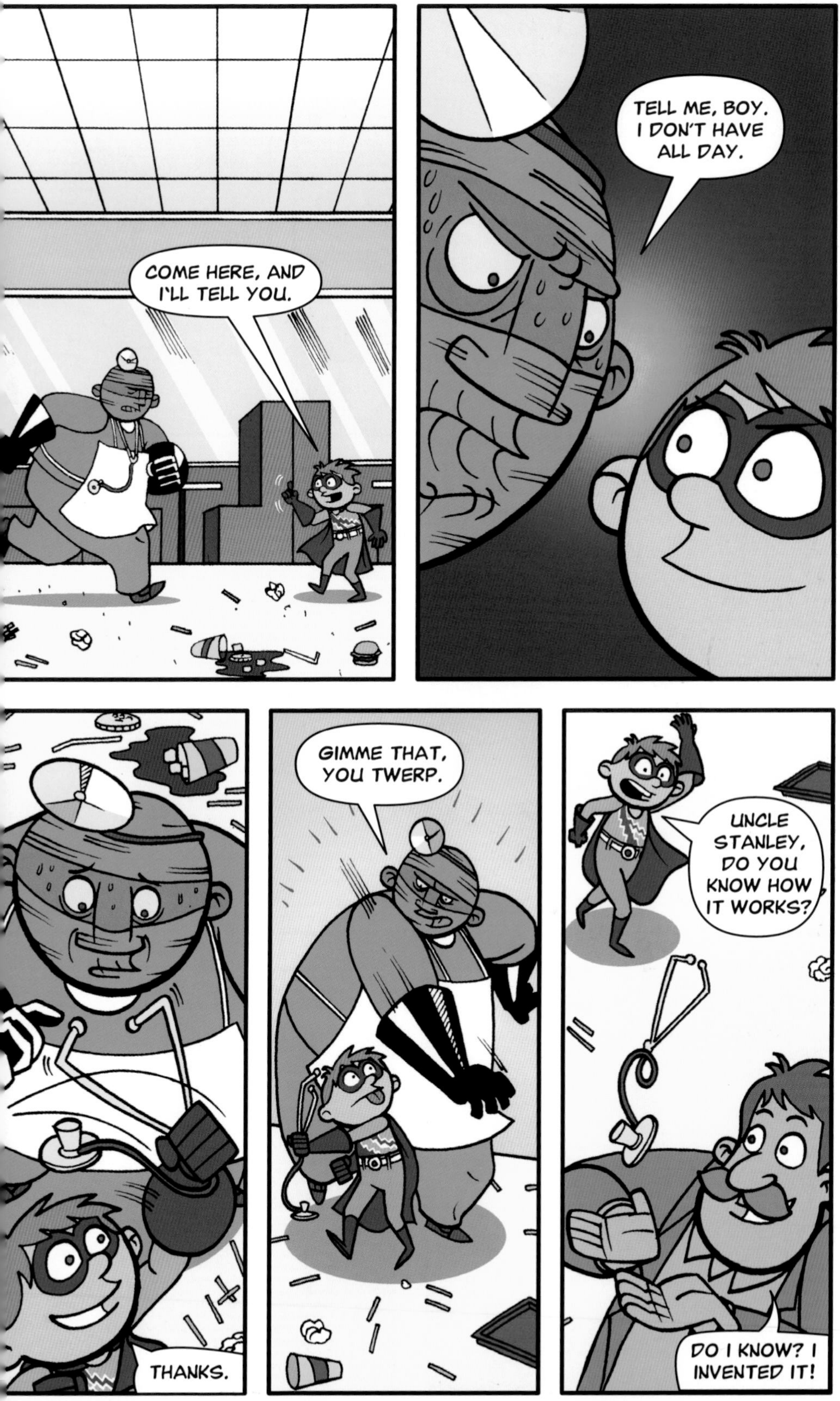
COME HERE, AND I'LL TELL YOU.
TELL ME, BOY. I DON'T HAVE ALL DAY.
THANKS.
GIMME THAT, YOU TWERP.
UNCLE STANLEY, DO YOU KNOW HOW IT WORKS?
DO I KNOW? I INVENTED IT!

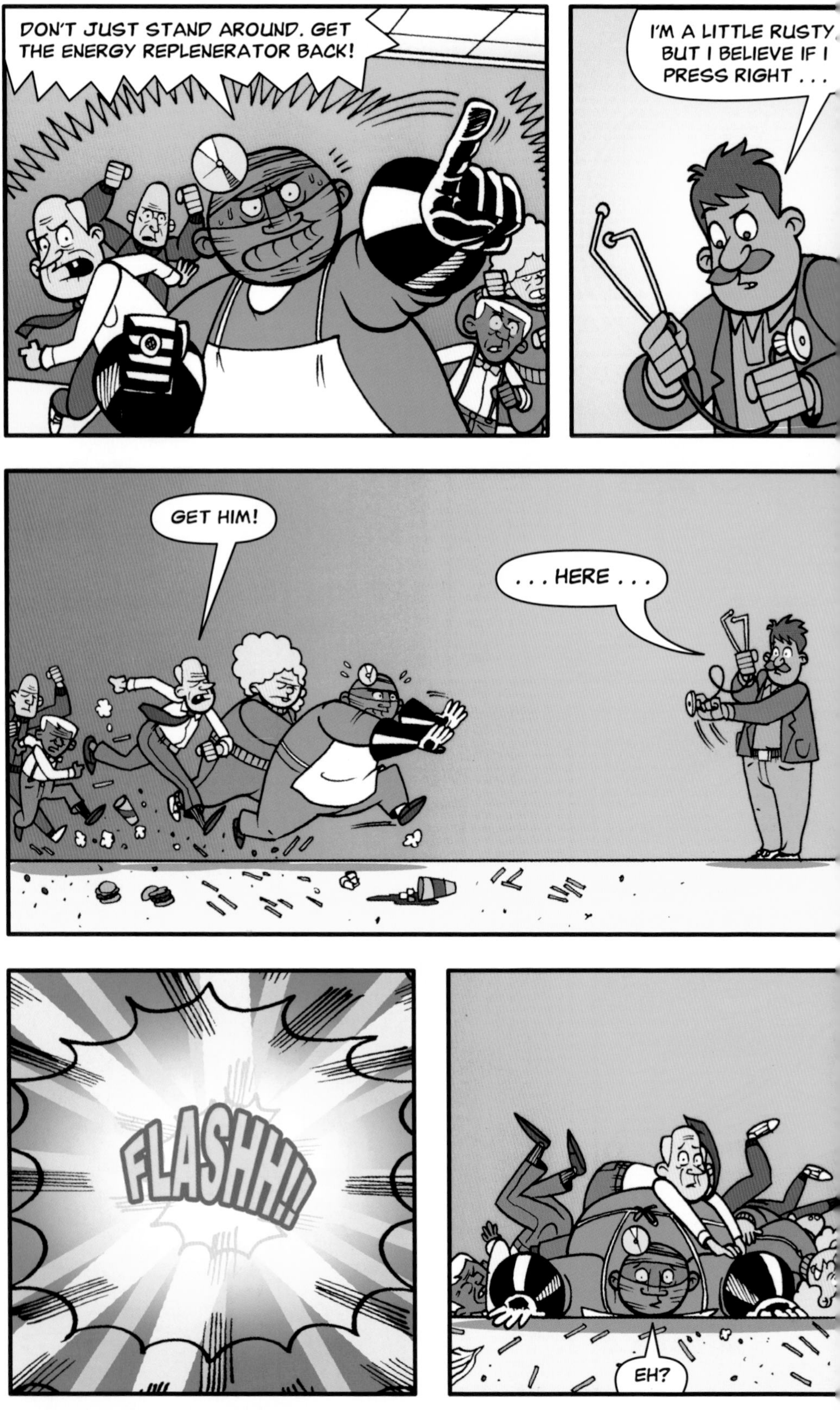
DON'T JUST STAND AROUND. GET THE ENERGY REPLENERATOR BACK!
I'M A LITTLE RUSTY, BUT I BELIEVE IF I PRESS RIGHT . . .
GET HIM!
. . . HERE . . .
FLASHH!!
EH?

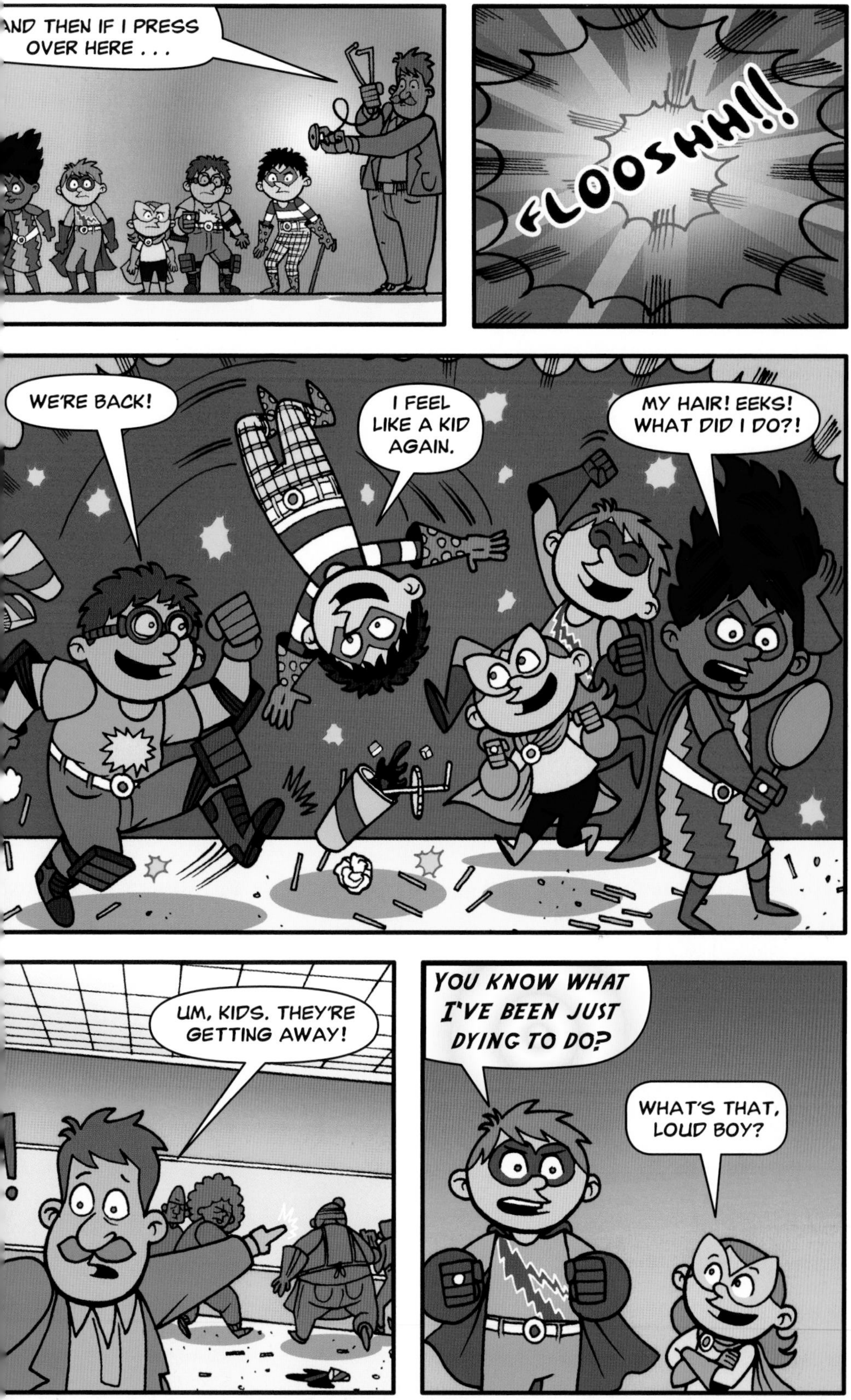
AND THEN IF I PRESS OVER HERE . . .
FLOOSHH!!
WE'RE BACK!
I FEEL LIKE A KID AGAIN.
MY HAIR! EEKS! WHAT DID I DO?!
UM, KIDS. THEY'RE GETTING AWAY!
YOU KNOW WHAT I'VE BEEN JUST DYING TO DO?
WHAT'S THAT, LOUD BOY?

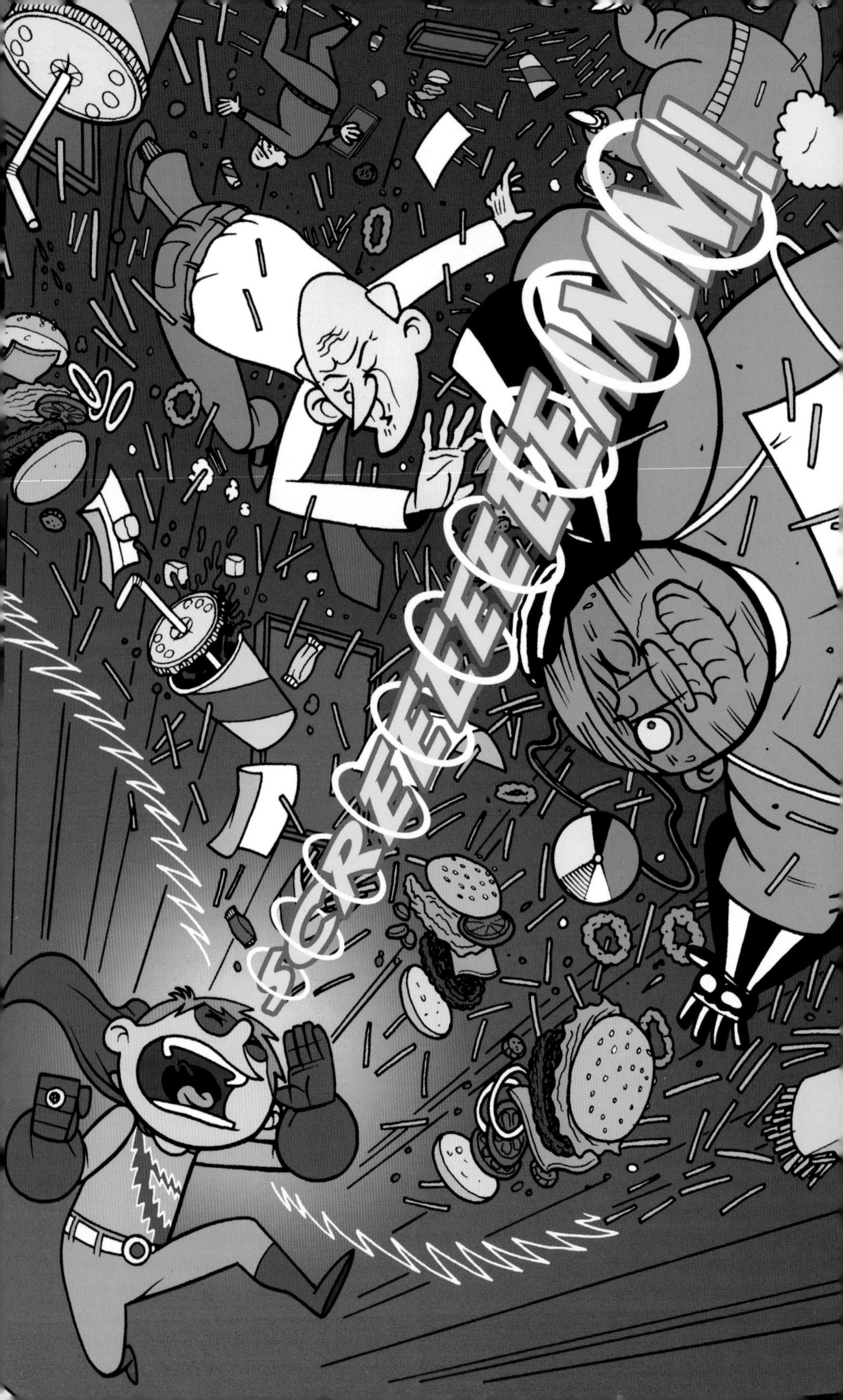
SCREEEEEEEAM!!

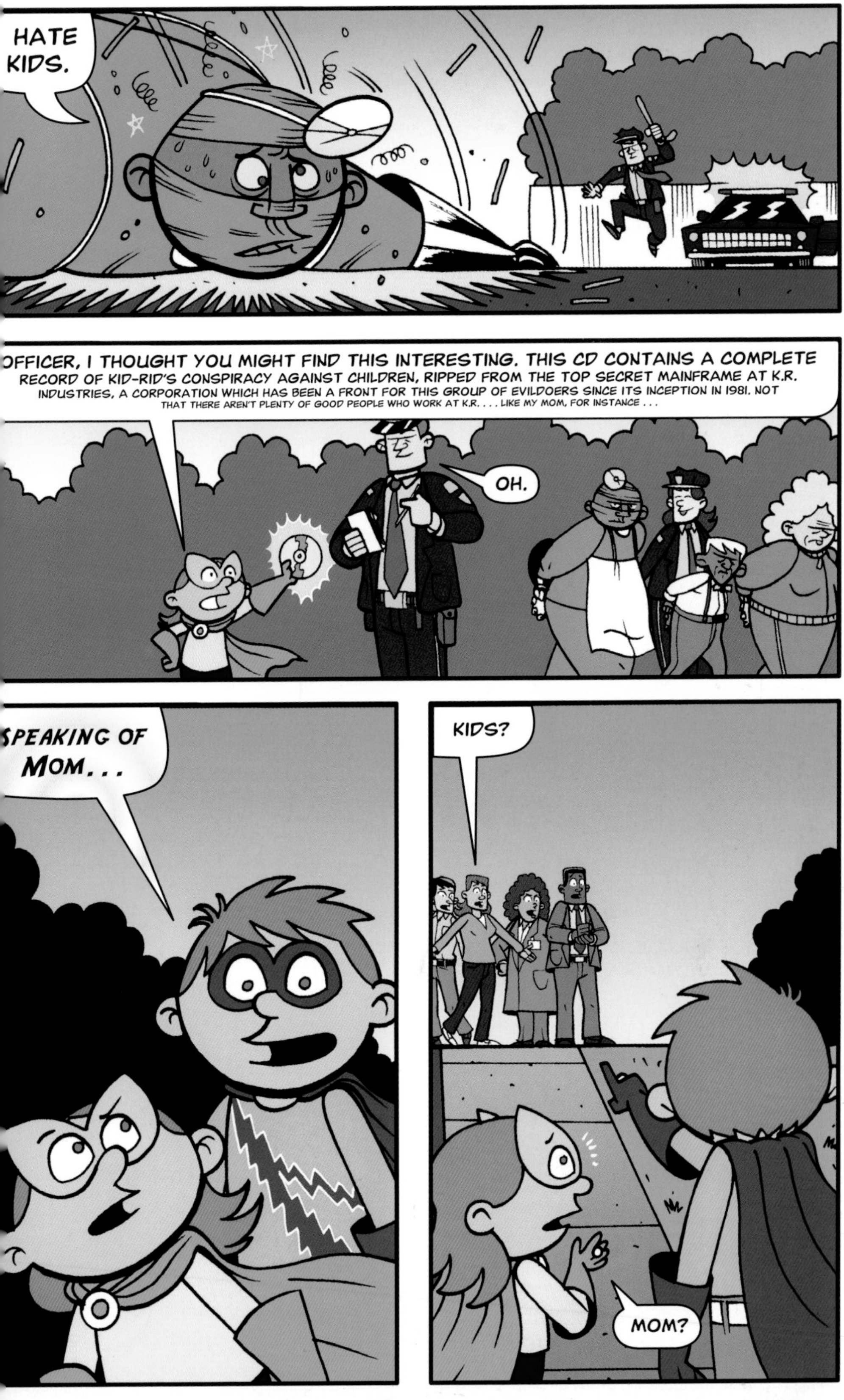
HATE KIDS.
OFFICER, I THOUGHT YOU MIGHT FIND THIS INTERESTING. THIS CD CONTAINS A COMPLETE RECORD OF KID-RID'S CONSPIRACY AGAINST CHILDREN, RIPPED FROM THE TOP SECRET MAINFRAME AT K.R. INDUSTRIES, A CORPORATION WHICH HAS BEEN A FRONT FOR THIS GROUP OF EVILDOERS SINCE ITS INCEPTION IN 1981. NOT THAT THERE AREN'T PLENTY OF GOOD PEOPLE WHO WORK AT K.R. . . . LIKE MY MOM, FOR INSTANCE . . .
OH.
SPEAKING OF MOM . . .
KIDS?
MOM?

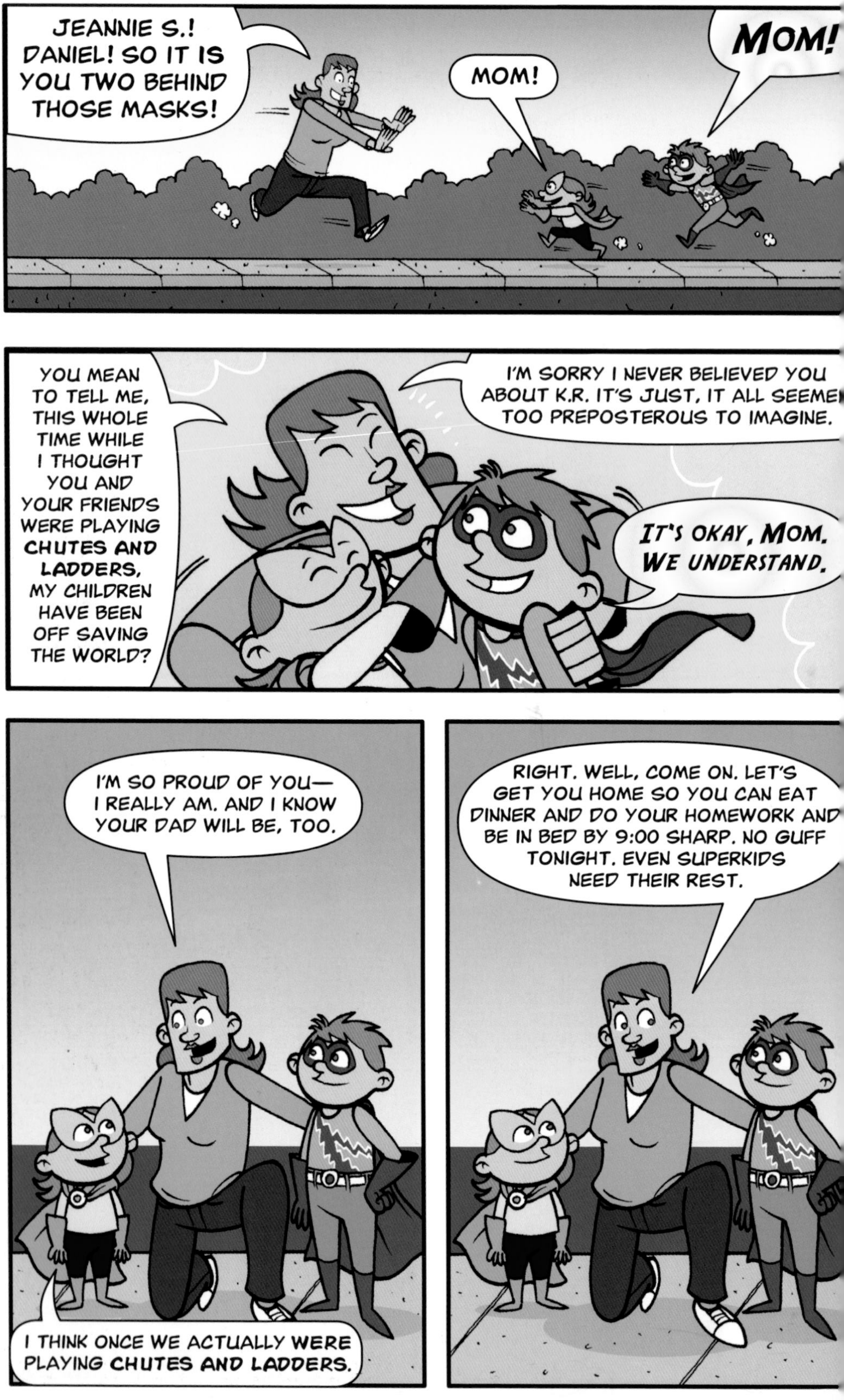
JEANNIE S.! DANIEL! SO IT IS YOU TWO BEHIND THOSE MASKS!
MOM!
MOM!
YOU MEAN TO TELL ME, THIS WHOLE TIME WHILE I THOUGHT YOU AND YOUR FRIENDS WERE PLAYING **CHUTES AND LADDERS**, MY CHILDREN HAVE BEEN OFF SAVING THE WORLD?
I'M SORRY I NEVER BELIEVED YOU ABOUT K.R. IT'S JUST, IT ALL SEEME
TOO PREPOSTEROUS TO IMAGINE.
*IT'S OKAY, MOM. WE UNDERSTAND.*
I'M SO PROUD OF YOU— I REALLY AM. AND I KNOW YOUR DAD WILL BE, TOO.
I THINK ONCE WE ACTUALLY WERE PLAYING **CHUTES AND LADDERS**.
RIGHT. WELL, COME ON. LET'S GET YOU HOME SO YOU CAN EAT DINNER AND DO YOUR HOMEWORK AND BE IN BED BY 9:00 SHARP. NO GUFF TONIGHT. EVEN SUPERKIDS NEED THEIR REST.

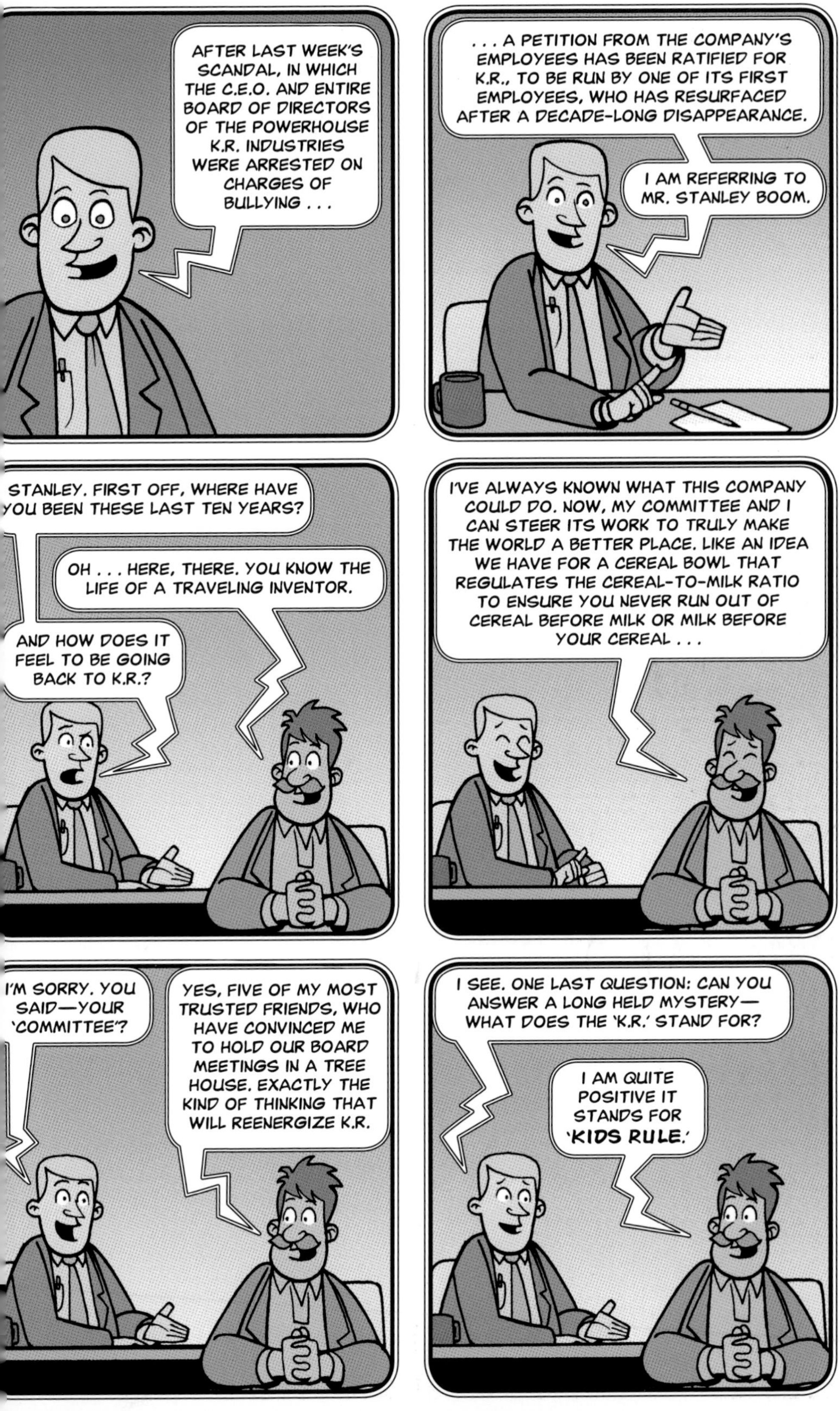
AFTER LAST WEEK'S SCANDAL, IN WHICH THE C.E.O. AND ENTIRE BOARD OF DIRECTORS OF THE POWERHOUSE K.R. INDUSTRIES WERE ARRESTED ON CHARGES OF BULLYING . . .
. . . A PETITION FROM THE COMPANY'S EMPLOYEES HAS BEEN RATIFIED FOR K.R., TO BE RUN BY ONE OF ITS FIRST EMPLOYEES, WHO HAS RESURFACED AFTER A DECADE-LONG DISAPPEARANCE.
I AM REFERRING TO MR. STANLEY BOOM.
STANLEY. FIRST OFF, WHERE HAVE YOU BEEN THESE LAST TEN YEARS?
OH . . . HERE, THERE. YOU KNOW THE LIFE OF A TRAVELING INVENTOR.
AND HOW DOES IT FEEL TO BE GOING BACK TO K.R.?
I'VE ALWAYS KNOWN WHAT THIS COMPANY COULD DO. NOW, MY COMMITTEE AND I CAN STEER ITS WORK TO TRULY MAKE THE WORLD A BETTER PLACE. LIKE AN IDEA WE HAVE FOR A CEREAL BOWL THAT REGULATES THE CEREAL-TO-MILK RATIO TO ENSURE YOU NEVER RUN OUT OF CEREAL BEFORE MILK OR MILK BEFORE YOUR CEREAL . . .
I'M SORRY. YOU SAID—YOUR 'COMMITTEE'?
YES, FIVE OF MY MOST TRUSTED FRIENDS, WHO HAVE CONVINCED ME TO HOLD OUR BOARD MEETINGS IN A TREE HOUSE. EXACTLY THE KIND OF THINKING THAT WILL REENERGIZE K.R.
I SEE. ONE LAST QUESTION: CAN YOU ANSWER A LONG HELD MYSTERY—WHAT DOES THE 'K.R.' STAND FOR?
I AM QUITE POSITIVE IT STANDS FOR 'KIDS RULE.'

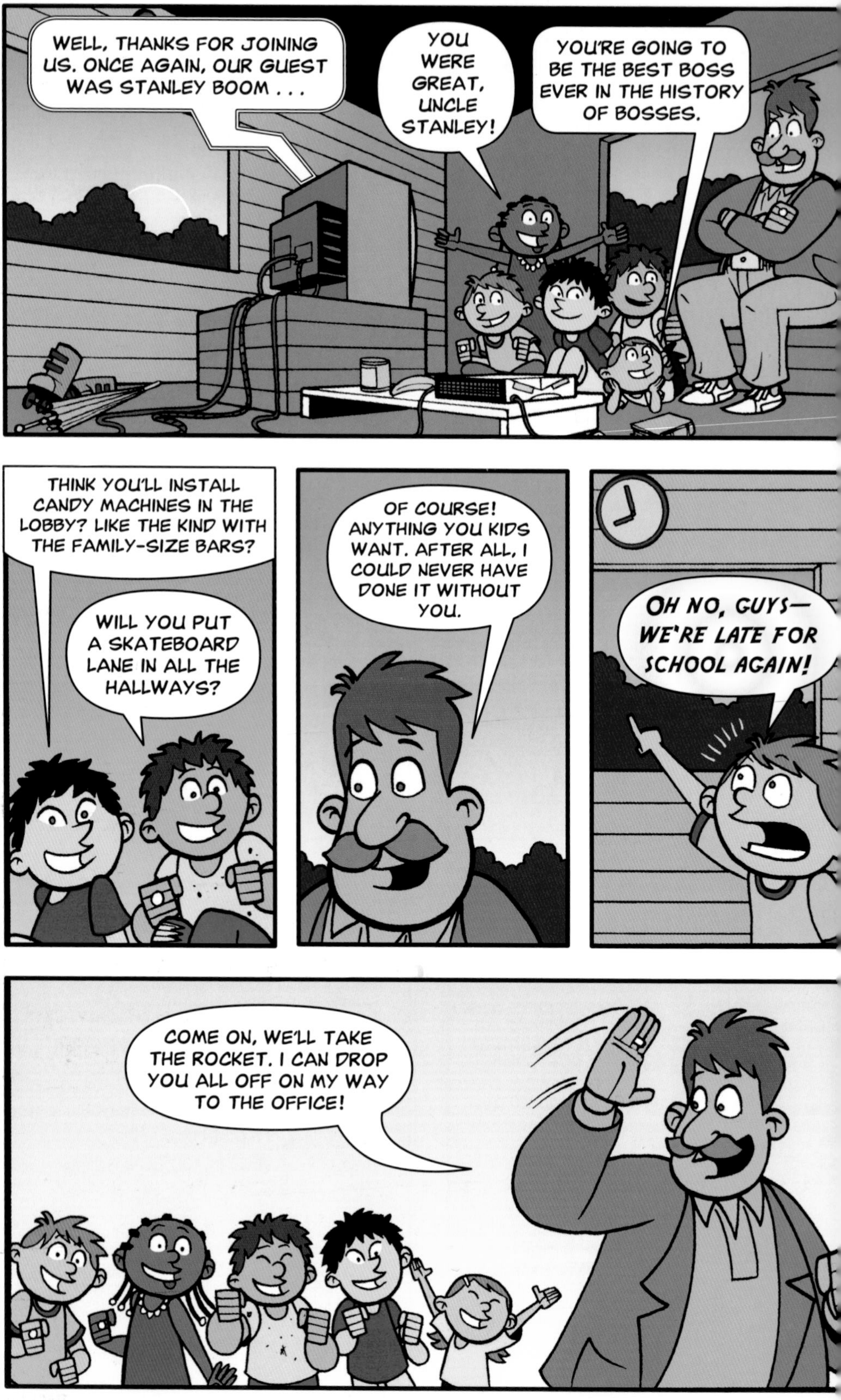
WELL, THANKS FOR JOINING US. ONCE AGAIN, OUR GUEST WAS STANLEY BOOM . . .
YOU WERE GREAT, UNCLE STANLEY!
YOU'RE GOING TO BE THE BEST BOSS EVER IN THE HISTORY OF BOSSES.
THINK YOU'LL INSTALL CANDY MACHINES IN THE LOBBY? LIKE THE KIND WITH THE FAMILY-SIZE BARS?
WILL YOU PUT A SKATEBOARD LANE IN ALL THE HALLWAYS?
OF COURSE! ANYTHING YOU KIDS WANT. AFTER ALL, I COULD NEVER HAVE DONE IT WITHOUT YOU.
OH NO, GUYS— WE'RE LATE FOR SCHOOL AGAIN!
COME ON, WE'LL TAKE THE ROCKET. I CAN DROP YOU ALL OFF ON MY WAY TO THE OFFICE!

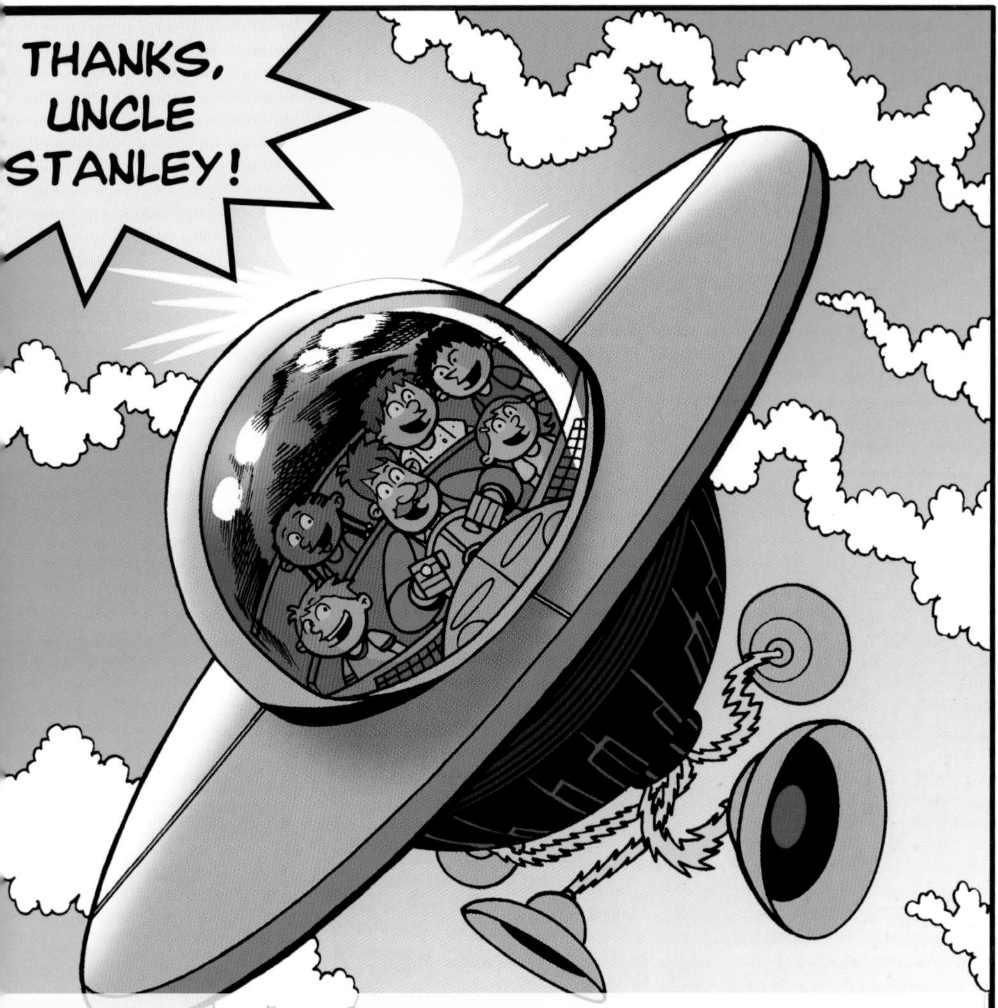
THANKS, UNCLE STANLEY!

**And that, dear friends, is how Doctor Docter and his evil corporation were undone and a new day was born for our five friends and the man they called "uncle." But what, you may ask, happened to the legions of Kid-Rid followers all over the world? Can a force of evil that deep and dark truly be vanquished? Perhaps we both know the answer. But perhaps we also know that, whatever may come, no force in the world can be greater than that of pure and unapologetic youth.**

**THE END . . .***

* PERHAPS?